For Phyllis A. Whitney

Death in Dark Blue

Julia Buckley

BERKLEY PRIME CRIME
New York

BERKLEY PRIME CRIME
Published by Berkley
An imprint of Penguin Random House LLC
375 Hudson Street, New York, New York 10014

Copyright © 2017 by Julia Buckley
Excerpt from *The Big Chili* copyright © 2015 by Julia Buckley
Penguin Random House supports copyright. Copyright fuels creativity, encourages
diverse voices, promotes free speech, and creates a vibrant culture. Thank you for buying
an authorized edition of this book and for complying with copyright laws by not
reproducing, scanning, or distributing any part of it in any form without permission.
You are supporting writers and allowing Penguin Random House to continue to
publish books for every reader.

BERKLEY is a registered trademark and BERKLEY PRIME CRIME and
the B colophon are trademarks of Penguin Random House LLC.

ISBN: 9780425282618

First Edition: May 2017

Printed in the United States of America
1 3 5 7 9 10 8 6 4 2

Cover design by Alana Colucci

Acknowledgments

Thank you very much to all those who read and reviewed *A Dark and Stormy Murder*. It's good to know how many readers admire the great Gothic writers of the 19th Century, and who appreciated my efforts to pay homage to their wonderful books.

Thank you to all the folks at Murder By The Book in Houston, and to Dean James, for their help in promoting the first novel. Thanks as well to the reviewers and bloggers who gave the book special attention and helped to find it a readership.

Thanks especially to all the readers who wrote letters to me after reading about Lena London and Camilla Graham, telling me that they wanted to travel to Blue Lake and meet my characters in person. This is only possible in a fictional world, but here is a second book in the same setting so that, for a few hours, you can visit them again.

Bestselling books by Camilla Graham

The Lost Child (1972)
Castle of Disquiet (1973)
Snow in Eden (1974)
Winds of Treachery (1975)
They Came from Calais (1976)
In Spite of Thunder (1978)
Whispers of The Wicked (1979)
Twilight in Daventry (1980)
Stars, Hide Your Fires (1981)
The Torches Burn Bright (1982)
For the Love of Jane (1983)
River of Silence (1985)
A Fine Deceit (1987)
Fall of a Sparrow (1988)
Absent Thee From Felicity (1989)
The Thorny Path (1990)
Betraying Eve (1991)
On London Bridge (1992)
The Silver Birch (1994)
The Tide Rises (1995)
What Dreams May Come (1996)
The Villainous Smile (1998)
Gone by Midnight (1999)
Sapphire Sea (2000)
Beautiful Mankind (2001)
Frost and Fire (2002)
Savage Storm (2003)
The Pen and the Sword (2005)
The Tenth Muse (2006)
Death at Seaside (2008)
Mist of Time (2009)
He Kindly Stopped for Me (2010)

(a four year hiatus)

Bereft (2015)
The Salzburg Train (2016)

An Excerpt from *Death on the Danube*

"*Margot knew the boat was there, floating just beneath the Széchenyi Lánchíd, the bridge which separated Buda from Pest. She made her way down a hillside fragrant with windflower, certain that she'd heard the signal from the man who waited. Her heart hammered in her chest, but she told herself she only had to find a path through the dark and climb into the vessel before morning, when they would certainly learn that she was gone. The chilly night air had a hint of mist, and she pulled her cloak more tightly around her. She never saw the man until he loomed up before her and blocked her path, and she screamed before she realized that she needed to remain silent . . .*"

Perhaps it would never have happened if the weather had not been so cold.
—From *Death on the Danube*

I OPENED MY eyes to see that ice had formed on my bedroom window, as though a delicate, artistic finger had traced complicated swirls and spires on a glass canvas. So lovely—but so cold. Blue Lake in winter was not for the weak, and certainly not for someone who had never experienced the occasional extremes of Midwestern weather. I pulled my quilt more securely around me, wanting to steal a few more moments of warmth before I darted to the bathroom, with its cold floor and colder countertop.

Beside me lay a warm ball of fur called Lestrade, who had taken to Blue Lake from the start. I had always heard that cats resented relocation, but Lestrade had proved to be quite flexible, not only about his new abode, but also about the two large German shepherds who wandered its halls and stairways. The three of them had become unlikely friends, and this camaraderie usually took the form of them sleeping in one big pile in some sunny spot or other, competing to see who could snore the loudest. I had taken video to prove it and posted it on my father's Facebook page. He had given me Lestrade as a present when he was just a tiny ball of fluff with curious eyes and a deceptively meek meow; now my dad enjoyed receiving updates about the fully grown and eternally confident feline.

"Okay," I told my cat. "Time to get up."

He did not agree. He remained curled into a ball, his eyes closed, his whiskers twitching slightly in some dream mouse pursuit.

I slid out of bed, darted across the cold wood floor, and into the bathroom. I raced through my morning routine, although I did linger a bit in the hot shower; then I bundled into brown corduroys and a wheat-colored sweater. I tucked my socked feet into high boots and marched out of the room feeling prepared for the weather and the day ahead.

It was early; I had set my alarm for eight but had woken before then, perhaps with a sense of anticipation. I crept down the stairs to find Camilla Graham already at her breakfast table, having tea. I never tired of the sight of her, as graceful and lovely as she looked on every book jacket, sitting at her own table in her own house—which was, for the time being, my house, too.

"You look pleased with yourself," she said, smiling at me. "Would you like some tea and toast?"

"Maybe something to go. I have—some errands to run."

"Of course you do," she said, smiling serenely into her

teacup. She took a sip, then set it down in her saucer and said, "While you're out, I wonder if you'd pick up some mail that I have waiting at the post office?" I noticed then that her dogs lay under the table at her feet, motionless as inanimate objects.

I nodded. "I have to go to Bick's anyway. Will Marge give it to me, or is there some law that she can only give your mail to you?"

"I'll call ahead and ask her to release it. I can't imagine there will be a problem."

"Sure. Well, I'd better get going."

"Your cheeks are flushed. Do you have a fever?" she asked, her eyes twinkling slightly.

"Haha. I'll be back by noon, I'm sure. I have the notes you asked for upstairs. We can look at them today, if you'd like."

"Perfect. Perhaps right after lunch."

"See you later, then." I waved, grabbed my coat from a hook, took precious moments to button it on and tie a scarf around my neck, and moved quickly out the door. The front porch was coated with a thin sheet of ice. I grabbed the bag of eco-friendly de-icing pellets that sat near the door and sprinkled them on the stairs and landing. The last thing we needed was Camilla with a broken leg.

Down the steps then, and to my car. I climbed in, enduring its wintry depths and waiting for the heater to kick in with the warming engine. Finally, I pulled toward the end of the long drive. To my right was a short road that led to a scenic overlook and a path that curved all the way around the bluff. Camilla's place was at the top of the bluff, so her view was the best of all. To my left was the same road leading down; I turned and descended the graduated path, lined today with bare and solemn trees that bent over the road like protective grandfathers with worry lines scratched into their bark. At the foot of the bluff I turned left onto Wentworth Street, which curved around and intersected with Green Glass Highway. For fifteen minutes I admired the scenery, bare and white, yet beautiful in its elemental reality, and then I turned into a well-appointed subdivision with charming stone and brick homes. I pulled up in front of a corner lot where a stone sign on the lawn read "Branch House." I got out and, digging in my coat pocket, retrieved the key that had been entrusted to me. My friend Allison lived here with her husband John; they were both at work now.

I moved across the grass, crunchy with ice, casually looking around to be sure no one found my presence unusual, if they noticed it at all. The wood entry door opened easily, and once I stepped into the warm, pine-scented house, I locked the knob behind me. The room I stood in was empty. I admired its beauty: hardwood floor, brown patterned rug in front of the hearth, striking and colorful seaside painting above the fireplace, and Allison's knitting bag tucked against the brick jamb. Slowly, I pulled off my coat and scarf and set them on the couch. The kitchen was just around the corner; my footsteps seemed loud in the silence. I could hear the nervous sound of my own breathing.

The kitchen, too, was empty. I stood, my mouth open slightly with surprise, and then jumped when someone grabbed me from behind, curling his arms around my waist. I turned, staying inside his embrace. "Where were you hiding?"

His eyes, blue and familiar, locked onto mine. "Not far. Did anyone see you?"

"No. I'm pretty sure I wasn't followed, either."

"Good." He smiled at me, and his arms tightened ever so slightly.

"You were in New York forever," I complained.

"I missed you."

"Did you find her?"

"No," he said. "We'll talk later." He bent his head and pressed his mouth against mine; I went pleasantly blank for a time, kissing Sam West in the secret hideout we'd arranged for our reunion, but a part of my mind wandered into a reflection of the ironies that had brought us together.

Not two months ago he had been suspected of killing his own wife, and then he was arrested on that suspicion. Now he was free because we had determined that his wife was still alive, but we didn't know where she was.

Since then we had all worked on finding her—the police and the FBI with whatever resources they were allotting, Camilla and I through online searches, Sam and his private detective, Jim Harrigan, through more specific means. Sam had been in New York for more than a month, talking with investigators, neighbors, anyone who might have had some sort of information about the missing Victoria. He had gone to New York at the end of November and had still been there at Christmas. It had been a lonely time, sitting in a snowbound Blue Lake and wondering what Sam was doing on the East Coast. Any future the two of us might have, we knew, was in limbo until we knew more about Victoria. We needed to know she was safe; we needed to know why she had left and allowed Sam to take the fall for her "murder," and we needed to know that Sam was fully divorced and able to start his life anew.

But all that was forgotten for a brief time as I nestled myself against Sam's chest and remembered the feel and scent of him. "Your hair is longer," he said, pulling far enough away to study my face. "I like it."

"I saw you on television last night," I said. "That reporter cornered you at the airport."

He nodded. "They wanted a response to Taylor Brand's blog post. Thanks to her, I'm news again, and so is Blue Lake."

I lifted a hand to smooth the frown line between his brows. "At least she apologized to you." Taylor Brand was a New York blogger who happened to be one of Victoria West's best friends. For a year Taylor had darkly hinted that Sam West had done something to his wife. Now that she had seen the evidence—that recent photograph of Victoria on a yacht, alive and well—she had no choice but to apologize to Sam, which she had done in an open letter on her blog. This had been picked up by the news media, and Sam's name was back in the headlines. At the end of her post, Taylor had written, "I hope that you'll accept my apology, Sam, and I plan to make it in person soon. I've always wanted to see Indiana."

"Ironically, she could have just looked me up in New York," Sam said now.

"Except you didn't want people to know you were there."

"No. I'm a bit gun-shy about being in the public eye."

I pulled him down for another kiss, then sighed. "If they're going to be following you anyway, then let's just get it over with. We'll be seen together in person, announce ourselves as a couple, and then it will be over."

"No. It would never be over. Lena, you know my feelings about this. They're horrible, and I won't let them anywhere near you. It's bad enough the way they stalked and tormented me."

"But—"

"Please," Sam said, touching my lips with a gentle finger. "You're the one sweet thing in my life, and you've kept me sane for two months of craziness. I want you to be separate from all of that. My haven in the storm."

I must not have looked convinced, because he said, "The headlines alone would hurt your feelings. I can tell you what they would say: "Dark-Haired Siren Lures Sam West Away from Hunt for Missing Wife." Or "West's Indiana Lover Lives in Home of Camilla Graham.""

"Oh. They *would* drag Camilla into it, wouldn't they?"

"They'll do whatever they can think of. They'll follow you around. They'll watch you buy coffee and turn it into some weird story. They'll look at what you choose in the grocery store; they'll spy on the clothes you wash at the Laundromat. They'll try to get pictures of you doing anything that could catch a reader's eye—walking those big dogs of Camilla's or trying to meditate down on the beach. You'd be a hunted woman."

I sighed again. "There's no way we can know if they'd even show up here."

"They're already here. I stopped at Bick's Hardware to pick up my mail, and Marge told me that two reporters are staying in town—for an indefinite period. If there are two now, there will be more soon. They're like the scouts before the army. They'll be coming back."

"Because Taylor's blog went viral."

"Exactly. I don't know what these reporters look like,

but I'm sure I will soon. And then I can warn you away from them." He saw my dejection and stroked my hair. "We'll find ways to be together. We just have to be sneaky for a while. You didn't tell anyone about us, did you?"

"There's no one to tell. I mean, Camilla knows, but that's just because she has eyes. She was smirking when I left this morning, so I'm sure she knew I was going to meet you. And Allison knows, because I had to get her permission to use her house. Now that she believes you're not a murderer, she thinks our story is very romantic."

"And our town police hero knows, because he wanted you himself. Though I admit he was relatively gracious in defeat," Sam said.

"Doug didn't want me, exactly," I said.

Sam sent me a disbelieving look.

I shrugged. "You would think I was a supermodel, or something."

"You're better than a supermodel. You're lovely in a very real way, with your silky chocolate-colored hair, and those big brown eyes. And you have a large, beautiful heart."

I batted my lashes, and he laughed. Then he grew sober. "Will Allison keep quiet about us?"

"She wouldn't tell them if they camped out on her lawn. She's beyond loyal."

"Great. And I know Camilla won't. And believe it or not, I trust Doug Heller to be discreet, too."

"Of course he will. He's a cop; they don't like the press nosing into their business as a general rule."

I moved away from him for the first time, reluctantly, and went to Allison's kitchen table, where I sat down. "So why didn't you find Victoria? I thought you said you and this detective of yours had a lead."

He followed me and took the chair opposite mine. "We did. We were working on the assumption that Nikon was the name of the yacht, and we actually found a yacht called *Nikon*; we traced it to the Canary Islands. We made a variety of complicated arrangements with authorities in that region. Essentially we lied and said that we had to get news to someone about a death in the family. They finally boarded the yacht, only to find that Victoria wasn't there—just a rich family and some of their friends. That took more than a month: hunting it down and getting that close, and then . . . nothing."

"Could there be other ships called *Nikon*?"

"Probably. That was the only yacht we found. Jim is still in New York, pursuing more leads. He's spent endless time on this, and it's really become an obsession. I trust him to stay on it, and to keep me informed. There are only certain places that yachts can even travel right now—the Bahamas, the Caribbean, Thailand, Malaysia, Australia . . ." He ticked them off on his hands.

"But in Greece too, right? My father and Tabitha went out there for their honeymoon, and that was in winter. And they sailed. It was the Alkyonides—supposedly a time during December and January when the weather is surprisingly warm and mild."

Sam raised his eyebrows. "So right around now, huh?"

"Yes. You can sail, and my father said that it was much better than sailing in the summer, because the weather was less hot and just very pleasant."

"I'll talk to Jim about that." He had a certain urgent look that worried me.

"But you'll stay here now, won't you?"

He reached across the table and took my hand. "I will.

Because I have a girlfriend, and I really need to devote some time to getting to know her better. God knows I think about her just about all the time. I have a lot of questions. I wrote them down while I was in New York."

I smiled. "Yeah? Tell me one of your questions."

He took a little notebook out of his shirt pocket and opened it. Sure enough, there was a list written there, with numbered items jotted in small, neat script. "We'll start with an easy one. Number thirteen: did you ever have a pet?"

"Besides my cat, Lestrade, you mean? I don't think you've met him yet, but you need to! And then there are my surrogate pets, Rochester and Heathcliff." Those were Camilla's big German shepherds. "As a matter of fact, I did. When I was seven I received a kitten named Smoky for my birthday. My mother gave in to my endless pressure to get me a feline friend. And later we found a stray dog who won our hearts, so he ended up living with us for ten years. His name was Faust, because my mom loved literature and was a fan of the play."

"You have some great memories of your mom," he said gently. He knew that my mother had died when I was a teenager.

"Only happy memories. Give me another question."

He consulted his notebook. "Name of your first boyfriend?"

"Sam West," I said.

He shook his head. "I know I can't be the first, so just break it to me gently."

"Okay. Charlie Baird. I chased him until he agreed to kiss me, and we held hands all through recess. That was in the first grade. After that day I think we agreed to see other people."

Sam laughed. "I don't feel too threatened by Charlie Baird."

"You don't need to feel *threatened* by anyone."

"Who was there before me? *Just* before?"

I sighed. "His name was Kurt Saylor. He's a botanist and researcher. We were together for a year, and then he ended it."

"And do you miss him sometimes?"

"When I think of him at all, I wonder what drew me to him in the first place. Now he just strikes me as cold and mean."

Sam absorbed this, and I poked his leg with my booted foot. "Get to a fun question."

He smiled into his notebook. "Okay. What's your secret indulgence?"

I thought about this, admiring his blue eyes. "You are my indulgence, and I am being forced to keep you a secret."

"True. What else?"

"Um. I would say chocolate, but that's not a secret."

"And waffles," said Sam West. He had won me over with waffles, as we both knew.

I reached out and played with the tips of his fingers. "I suppose my secret indulgence is reading in bed. And sometimes eating when I do it."

"That's cute."

"What's yours?"

He thought about this. "Salted pretzels. I keep bags of them in my desk drawer. I have trouble stopping at one bag. Oh, and this." He took out his phone, clicked a few buttons, and then held up a photograph of me. He had taken it before he left for New York; I was standing under one of the trees that lined his long driveway. We had met in this very spot and disliked each other on sight. In this photo, though, I was smiling and shading my eyes with one hand. "I probably look at it one hundred times a day," he said lightly.

I studied the picture for a minute, then saw that he was looking at it, too, with an expression that made my heart beat faster.

"Sam?"

"Yes."

"Will we ever find her?"

"We will. And soon. Doug says the CIA is involved. They're concerned about fraud."

"All these people looking for one woman, and yet somehow they can't seem to succeed."

"They will. We will. Very soon, Lena." He stood up and walked into the hallway; when he returned he was holding his coat. "But I have to go, and we have to stay away from each other. Maybe we can arrange a few clandestine meetings, but we have to be very careful about it. Even this one—I have a bad feeling."

"Why?"

"I don't know. I parked my car far enough away, and your car shouldn't matter, because Allison is your friend and you've been seen here before. I just worry about those watching eyes."

"I didn't see anyone at your house when I drove past."

"It won't last."

"You've become a cynic. That's what they've done to you."

"I've become a realist. And I know what reality is, because I've lived it." I went to him, and he pulled me into his arms. "I am so very glad to see you. You know that, right?"

"I know."

He kissed my head, then put his nose in my hair. "What is that fragrant shampoo? You smell like some rare flower."

"I don't know. Camilla put it in my shower stall. It has a French label—*Amour Interdit*—whatever that means. I don't know; I took Latin in high school."

Sam's laugh had a tinge of sadness. "I minored in French. Your shampoo is called *Forbidden Love*. Apropos."

I sighed and watched him put on his coat. "Before you go," I said. "Let me take a picture of you that will be *my* secret indulgence."

He smiled at me, and I captured it with my cell phone camera. I looked at the picture to make sure it wasn't blurry, and found that it contained the essence of everything that made Sam attractive—his blue eyes, his messy brown hair, his slightly dimpled smile.

"We'll text each other," he said, blowing me a kiss. "That will make it easier."

He went out the back door and slipped into the trees behind Allison's house. In a moment it was as though he had never been there.

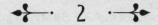

· 2 ·

Her mother had always quoted an expression
which, loosely translated, meant "Danger wears a
cloak of silence." And it was true that she did not
hear danger approaching.

—From *Death on the Danube*

I STOPPED AT Bick's Hardware in town, as I had promised,
to pick up Camilla's mail. Naturally Marge Bick was full
of her usual gossip about reporters and Sam West and
various scandalous townspeople. She paused as she
handed me the bundle of envelopes. "I hope Mrs. Graham
isn't sick or anything?"

Always looking for information, I thought darkly. And
yet Sam and I both acknowledged that Marge Bick could
be quite handy for our purposes. "No, just not willing to
come out on such an unfriendly day. I don't mind it so
much because I just got these nice warm boots, and it
keeps the snow and moisture away."

"Nothing like the proper clothes for the weather,"
Marge said, nodding her approval. "Oh, and I almost
forgot. There's a box, too. Now I'm not sure you can carry
it all." She went into her back room and returned with a

medium-sized parcel. She set it on the counter with a bang, and said, "It's a bit heavy."

I glanced at the return address and saw that it was from Camilla's New York Publisher, Carthage House. My hands shook slightly as I reached for the package.

"Are you okay, hon?" Marge Bick's eagle eyes had noted my trembling.

I hefted the box. "Oh, yes. I can carry this with no problem. My car is right out front."

"All right then. Shaky hands mean not enough food— didn't you eat breakfast?" she asked.

"As a matter of fact, I forgot to do that this morning. I guess I need some protein, huh? Okay, thanks, Marge." I put the letters on top of the box and started to turn away, but then had a thought and turned back. "Hey—those reporters you saw in town—what did they look like? In case one of them comes snooping around Camilla or me, I want to be prepared."

She nodded. "One was a bald guy. Sort of good-looking. Older than you, but not old. Maybe fortyish. The other one was kind of medium—not noticeable—what's that word?"

"Nondescript?"

"Yeah, that's it. He almost looked like a guy wearing a disguise. A thick head of brown hair, medium build, glasses, mustache. Hard to see his eye color behind the glasses. They both asked a lot of questions about Sam West." She held up a hand before I could say anything. "Which I did *not* answer. I told them they were reporters and they could figure it out for themselves. I did say that we all felt really bad for being suspicious of him, and that they should leave him alone."

I nodded approvingly. "Thanks for that, Marge. Camilla and I feel the same way." I waved and lifted the box again. I wanted to toss it in the car and rip it open, but it was Camilla's to open, not mine. She had told me that the advanced readers' copies of her book *The Salzburg Train* would be coming soon—that they had in fact been rushed through for Camilla's approval in a matter of two months. I wanted so desperately to hold one of those books in my hands—not only because I had read it and had helped Camilla edit the whole thing, nor because she had long been my favorite author and this was a much anticipated new book, but because she had put my name on the cover as a collaborator. "With Lena London," the books would say. And suddenly there would be people all over the world who would see my name, in large, mysterious font and purple-blue letters.

My hands were still shaking slightly when I got back to Camilla's and bounded up the stairs. I barely managed to get the door open while still holding box, mail, and purse, and then slammed the door with my foot and ran to Camilla's office. She was there, at her desk, massaging her forehead. "Hello, Lena! How was your—I mean, how were your errands?"

"You can stop pretending; I know you know where I went."

"Well, I don't know exactly *where* you met him, but yes, I figured you would be hunting down our handsome neighbor once he was back in town."

I sniffed. "I didn't hunt him. I'm not a stalker. I went to see him in secret only because he doesn't want reporters knowing about me."

"Very wise, I must say. Ah—do you ever get headaches

between your eyes? I believe it's from removing my glasses and then replacing them all day long. Curse my nearsightedness."

"I'll get you some Advil," I said. "But first, I have a present." I set the mail and the package down on her desk, and she smiled.

"Oh, lovely. But to be honest, dear, I've gotten so many of these, they're not as exciting as they used to be. You open the box. In fact, I'm going to film you doing it on this ridiculous phone Gabby sent me, and she can have the footage for the website."

"Gabby" was Gabriella Carr, Camilla's publicist. "Thank you," I said. "I'd love to!"

Camilla handed me a pair of scissors and got out her phone. She had recently learned to use it much more effectively because she'd been dating a man who was tech-savvy, and he showed her all kinds of things that she had previously dubbed "stupid."

I opened the scissors and slid one blade slowly along the tape line, making sure not to press too deeply and potentially gouge a precious book cover. I opened the box flaps, moved some tissue paper aside, and saw them, gleaming like amethysts in a treasure chest. The cover was purple-blue, and in the center image, a black train barreled through the Salzburg twilight; in the backdrop were the twinkling of city lights; in the foreground, mysterious blue-black scenery and glowing fireflies. "Oh, my!" I said, slipping my hands into the box and pulling out a thick paperback book. "It's beautiful!" I sniffed at the cover, breathing in that new book smell.

"Read us the cover," said Camilla, grinning and holding up her phone.

"'The latest suspense novel from the great Camilla Graham doesn't disappoint.' That's the blurb from *Kirkus Reviews*. And under that is the quote from *Publishers Weekly*: 'Gripping and riveting!' And then, of course, it says *The Salzburg Train*, by Camilla Graham."

"And what does it say at the bottom?"

"'With Lena London,'" I said, grinning at her.

"Look at the biography page. How do you like that?"

I flipped to the back, to a page that read About the Authors. At the top there was a recent photograph of Camilla; she was sitting at the very desk where she stood now, with the sun on her face, contemplating her computer. It was a great shot. "That's a nice picture of you," I said. The photography credit read Adam Rayburn. He was Camilla's boyfriend, and the proprietor of one of the best restaurants in Blue Lake. "I didn't know Adam was such a good photographer."

"He manages to make me not feel self-conscious," she said.

"And then there's this bio of you that we signed off on last fall."

Further down was a picture of me, posed on the bluff just beyond Camilla's driveway, with a backdrop of vibrant autumn color. I was smiling slightly, almost mysteriously, and my eyes looked just to the left of the camera. It was a good photograph; Camilla had insisted on hiring a local photographer to take a series of shots, and we had both liked this one best.

I felt a sudden burst of good feeling. "Oh, it's just beautiful. A wonderful book, a genius of an author, a great title, a beautiful cover . . ."

"You're going to run out of adjectives," Camilla said wryly.

"May I keep one, Camilla?"

She clicked off the camera and set the phone down.

"Of course, Lena. That box is half yours. We'll have to decide what to do with them all. The publicist will send them to all the likely places, of course."

"I'd like to send one to my father."

"Naturally. You must send it out today."

"And—can I give one to Sam?"

She came around the desk and gave me an impulsive hug—a rare thing for the reserved Camilla Graham. "You are adorable, with your wide shining eyes. You help me remember the old days, with my first sales and first publications. How bright everything was then."

"Well, there must be a lot of joy in being who you are now—a queen of suspense with millions of readers who wait on every book. I'm one of them," I said.

She shrugged, amused, and went back to her desk. "To be honest I don't think of myself very often as the author Camilla Graham, even though I spend so much time writing. And, not to be a joy killer, but I've been focusing on the work we have to do."

"Of course," I said.

"I'm more and more concerned about Victoria West." She looked up sharply. "Is this too hard to think about—given your feelings for Sam?"

"No, of course not. I feel badly for her, if in fact she is in some kind of trouble."

"Yes, that is my fear. I wonder what the police think."

"Sam said the FBI is involved. But it doesn't sound as

though they're communicating much with him. I suppose they all still vaguely suspect him of being involved in her disappearance."

"It seems to me we've been wasting time with all of our phone calls and e-mails in the past few weeks," she said. "Perhaps it's time to return to your original searches—the ones that helped you find Victoria West in the first place."

"A bit more Internet investigating?"

"Yes, I think so." She rubbed her forehead again. "There, it's getting bit better. I'll also need you to look at the first draft of the new book."

"Oh, Camilla! You finished it?"

"Yes. It was a pleasure to write, actually. I've set it in Budapest, for the most part. James and I spent a summer there once. So many memories, and many of them came back as I was writing this, exploring the landscape of my past."

"You have had a remarkable life."

"Yes. I'm lucky." She turned to her desk and rounded it again, finding her seat and the work she had left to congratulate me.

"Camilla, before we get started—I wonder if I can just put one of these copies through Sam's mailbox? He told me to stay away, so I won't talk to him, and if anyone asks, I'll just say I'm delivering it for you."

"Of course you can. He'll be very proud of you, I know."

"And I'll mail one to my father tomorrow morning. He won't believe it. He told me he already saw the image online, but this will be a first—holding it in his hand."

"My parents were most proud of my first book. They had the cover image framed, and then I was asked to send another so that they could bring it to the local pub for their celebrity wall."

"Oh, wow! And who were the celebrities on the wall?"

"Just me," she said, smiling. "My parents started the idea, you see. But it never really took off. They just kept adding my book covers. Quite flattering."

"I want to go to that town and eat lunch in that pub," I said. I wasn't joking.

Camilla nodded. "When we go on tour, we'll visit there, and I'll show you."

"That would be the most amazing thing that has ever happened to me."

She looked wry again. "Go and deliver your book. Then we'll get to work."

"Someday I will make you accept my hero worship. You'll sit up on a big float in a Blue Lake parade, and I'll toss confetti at you and people will kneel along the pathway to acknowledge your genius. And then, in the park, I'll erect a giant screen and show images of all of your books, and we'll hire voice artists to read passages to the crowd."

My mentor sat up straight in her seat and glared at me. "I could not imagine anything more horrifying."

I laughed, and she said, "Go, Lena."

I jogged out of the room and put my coat back on. I still wore my industrial strength boots, and these took me safely down the stairs and along the carefully shoveled path. Camilla hired a local company to plow the road up the bluff and our whole driveway, so the walking was fairly easy all the way to Sam West's place. I stood at the foot of his drive, noting that the trees, burgeoning with colorful leaves when we first met, were now dark and bare, and his house was visible between the branches. It, too, looked dark and rather forbidding. I tromped up the driveway, ready with my excuse: *I'm Mrs. Graham's assistant. She asked me to deliver this to Mr. West.* But there was no one along the path; no paparazzo with a camera, no reporter hovering in the trees, no spy with a telescope. Just winter silence, and snow crunching under my feet.

I climbed Sam's steps and opened the little swinging door to his mailbox. I shoved the book through and heard it plop satisfyingly into the box in the porch. Then I turned around and paused, scanning the scenery as Sam would see it each day as he left his house. Blue Lake was visible as a line on his horizon, across the street and beyond Camilla's house. The rest of the scene was elemental and satisfying: white snow, dark branches bending in a cold wind, clustering clouds of grayish white against a blue-gray sky, and a rocky path that led upward. I scanned the forest around me, wondering if he ever saw deer, and noted that there was something in the woods to the west of his house, bulky and still.

Could I have stumbled upon a sleeping deer? Surely there were no bears here in Blue Lake, and yet the hide of this animal seemed black and furry. Fearful, yet curious, I crept closer, my boots squeaking slightly on the snow. Ten feet away, I saw that this wasn't an animal. It was too still. Inanimate. And there was something broken about it, like a sack of garbage had been thrown from the top of the bluff that rose majestically behind Sam's house. Various thoughts flickered through my mind. Rotted, molding trash? Rejected swatches of material? Some sort of fur-covered piece of furniture?

My curiosity got the better of me, and I pushed myself to walk those last few feet. Then everything came into perspective, and I let out something between a gasp and a moan. The black furry thing was a long woman's coat, not black after all, but dark blue; it looked both warm and expensive. Underneath it was a woman, or what had been a woman when she lived. She was clearly dead now, lying broken, unnatural, a dark and terrible contrast against the bright white snow.

"Oh, God," I moaned. I think I added, "I'm sorry," to her because her eyes were open and staring at the pale sky. I felt her loss strongly in that instant before I fumbled for my phone and pressed a name that, thankfully, had already been entered into my directory.

He answered in a moment, his voice casual. "Hey, Lena. What's up?"

"Doug," I whispered.

"Lena?" He was alert now.

"There's a dead woman." My voice croaked away into nothingness.

"Who's dead? Where?"

"She's in the forest behind Sam's house. She's not from Blue Lake."

"Don't cry, Lena. Go to the road. I'll be there in five minutes, and you can show me where."

"Yes. Oh, God."

He hung up, and I stole one last look at her; I don't know if I was torturing myself or just feeling curious, or if perhaps I was making sure of something. "I'm sorry," I whispered again. "You didn't deserve this."

I turned and walked toward the road, forcing myself to breathe deeply while I waited for Doug Heller and his team.

I did not look at her again, but I didn't have to. I knew who she was.

3

*She realized, soon enough, that she could rely only
upon herself for a way out of trouble, and yet she
had no idea what that way might be. She decided
to put her faith in ingenuity and the spirit of inspi-
ration.*

—From *Death on the Danube*

I STAYED ON the side of the road while they worked;
Doug came to me eventually, in note-taking mode, his
little tablet device in his hand. "I know it's cold out here.
I'll let you go soon. But we want to get this done in day-
light."

"People will come sooner or later. They'll see her," I
said, feeling protective.

"No. We closed off the road at the foot of the hill. No
one's getting in."

"The reporters are here. From all over, probably.
Marge Bick told me about two of them. They have no
respect. They'll hike in through the trees."

He put an arm around me. "You're trembling. Are you
okay?"

"I've been better. I'm just—really offended. That she
had to go through that. That she had to die at that young

age. And it looks as if it was such a violent parting from the earth."

Doug nodded. "You're getting poetic, so I know this is upsetting you. I'll send you home with Officer Goggins, and Camilla will make you some hot chocolate or something."

"Ask me your questions first."

He studied my face, then nodded and looked at his iPad, lifting his stylus. "You were right. She's not from around here. But she has no purse, no ID on her. Have you ever—"

"She's from New York," I interrupted.

His head shot up, and his brown eyes locked onto mine. "You know who she is?"

"Yes, I think so. I've never met her."

"Who is she, Lena?"

"Remember when we had our sort of round table at Camilla's house, and we talked about Victoria West and how we realized she was in trouble?"

"Yes, of course. Camilla knows I've been working on it in my spare time. So does Sam."

"Well, at the time you asked how I knew about Victoria, and one of the puzzle pieces was that photo of Victoria on the blog. It's what helped us identify her on that yacht."

"Yes, yes, I remember."

I pointed in the direction of the dead woman, covered now with some kind of tarp. "*Her* blog."

"What? You mean that's Victoria's friend?"

"I think it's Taylor Brand, yes. It looks like her. I've read her blog a lot since I first discovered it, looking for clues or ideas about Victoria. Taylor had a certain style, and even if I didn't recognize her face, I'd recognize that coat. It's the sort of thing she's always wearing in the photos."

Heller did some clicking around on his computer; I peered over his shoulder and saw that he had pulled up the blog. There was Taylor Brand's photograph. "Ah," he said. "I'm afraid you're right, Lena. We'll try to get someone in New York to come down and make a formal identification."

"Or they can give Sam permission to make it. He knew her, right? She was his wife's best friend."

"Yes," Doug said, and his face grew troubled.

"This will be bad for Sam, won't it?"

He put the iPad in his big coat pocket. "As you said, she's his wife's best friend. He's just been cleared of killing Victoria, and now her friend is dead in his yard. Yeah, it looks bad. But it also looks convenient."

"Meaning what?"

"Meaning if I were going to kill someone in this town, I might want to make it look like Sam West did it. It sure would get the attention away from me, whomever I might be."

"Are you sure someone killed her? Maybe she just had some kind of attack, or tripped and fell, or . . ."

Heller shook his head. "She was murdered," he said.

"How do you know?" Again, I felt a mixture of dread and curiosity.

Doug looked back at his team; he clearly wanted to join them. "I can't really go into it, but the evidence suggests that she was pushed. From up there." He pointed to the top of the bluff, where a scenic overlook curved around right over Sam's property and all the way down the giant hill. If she had fallen from the path, it meant that she had plunged perhaps forty to fifty feet.

"I think her legs were broken," I said.

"Yes." His voice was grim. "But so was her neck, so she likely didn't feel any pain."

"What is happening? This can't be real. She was just some woman in a picture on the Internet, and now suddenly she's here, and—Oh my God."

"What?" He leaned toward me, alert.

"She had posted something about how she was going to come here. She intended to apologize to Sam. Look at her blog."

He tapped the computer again and found the post. "*I owe you an apology, and I plan to make it in person soon . . .*" Doug looked grim. "She posted this three days ago. Which means anyone in the world could have read this and known that she might show up in Blue Lake."

"This is scary, Doug. What's going on here?"

"I don't know." He put a hand on my shoulder. "Go home. I'll come to see you and Camilla tonight, and we'll talk. We'll ask Sam to come, too."

"I thought this was over. I thought it was all over."

Doug wanted to comfort me, but I could see that his eyes were darting back to the scene, where he felt he should be. "I'm sending you home." He lifted a hand. "Darrell! Come and see Miss London back home to Graham House."

The officer put a hand under my elbow and walked me home; my mind was darting around to various thoughts, and I was barely conscious of the journey. Soon I was climbing Camilla's steps and thanking my escort, and only when I was in the warmth of Camilla's living room did I realize what had been bothering me: Sam had never returned home.

"WE'VE MISSED SOMETHING," Camilla told me, her expression brooding as she frowned into her mug of hot chocolate.

"Doug saw the blog. He said anyone could have read it and realized that Taylor Brand was going to show up in Blue Lake. They could have been watching for her."

"But why?" Camilla asked.

I shrugged. "Maybe—I don't know—someone has a grudge against Sam and Taylor both?"

She shook her head. "There should be no connection to Blue Lake, none at all. And yet this is where that poor woman has died. If this were a book, Lena, we would know that there was some association that we had not seen before—something linking her to this town."

"Well, Sam does. I mean, he was her best friend's husband, and she wronged him and wanted to make it right."

"But that doesn't give anyone motive for murder, does it? Which means there's something else."

Camilla's mind was working, too, and her brown eyes moved from her hot chocolate to the window that provided a view of the wintry front yard. Her gaze stayed there, as though she could read the truth in the scenery. "What did Sam say?" she asked, shifting her gaze to me.

I cleared my throat. "He never came home. I assumed he was going straight there after we met at Allison's house, but . . . I never saw him. Doug wanted to talk to him, I could tell."

"He'll be a suspect, of course."

"Doug said it was convenient. He's not going to be as quick to suspect Sam this time, not after he ended up being wrong last time."

"Yes. I see." She took a sip of her drink, and we sat in silence. She roused herself enough to say "Lena, are you sure you don't want some hot chocolate?"

"No, no, thank you." My throat felt tight, and my heart was still pounding a bit too quickly. I moved restlessly in my seat. "Camilla, what can we do?"

She nodded her approval. "You're like me—a woman of action. And there are things we can do. Yesterday this woman was not a part of our equation, nor was she an element of our research. Now she is. We'll return to her blog and read it more carefully. We'll look into any connections she may have had to Sam and his wife, other than friendship. We have to find that missing piece. Puzzles are so frustrating when you don't know the final picture, aren't they? But it's getting clearer. Yes, it is."

"I guess I'll start reading the blog," I said.

"If you're willing, Lena, there's something else I'd like you to do."

"Of course."

"I'll start on the blog right now, but I wonder if you would go to the library. Perhaps they have some methods of research that haven't occurred to us. Focus on Taylor Brand, the Sam West trial coverage, Victoria West. And, of course, *Nikon*, our ever-elusive *Nikon*."

"Sam said that he and his investigator had found a yacht by that name. They worked for weeks to contact authorities and have it boarded. It was a dead end."

"Don't look so bleak. As long as we're hunting, we

have hope. And we have not yet begun to hunt." Camilla's face was intense, full of lively intelligence and a tiny gleam of enjoyment. She couldn't help the fact that she loved puzzles; she had been genuinely grieved to hear about Taylor Brand's death.

"I'll be happy to go to the library. I've only been there once since I've been in Blue Lake, and I would like to explore it further." I stood up and stretched in the warmth of her living room. "I'll get my gear back on."

"Do you want to lie down first? Have a quick nap? The cold tends to sap a person's strength, and you've had a difficult day."

I patted her affectionately on the arm. "Maybe when I get back. First things first."

I put my coat and scarf back on and slipped my feet back into my boots; then I made my way out the door and crunched through the snow, bound for the library on North Wentworth Street. When I spied it on the snowy horizon, I was impressed with its rather Gothic look against the gray-blue winter sky. I marched toward the building with a quickened pace, feeling an inexplicable sense of urgency. By the time my feet hit the well-shoveled stone stairs, I was determined to accomplish something—anything— that could help in the investigation.

It was quiet in the library today; that hadn't been the case at my last visit, which had coincided with a story time event, for which about twenty little children had assembled with their parents. They had a lively, loud discussion of *Skippyjon Jones*, and then they drew their own versions of Siamese cats and Chihuahua dogs to hang in the library windows.

Today no children were visible, and the few people I saw were either engrossed with computers, their heads covered by giant earphones, or scanning the enormous shelves of books. I hesitated, wondering where to start. Claim a computer myself? But I could do online work at home. Look for books? Journal articles? Something on microfiche? The newspaper morgue? But what, exactly, was I looking for?

"May I help you?" The woman before me, whose nametag said "Janet Baskin, Librarian," looked nothing like a typical librarian you'd find in a little Indiana town. She was tall and thin and wore faded blue jeans with a man's white shirt and tie, over which she wore a black leather vest. Her dark hair was pulled back into a pony-tail, and she had a number of piercings—two in each ear, one in her nose. This last was a small diamond chip, and to my surprise I thought it looked rather good with the rest of her ensemble. She was perhaps thirty years old. I might have thought she was in some sort of a cappella group or a stylish motorcycle gang, but when she talked she gave herself away. If a voice could sound intellectual and bookish, her voice did.

"Uh I wish you could. I don't actually know where to start. I have some things I need to research, but it's kind of a big task, and I have no idea how to go about it. I'm sure that sounds ridiculous."

She smiled. "Not at all. And I have the solution to your problem."

I stared at her. "Um. Okay."

She was still smiling. "Not a physical solution—a human solution." She pointed to a corner where a sign suspended from the ceiling said *Research Desk*. "You need Belinda. She's magical. No one leaves here unhappy, that's all I can tell you. She's a research witch."

"That's exactly what I need," I told her, summoning a smile in return. "Thanks."

I walked across the slightly moldy-smelling carpet and approached the big brown desk. A blonde woman sat there, typing something on a laptop. She wore a caramel-colored knit dress and a red nametag that said "Belinda Frailey, Research Librarian."

I waited for her to notice me and ask "Can I help you?" as the nose-piercing woman had done. This seemed to be a very polite establishment. When her green eyes looked up to study me, they widened in surprise. "Oh, my! I know you. Wait—I'll remember—you're Lena London!"

I stared for a moment, nonplussed. Then I said, "Yes, uh—?"

She stood up and held out a hand. I shook it. "I'm the research librarian, so naturally I keep up with all the news, including local news. I read all about you in the *Blue Lake Banner* a couple of months ago. How you're working with Mrs. Graham, our local celebrity, and how you confronted that horrible man who tried to kill you both in your own house."

"You make it sound very flattering. I did almost everything out of basic fear."

"You are modest, Lena." She pushed her glasses up on her nose. She was my age, maybe a little older, certainly not even thirty yet. She was one of those women who looks good in glasses, although she didn't seem to fuss with her appearance. Her hair was yanked back into a utilitarian ponytail, and she wore no makeup that I could discern. "Because I know something else about you. When the papers broke that story about Sam West's wife and hinted that 'a local woman' had unearthed the photograph of her, I figured that was you."

"Why did you think that?"

She shrugged. "A lot of things happened all at once. A man was found dead on the beach. Then the local police found a drug lab in a secret tunnel. Then they caught a murderer, and right after that it was revealed that the whole town had been maligning Sam West for no reason. Kind of a domino effect, right? And who came from the outside and started those dominos falling? You. I'm so excited to meet you, to be honest."

"Wow. Okay, thanks. I happened to believe in Sam West's innocence from the start."

She leaned forward, looking conspiratorial. "Did it have anything to do with the fact that he's dreamy?"

My mouth opened, then closed, and she laughed. "I'm just kidding. He is good-looking, but I'm sure you noticed that there is someone far better-looking in town. And you had to work with him a lot. Janet and I call him Inspector Wonderful."

"What?"

"Janet is the head librarian. You met her when you walked in, probably."

"No, I mean who is Inspector Wonderful?"

"That cop that you helped solve the case. Detective Heller."

"Oh, Doug," I said.

She leaned even closer. "You call him *Doug*?"

"Oh. Well, he's friends with Camilla, and so we just became friends, too."

"Friends?" Her expression was almost childlike, as though I'd told her I met a Disney prince.

"Yes. Anyway, back to the research."

She nodded and pushed up her glasses again. "What can I help you with, Miss London?"

"Lena is fine."

"Great. I'm Belinda."

"Belinda, I don't know where to start. This puzzle makes the crimes of a couple of months ago look sophomoric."

Her eyes gleamed with a new interest. "Let's go in the research room. We can sit at the table and take some notes." She lifted a little bell and put it on the counter. "If someone needs me, they can ring."

She led me to a small room behind the research desk, which contained a long wood-plank table and several chairs, along with shelves filled with boxes of periodicals. The lower shelves were lined with phone books from, as far as I could tell, everywhere in the world.

"Have a seat there." She sat across from me and set down her laptop. "Let me just open a little file. I'll call it *The London File*. Doesn't that sound like a spy novel? Like something your boss might write. Or you, correct? I saw the new book on Amazon, with your name on it. I preordered it for the library."

She talked very rapidly, I noticed. "Oh—thank you. That's very nice."

"Okay. Shoot. Why is it that you don't know where to begin?"

There were certain things I was not going to tell her: that I was Sam's new girlfriend, or that Taylor Brand was dead. That was classified information. I hesitated, choosing my words with care. "I found Sam West's wife because I believed that he was innocent, and I happened to be doing research for Camilla on yachts. But as I was doing that research, I slipped some other search terms into my searching, and some of them had to do with Sam West. I guess I felt there was some kind of connection, and so I just combined words—"

"In a Boolean Search," she said.

"Uh, I guess."

"A Boolean Search allows you to combine search terms with words like AND or NOT or OR and then to retrieve documents linked by those particular conjunctions."

"Oh. Okay, yes."

"So the search brought the unexpected result of this picture."

"Yes. But I didn't know it was Sam West's wife at first, not until I saw Taylor Brand's blog."

"Yes—I remember reading about this in the *New York Times*. Taylor was Victoria West's friend, right?"

"Yes."

"So why is this important now?"

"For reasons I won't go into, Camilla and I are still working hard to find Victoria West. Apparently the— authorities—recently had a yacht searched because it was named the *Nikon*."

She typed a few things into her word file. "And why is this important? Is it one of the terms you searched?"

"Yes. It somehow brought up her image, but I don't know why. It's not the name of a yacht, as far as I know."

"Why search Nikon?" Her green eyes were curious and smart.

"Because Sam West told . . . Camilla . . . that it was one of the last things he'd seen his wife type into her phone, and that she'd been defensive about it. This is classified, okay? Just between us."

"I am discretion. I am the *quiddity* of discretion."

"What's quiddity? That game from Harry Potter?"

She sniffed. "The quiddity of a thing is its very essence. You are the quiddity of intelligence: you write books, you solve mysteries, you delve into research."

"You're full of compliments. I'm going to start suspecting you of a hidden agenda."

She shook her head and tucked a blonde strand of hair behind her left ear. "I just like people who dig research as much as I do. I get kind of euphoric. Sorry. The whole town thinks I'm weird."

"I doubt it."

"Okay, *Nikon*. Interesting. So you are searching for—what? What it means, still?"

"Yes—and how it relates to Victoria West in particular. We need to find her."

She raised her eyebrows, but said nothing. "And what else?"

"Somehow Taylor Brand is connected to my puzzle, as well. She was Victoria's good friend and she wrote that daily blog. So I need to look at that, but I also need connections. How is she connected to Victoria? Were they always friends? Did they go to school together? Does she have any other connections to Sam West? How did they all end up in New York? I keep feeling that if I just ask the right question, I'll get the right answer."

She typed for a moment. "So our bottom line is finding

Victoria West, but we're also looking for any background information we can find—kind of like a CIA file."

"Yes. In fact the CIA is looking for the very same stuff."

Her hands froze on her computer. "So why are we doing it, too?"

"Camilla and I feel—well, it doesn't matter who finds her first, it just matters that she's found. We're not totally convinced that poor Victoria is going to be allotted the resources that the police or the Bureau might give to a more high-profile crime. They may well be doing this case on an as-available basis. I really have no idea."

"So we're all working toward the same goal, but we're also sort of racing each other?" Her expression was awed, as though she had seen an angel.

"I guess so. You're a little bit competitive, aren't you?"

She shook her head, dismissing this. "No. It won't even be close. We'll be the ones who find the answers."

"How can you be so sure?"

Belinda Frailey pushed her glasses up on her nose and sent me a bright green glance. "Because there is no one in any organization who can match the skills of a truly talented research librarian. And everyone underestimates the amount of information they can get in a library."

"You're awfully confident." I softened it with a smile.

She grinned back. "I wouldn't say it if it weren't true. You mark my words. I will help you solve your research problem, and I'll start right now. How about if we meet tomorrow, and I'll give you everything I've found?"

It felt so good, suddenly, to have an ally, especially an ally this optimistic. Belinda Frailey would apply her intellect to the problem; she would wield the library witchcraft that her colleague had said she possessed, and she would see the obvious answers that we somehow missed. "That sounds great. To be honest, I've been over it in my mind so many times, I think I'm just blind to the clues now, if they're there."

"They *are* there. If there's a connection, we can find it. I'm off duty soon, and then I can spend all my time on it and really get to work back here."

"Hey, I'm not asking you to work overtime."

She typed something else, then closed her laptop. "Work is like play to me, and you just gave me the biggest toy, I can't even tell you."

She reminded me a little bit of my friend Allison, although she was a bit more intellectual and eccentric. Still, I liked her, and her confidence was alluring. "I'm glad I found you, Belinda. Right now I feel that if you can't help me, no one can."

"You're right about that." Her ponytail had crept over her shoulder, and she flung it back with a careless gesture. "Would you like a library bookmark?"

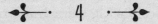 · 4 ·

*When a man came to the door, she was tempted to
hide. It was only with great reluctance that she
turned the knob to let him in.*

—From *Death on the Danube*

ON THE WAY back toward the dirt road that led up to the
bluff I was passed by a hiker with a backpack who seemed
bent on going to the scenic overlook—the one from which
Taylor Brand had fallen to her death.

"You can't go that way," I said. "It's been blocked off by
the police." I pointed to the end of the street, where some
orange cones and a couple of uniformed officers were visible.

He stopped walking and turned toward me. He had thick
brown hair and a brown mustache; he reminded me of Ned
Flanders from *The Simpsons*. "Oh—it is? Darn it. I wanted
to get some photos. This place looks amazing in winter."

"Doesn't it? Are you vacationing here?"

"For a short time, yes." He stuck out his gloved hand.
"I'm Ted."

"Hi. I'm Lena. I live in the house at the top of the bluff,
so I think they'll let me go by."

"Lucky you. So why is it blocked off? It seems like an obscure road."

"There was—some kind of accident. I don't really know a lot about it." I felt strange lying to a tourist, but I wasn't going to be indiscreet after Doug had trusted me with certain details.

His gaze wandered back to the police officers, standing sentry in their uniform coats. "Huh. Well, not to be overly curious, but did you see anything? You must have passed whatever it was on the way down."

"Not really. Just the police."

"Hopefully all your neighbors are okay," he said with a concerned expression.

"Yes—I hope so, too. I actually haven't talked to any of them today."

"I really wanted to get to the overlook—the lady in the hardware store told me it had the best view of the lake. I don't suppose I could walk up with you? Maybe they'd let me by if I was your companion."

This seemed highly presumptuous, and yet his expression was friendly and slightly conspiratorial. His nose was red from the cold.

"Are you a photographer or something?" I asked.

"Just an amateur. But I like to think I'm pretty good. Tomorrow I'm going to head over to Westvale and get some shots of their coastline."

"Ah. Well, I'm afraid you'll have to try your luck with the officers up there. I don't want to break any rules."

He shrugged, his face still cheerful. "Fair enough. Have you lived here all your life?"

"No. I'm a relative newcomer, but I do live here now. My employer lives at the top of the hill; I live with her."

He laughed. "You live with your boss? That could be a really bad scene. I would jump off a cliff before I lived with mine. Sorry—was that a bad thing to say?"

"No, I—it just reminded me of something. It was nice meeting you, Ted."

"You too. Maybe we can have a drink sometime and you can tell me about your job."

"Maybe. I'm sure I'll see you around town."

"Yeah—I'm staying at the Red Cottage Guest House."

"That's a nice place. Very homey. I've got to get back."

"See you around, Lena." He gave me a friendly wave and crossed the street.

I walked toward the bluff and the police officers consulted their list of residents on the hill. I showed them my identification, and they let me pass. I looked back once over my shoulder, but Ted had not tried to get permission to come up after all. Apparently he planned to take his picture after the commotion died down.

Camilla had been reading the blog while I was gone, and she had jotted down some notes. "All right, I have some things to share."

"Good. I think now I will have some hot chocolate. Would you like any more?"

"No, thank you. Go get some, it will warm you up."

"Hang on." I went into the kitchen, where a big coffee pot had been filled with the sweeter beverage. I poured some into a mug and warmed it up in the microwave. Then, in a fit of self-indulgence, I found canned whipped cream in the fridge and squirted some on top of my drink. Then I went back to Camilla. I sat in the purple chair across from her desk, and she sat behind it; we had done this all through our working relationship, and I had come to love the dynamic. These were our spots, and we never opted to sit on a couch or at the dining room table. When we were working, we sat like this.

"Ah." I took a careful sip. "That hits the spot."

"Warm beverages soothe the soul." She pulled her sweater more tightly around her. "I fear it's a bit drafty in this old place."

I took another bracing sip. "Okay, shoot."

She consulted a legal pad in front of her, where she had jotted notes in her graceful handwriting. "I have learned the following things after reading about three months of blog posts, starting before Victoria went missing: first, Taylor Brand is—was—thirty-four years old."

This silenced us for a moment. I sighed. "What else?"

"She had never been married, but she seems to have gone through several relationships, some with high-profile people. She last dated the son of Philip Winters, the New York banker. Alexander is his name. But that appears to have ended months ago."

"That might be interesting; I don't know why, exactly. But when money enters the picture, it's always noteworthy, right?"

She nodded. "At least in a mystery novel." She consulted her notes. "She and Victoria West had been friends for about ten years. At one point she was a model for West's fashion line."

"That makes sense. She looked like a model on her blog. And there were so many pictures of her." She had been a model-tall woman, but I hadn't realized that until I'd seen her poor broken body in the snow.

Camilla tapped a finger on her pad. "She mentions a brother in several of her posts. It seems he was also in New

York or near there. His name is . . . Caden. Perhaps we can reach out to him, if we ever come up with concrete questions."

"We should tell Doug. He'll need to notify her family." I sighed. "I don't know how he does it. Why would anyone want to be a cop? So many grim obligations."

"You're right. I prefer to keep those things in the pages of my fiction." She watched as I took some bracing sips of hot chocolate. "What did you find out at the library?"

"Well—nothing. But the librarian in charge told me that all my problems could be solved by some amazing research wizard named Belinda Frailey."

Camilla sat up even straighter. "Oh, yes! I haven't met her—she's fairly new—but Adam mentioned her once. She researched the history of his building—the one that Wheat Grass is in."

Adam Rayburn had been one of the first people I met when I arrived in Blue Lake. He was the proprietor of the nicest restaurant in town, Wheat Grass, and he had recently revealed his secret feelings for Camilla—feelings he had kept hidden since the death of her husband, who had once been his friend. Now Camilla and Adam were dating, and they seemed happy. "What did she find out?"

"Well, apparently it's close to two hundred years old— even older than our Graham House here—and was once a fulling mill that specialized in homespun goods. It had stone walls and a high, barn-like ceiling. Some of it crumbled away, which is why Wheat Grass has that lovely back stone wall but also has the far more modern construction at the front. Adam says that it was fascinating, not just what she found, but the detail in which she found it. He had tried to look into it on his own and failed to get far."

"Yes, well, the other librarian raved about Belinda and

called her a witch and magical and things. I'm hoping she is as gifted as her legend suggests, because we need a break."

The doorbell rang, and Camilla's dogs rose from their torpor and ran to the front door, slipping and sliding on the wood floor in the foyer. "That will be Adam," she said. "Speak of the devil. He called and asked if I would accompany him to the play at the community theater. I don't normally go in for amateur drama, but Adam's niece is in the production, and he wants me to see her."

"Oh—of course. I have to apologize; we had a schedule of work, but then this whole thing happened at Sam's—oh, and Doug said he would come over tonight. Will you be back by then?"

"Certainly. Adam will come, too."

"Okay. Should I tell Rhonda to make dinner for everyone?"

Camilla thought about this. "We won't be back until later in the evening. Mention that to Doug. Let's say we'll meet at eight o'clock, and ask Rhonda to just make a few snack-like things. Normally I would feel badly asking her that on the spur of the moment, but Rhonda can do that sort of thing with her eyes closed. She really is a gem."

"Okay." I set down my empty mug and grasped the edge of her desk. "Camilla."

"Yes?"

"It's bothering me that Sam never came back. This morning, we met and we both left, and I stopped at Bick's. Then I came here, and we looked at the books, and then I went to his house. He didn't mention that he'd be going anywhere—just told me to be on the lookout for reporters. But he never returned, and I'm wondering where he was."

"Just call him, dear. It doesn't have to be a mystery."

"Right. Of course." She walked out of the room to answer the door, and I sat staring at a pillow on the window seat. It was true that I could have called him at any time; my hesitation surprised even me.

I was roused from my contemplations by Camilla's voice, strident with indignation. "I most certainly will not!" she was saying. "And I don't want to ever see you on my doorstep again!"

I jogged out of the room and walked up behind her. The man on the stoop was a stranger to me; he was perhaps forty. His head was covered by a longshoreman's cap, but when he scratched underneath it I noted that he was entirely bald; he wore a navy blue pea coat and jeans. He was smiling, as though Camilla hadn't just yelled at him. "I understand your reluctance, Mrs. Graham, but the fact is that people are going to write about him one way or the other. I'm not the only reporter in town. And now they've found a dead body in his backyard. If you think that's not news, you're mistaken."

He said it in a mild enough tone, but it was vaguely threatening, and I felt as defensive as Camilla did. I stood beside her, showing solidarity, and Camilla said, "This is my assistant. Mr. West has been a friend and confidant to us for a long time, and we never once believed in his guilt, nor do we think he has anything to do with the body found in Blue Lake today."

"Even though it's in his yard?"

"A person can die anywhere, Mr. Elliott. I could walk into your yard and die there. Would that make you guilty of my death?"

"If I had murdered you, yes." He smiled again; he had straight teeth, but they were rather long, and made me think of a predator.

"I am not privy to police information," Camilla lied, "but I don't think you should be jumping to the conclusion that every dead body has been murdered."

"No. But when I hear the word 'homicide' on the police scanner, I feel confident that it has." He smiled again. I had to hand it to this guy—he was tenacious and smooth. He turned to me and stuck out his hand. "Jake Elliott. I'm with the Associated Press."

"Uh," I said. The Associated Press. Not some little Indiana paper, as I had hoped. "I'm Lena London."

"Are you from Blue Lake, Ms. London?"

Camilla's voice was crisp. "We don't have to tell you one word about ourselves, nor do we need to subject our good friend Sam West to any more media intrusions. I will call the police, Mr. Elliott, if I think you are harassing Mr. West in any way."

Jake Elliott shrugged. It was cold out, but he looked somehow comfortable in the icy air. "Mrs. Graham, I am not some crazy paparazzo who is willing to do anything to get a story. However, it is my job to find out what's happened here. It would be better for me, and frankly for Mr. West, too, if that story were told by someone who is intelligent, someone who likes and respects him, someone who understands the nuances of the situation. Do you see what I'm saying?"

Camilla hesitated. Jake Elliott made a convincing case; one way or another, Sam's name was going to get back into the papers. Would it, in fact, be better for us to confide in Elliott now rather than let the gossips have at Sam, especially if this latest murder made the pendulum of public opinion, which had only very slowly swung in Sam's direction, now veer back again in the face of fear and prejudice?

Before she could answer, Adam Rayburn came walking up the path behind Elliott. "Hello! Am I interrupting something here?" Adam asked, his eyes assessing. He watched Camilla, mainly, to gauge her reaction to her visitor.

Camilla sighed. "Adam, this is Jake Elliott, a reporter from the Associated Press. Mr. Elliott, this is Adam Rayburn, the owner of Wheat Grass."

Elliott stuck out a gloved hand. "I had lunch there. You run an excellent establishment." With just two sentences Elliott had won over Adam, whose face creased into a pleased smile.

"Thank you! We work hard to keep it that way."

Camilla nodded. "Mr. Elliott, I will speak with you tomorrow afternoon—perhaps around two o'clock? Tonight I have a previous engagement with Adam here. And I'd like to ask that you stay away from Sam West until that time, as well. If you can do that, maybe I can persuade Sam to join me for the interview."

Elliott's brows rose and his eyes gleamed with excitement. "Mrs. Graham, I would be most grateful—but I think it is a good opportunity for you and Mr. West to shape the narrative properly."

That one bugged me. "There is no need to 'shape the narrative.' We'll tell you the truth, and so will Sam, and you can tell it to the world. That's your job, isn't it? To determine what is true."

He studied me with thoughtful brown eyes; they held a hint of suspicion. Camilla seemed to sense this, because she said, "Oh, and before you go, I'm sure you wouldn't mind showing me some identification?"

His lip curled up on one side. "Not at all." He took out his wallet and retrieved a card, which he held up for our inspection. It looked authentic, and I wasn't sure if this made me feel annoyed or relieved. "You can also call the A.P. office in New York, if you'd like to verify my identity."

"We may do that." Camilla was still stiff, but her voice was grudgingly respectful.

Adam, on the other hand, shook Elliott's hand again and encouraged him to have more meals at Wheat Grass. "Mention my name to the waiter and tell him I said to give you the special discount," Adam said, ever the salesman.

Elliott grinned, nodded, and made his way down the path, looking like a mariner headed down a gangplank to a waiting ship.

"I don't know what to think," Camilla said. "I fear we can't avoid them anymore."

"Go inside before you catch a chill," said Adam, gently pushing us both backward into the warm hallway. He shut the door behind him and then kissed Camilla on the cheek. Her face grew rosy, as it always did when Adam romanced her. We walked into Camilla's office, where she had recently stoked the flames in the fireplace, and Adam sat down in another plush chair. "I'll just quickly change," Camilla said.

"I'll be here," Adam said, his voice cheerful.

I walked to his chair and touched his arm. "Nice to see you, Adam."

"You too, Lena."

"I hope you don't mind—Camilla asked me to make a few arrangements, and I have to do some of them from my computer upstairs."

"Of course not. Do what you need to do; I'm happy resting in front of the fire." The dogs came to sit beside him, sensing perhaps that he intended to stay awhile.

Rochester's ear was inside out, which meant that he and his brother had been wrestling. I tweaked it back into shape and smiled at Adam.

He did look content—far more peaceful and happy than when I'd first met him. Camilla's companionship had done wonders for Adam Rayburn. He even looked younger; I wondered if he was gradually dying the gray out of his hair.

I waved and jogged up the stairs. Lestrade, who had been so lazy that morning, was still lounging on my bed, although he had clearly taken a play break from a giraffe toy that lay nearby.

"Been having fun?" I asked.

He yawned hugely.

"That's how I feel, too," I said. I grabbed the phone from my desk, moved to the window seat and dropped into it, composing a text to Sam. *Where were you? Did you find Doug at your house? Do you know what happened? Where were you, Sam?*

It was repetitive, but it reflected my agitation, which was good. I hoped Sam would be forthcoming with the answers I sought.

I went to my laptop, where I had been researching anything I could think of to lead me to Victoria West. I tried to recall the search terms I had used months earlier when I had first stumbled upon the photograph that saved Sam from prison. I pulled out the notes I had taken initially about yachts and yacht culture. There were all sorts of interesting little facts and tidbits, but they were all random; nothing linked them to Victoria West or Taylor Brand or a yacht called *Nikon*.

I had a list of yachtsmen pulled from various Google

searches—American business tycoons and celebrities with names like Arthur Vandenhall III and Brace Lawrence Atkinson of the Atkinson Oil Company. I had accrued a list of foreign names from searches I'd done about Greek islands, some of which had popped up when I paired the search with the term "Nikon." I stared blankly at the list of nearly unpronounceable names like Vladislav Bogomolov, Zephyr Kalahalios, N. Leandros Lazos, and Albrecht Iverson. I had looked at this list before; it wasn't bringing me anything new, but of course I could show it to Belinda Frailey and ask if any of these people had appeared in her searches, as well.

I remembered what Camilla had said about Taylor's former boyfriends. One of them had been rich. What was his name? He was a banker's son, she'd said. I clicked a few search terms into Google and came up with the name Philip Winters. Ah yes: Camilla had said Taylor dated his son, whose name was Alexander.

On a whim, I searched "Alexander Winters" and "yachts." Several images and articles came up in response, one of which was a picture of a dark-haired man standing on a large white vessel called *Antigone*. I found the original page, linked to the *New York Times*.

The caption read: *Alexander Winters christened his father's yacht* Antigone *this weekend before the family took the vessel out to the Atlantic for a week-long journey.*

"Lah-dee-dah," I said. My phone vibrated next to me, and I picked it up. Sam had written, *I got home around noon. Doug was still there, and I heard the news. Still in shock. Do you want me to come over?*

I wrote back briefly, telling him about the meeting at eight o'clock. He agreed to join us, and I pushed my phone away. For some reason I didn't want to converse with him any further. I wasn't angry, but some lurking emotion made me want to avoid him.

I looked back at my computer and at Alexander Winters's smug face. I was tired of looking at rich people on yachts, tired of wondering about their secret lives, tired of fearing that some dark alternate reality lay behind these pictures, and that somehow Victoria West had been caught up in a web she had not noticed until she had stumbled into its very center, a relatively innocent fly.

If Victoria had been caught in some dark secret that took her to some far-flung island, then what had brought the sophisticated Taylor Brand to Blue Lake, Indiana? Had she indeed come to visit Sam West, or had someone lured her for reasons unknown?

Poor Taylor. She could not have known that she would meet her demise in the cold, anonymous woods of a town she had never been destined to see. Only Sam West seemed to link her to this place, and it was on Sam West's property that she had died.

How would the majority of people react once that fact became public? Might Doug consider keeping it a secret? Did Jake Elliott have to tell people where she died? Did the site of one's murder have to be shared with the general populace?

I sighed. Lestrade was still yawning on my bed, obviously bound for another nap before he played again.

"I think I'll join you," I said, and I climbed under my covers with the intention of sleeping away my worries.

To my consternation, I lay awake, and the image in front of my eyes was that of Taylor Brand, lying still and broken in the snow, her eyes directed at a sky she could not see.

· 5 ·

After the man left, thoughts of him lingered in her mind, especially the kindness in his expression contrasted with the urgency of his hand on her arm. He was afraid for her, but unwilling to say as much. She studied the gray sky outside her window and was reminded of his eyes.

It was then that she knew she trusted him.

She would run, as he advised.

—From *Death on the Danube*

WE MET IN what I had come to consider Camilla's war room: a formal dining room with high glass windows and a view of the bluff and the distant Blue Lake. The only other time I had been here had been two months earlier, when we four had met—Sam, Doug Heller, Camilla, and I—to discuss the idea that Victoria had not disappeared of her own volition. Camilla had showed us pictures, and she spoke persuasively of her theory that Victoria, for whatever reason, was afraid.

Two months later we were still pursuing that premise, and now we were faced with a new and terrible complication. Victoria's best friend had come to our very doorstep, and she had been killed here. Why? We sat solemnly around the table, along with Adam Rayburn, who had been admitted into our relatively secret society because Camilla trusted him implicitly, which meant that we trusted him, too.

I stole occasional secret looks at Sam, who tried to smile at me but instead looked miserable. He saw the writing on the wall, as did we all. The news would be out tomorrow, and Sam West's name would be back in the headlines for the third time in his life, and for the third time it would be unwelcome.

"Doug, I know you can't tell us everything, but this complicates matters greatly. We were operating on the assumption that whatever danger lurks out there affected only Victoria. Yet here is poor Taylor, who made no secret of the fact that she was Victoria's devoted friend, and now she is dead," Camilla said, warming her hands on a cup of coffee.

"She wrote on her blog that she was coming here to apologize," Doug said, wielding a toothpick and making a thoughtful set of circles in the mustard sauce on his plate. He'd eaten very few of the little chicken wings that Rhonda had put out, along with dipping sauces and various other hors d'oeuvres. None of us seemed to have an appetite except for Adam, who was clearly assessing Rhonda's cooking skills.

"She has a gift," he murmured. "I should have her at Wheat Grass."

No one paid any attention to this, and Adam grew silent, thinking his own thoughts and occasionally patting Camilla's hand.

Sam straightened in his chair. "Just to clarify, I never saw her. I didn't even know she was in town. How did she get here? Doug, do you know?"

Doug took out his phone and scrolled through some notes. "Her flight left New York yesterday morning. She landed in Indianapolis three hours later, then rented a car and drove out to Blue Lake. She checked in at the Red Cottage last evening, and had a bowl of soup at Willoughby's for dinner. She retired early. She wasn't up and around for long the next day before someone found her and killed her."

"Why?" I asked.

Doug sighed. "Listen, I'm investigating this murder as I would any other murder. After tonight, I'm not going to be able to check in with this group. I mean, I have to work independently of you."

"What about our search for Victoria?" Camilla asked.

"I'm still on board for that; but I can't be discussing an open murder investigation."

"Of course, we understand that," Sam said. "But I'll tell you all again—I had nothing to do with this. And I believe that someone wants all of Blue Lake—all of America—to believe just the opposite. It's diabolical, really, because the suspicion of me never really went away. It was forced out temporarily by the reality of Victoria's picture. But now people will be happy to retrieve it from those narrow little places in their hearts and cast me as the bad guy again."

No one said anything; it was clear that we all agreed with Sam, even if we didn't want to.

Doug studied him. "And you're sure that she didn't contact you in any way, or explain why she might have made such an effort to come out and see you?"

Sam shook his head. "No. I've had no contact with Taylor. I only knew about her blog because Lena and

Camilla showed it to me. I didn't make a habit of reading it, since she was yet another person who was willing to believe the worst of me." His lip curled slightly in apparent disdain for Taylor Brand. He realized too late that this might look inappropriate, and he held up a hand. "I know, I know—bad to admit that I didn't like her, but I didn't. She made a lot of trouble for me and that's hard to forgive. But I wouldn't murder her any more than I would harm any human being. I'm not the sort who could do that."

Camilla sighed. "Doug, what have you learned in town? Someone must have seen her."

Doug looked back at his notes. "I talked with Janey Maxwell at the Red Cottage, and she said the lady paid up front and was very quiet. Said she was friendly and tended to overdress. When Janey commented it was a cold time to come to Blue Lake, Taylor Brand said she had come to deliver an important message."

"An important message?" Sam sat up. "To me?"

"Sam," I said, leaning forward. "Did you check your mail? Could Taylor have put anything in your mailbox?"

He shook his head. "I went through the mail today. Just some letters and bills, and a parcel from you." Sam took a moment to smile at me. "Congratulations, by the way."

Doug turned away, making a point of studying his phone. He had liked me once, when I came to Blue Lake, and he still seemed jealous of my feelings for Sam, and Sam's for me. "Thanks."

Camilla was still in thinking mode. "A message. Assuming she wanted to deliver the message to Sam, that would explain why she was on his property. It doesn't totally explain why she was up on the scenic overlook; why wouldn't she have come directly to Sam's house?"

"Maybe someone lured her up there," I said. "Clearly whoever did this had ill intentions. Perhaps they persuaded her to look at the view, and then pushed her off the bluff when they knew they were right above Sam's property."

"They could have made her go up," Doug said. "Held a gun on her, whatever. It's just not clear why they did it. If they had a gun, why didn't they shoot her? Falling doesn't guarantee death."

"But guns make noise," I said, "and they're traceable. People wouldn't suspect Sam if it wasn't Sam's gun. This way it seems much more connected to him."

Adam Rayburn seemed to have finally stopped thinking about his restaurant and focused in on what we were saying. "This is unbelievable!" he said. "And so soon after another murder in Blue Lake. What is happening in this town?"

Camilla looked at him, her expression calculating. "Adam, she would have sought out the best restaurant. Did you happen to see this woman at Wheat Grass?"

Doug pulled up a picture of Taylor on his phone, and Adam studied it.

"I think I did see her, yes. With the lunch hour crowd, but later lunch. Perhaps around two or three o'clock. Must have been right when she got to town. She was sitting and doing a lot of texting."

We all turned back to Doug. "Do you have her phone?" I asked.

He nodded. "It was in her purse, which was in her hotel room, apparently untouched. I have someone going over the text messages; I'll meet with him tomorrow."

I looked past him to the tableau of cold night visible

through Camilla's window. The trees were tall black sentries against a dark blue sky; a few stars glimmered above the horizon, and the moon, a perfect half circle, was partially obscured by dark clouds. A thought occurred to me, and I brought my gaze back to the faces around me. "I met someone who's staying at the Red Cottage. His name is—wait a second—Ted! He was climbing the hill this afternoon, and he asked why the road was blocked off. He said he wanted to see the scenic overlook."

"Hmm." Doug said. He scrolled around on his phone and consulted some notes. "She has four guests staying there right now. And she's expecting another tomorrow; Taylor's brother is coming into town to meet with us and to make arrangements, I suppose. He's made reservations at the Red Cottage, since that was where his sister stayed. I presume he'll want to ask his own questions."

We were all silent for a moment. What a sad task to have to perform; I looked at Sam and wondered if he was thinking of his own family. Camilla had told me in the fall, when Sam had been arrested and things were looking extremely dark for him, that he'd already suffered greatly because his little family—mother, father, and sister—had been killed in a plane crash when Sam was just a young man.

Sam had been forced to put up with too much, and none of it had been his fault. Yet now, somehow, he felt it was his destiny to be hated by the world.

"Doug," I said. "Will you talk to that man, Ted? In retrospect it seems like he was really eager to get up the hill, to find out what happened. Maybe he already knew and just wanted to get close to his work."

Doug cleared his throat. "Let's not jump to conclusions. You know that we'll be talking to everyone, looking at everything, before we close this case. Trust that we will do that, and focus on Victoria. Sam needs you to find her more than he needs to know anything about Taylor Brand."

Sam stared at the table. "That would be true if she hadn't been found on my property. Tomorrow everyone will know that. Then what?" He looked up at Doug with a bleak expression.

Camilla touched his hand. "Sam, we were approached by a reporter today. He's with the Associated Press; I checked him out, and he's legitimate. He had initially come out here to do a follow-up story on you, but then he heard about Taylor's death, and he wants to talk to us. To you. I think it might be a good idea, Sam. He persuaded us that it might be better to have some authentic quoted responses from you and your friends than a lot of pointless chatter on the Internet. Nowadays people somehow believe gossip as news, and there's more and more of it available. He said that we need to shape the narrative, and the more I think about it, the more I think he's right."

To my surprise, Sam didn't even protest. "All right," he said with a shrug. "When does he want to do this?"

"I suggested tomorrow at two."

"Fine," he said. I could almost see the depression settling on him, heavy as the snow outside.

Doug drummed his fingers on the table. "I have to go," he said. "But I assume that you will all still be focused on finding Victoria, or any facts about her that we may so far have missed."

"We're on it," I said. "And I've got a research librarian on it, too. I didn't go into any specific detail—just gave her some topics to research for me. I'm meeting with her tomorrow."

"Great." Doug stood up. "I haven't heard any updates from the New York police, and the FBI isn't going to update anyone. So we have to just plug along and assume we're on our own unless they break something first. No matter who finds something, we win."

Adam held up a hand. "Sarah Jemmison, one of my waitresses, waited on this woman yesterday. I assume you'll want to talk to her."

Doug nodded. "I'll be around tomorrow morning. Thanks, Adam." He moved past Sam on the way to the door and patted him on the shoulder. "Hang in there, Sam," he said. Then he paused. We had all been waiting for this; we understood that Doug didn't have to speak to us at all, not while he was investigating a crime. "You will stay in town, right?"

"I will," said Sam grimly.

Doug thanked him and left the room. Moments later we heard the front door open and felt a blast of cold air make its way down the hall and into the room where we sat. "I should go, too," Adam said. He stood up, and Camilla did, too. "Let me get your coat, Adam."

They left the room, and Sam and I sat alone. "We'll deal with this," I said. "We did before, against all odds."

He smiled at me, but his expression was distracted. He was thinking private thoughts, and I realized with a pang how little I really knew about him.

"Sam? You don't have to retreat into some lonely place. You're not in it alone this time, not like before."

"I know." He pushed his chair backward; it scraped against the floor with a raw sound. "I need to find my coat, as well." He was up and almost out of the room before I realized that he didn't intend to say good-bye to me. I sat, stunned, and let him walk away. When I heard the door close behind him, I shook my head.

"No. I don't care if you are having a rough day—no." I grabbed my jacket off a nail near Camilla's door, slid into my snow boots, and moved swiftly past Camilla and Adam, who were saying their gentle and sweet good-byes.

I blinked in the shock of the sudden cold. Sam was halfway down the driveway. I ran until I caught up with him, and I grabbed his arm. "What was that?"

"Lena, go back inside. It's got to be five degrees out here."

"Sam!"

"I'm sorry. I don't know what to think, or how to deal with this. I feel like I need to go lick my wounds for a while."

"Stop it!" I said. Now I clasped both of his arms and shook him. "You want me in your life? Then let me be in it. Don't retreat into your solitary habits because you don't know how to let somebody care about you!"

He sighed, and his breath made a vapor cloud visible in the halo of light that came from Camilla's motion response security lamps. Every time the lights went off, one of us would make some slight movement that would cause them to flash back on; it had a strange and unnerving strobe effect.

"Maybe you shouldn't be in my life. Not for a while. Not until we figure out what's going on."

"Oh, sure. Let's wait another year, or maybe two years. Let's wait for a few more mysteries to crop up in the meantime. Whatever malignant force is eating away at your life is going to win, because you're letting it win." I studied his face, shadowy in the darkness, then illuminated by the ridiculous lights, its hard lines etched in the previous year giving him a closed-off look.

He didn't respond, so I said, "Fine," and turned away. I took one step and found myself spun around and facing him again. This time his face showed feeling: surprise and a bit of fear. He clutched my shoulders and put his face close to mine.

"Lena, don't be angry with me. You're the one person whose disapproval I cannot bear."

"Then *fight*. Fight against this. Talk to the reporter, go on television, talk to people in town, whatever action you want to take. As long as that action isn't sitting in your house and brooding about how your life went wrong. It didn't go wrong. It's started to turn back in the right direction, and you just don't see it yet."

The lights had gone off, and we read each other's faces in the darkness. Then with a jerking movement he pulled my head toward his and kissed me, hard. I sensed that the lights had flashed back on but I barely took notice because this kiss was more passionate than any we had yet experienced. I leaned into him, seeking his warmth, and touched his face with bare hands. "Let me come home with you."

His jaw tightened. "Not yet," he said. He saw my expression and said, "I want you there; you don't know how much I want you in my house, in my bed, Lena. I think about it every night. But they'll find us, and they'll photograph you walking out some morning, and they'll ruin it. I won't let them ruin this. You're all I have."

His stark words silenced me. The simplicity of his

request was something that I had to honor, much as I wanted to comfort him, and myself, with physical affection. "Okay. But I'm here when you need me. Whenever you need me, Sam. This will all be worked out."

"Of course it will. Now go in; your hands are freezing."

I gave him another kiss, and a hard hug. Then I turned and ran back toward Camilla's in the weird lamplight. At the stairs I turned back to see Sam's silhouette, hunched against the cold and outside of the halo of light, trudging down the rocky road that led to his house.

6

The day after she ran away, her name appeared in newspaper headlines. She became a convenient scapegoat for the crimes of her oppressors, and her absence, to the press, became an eloquent argument for her guilt.

—From *Death on the Danube*

SAM WAS BACK in the headlines the next morning; Camilla had pulled up the front pages of papers from Chicago, New York, and Indianapolis, and they all led with the death of Taylor Brand. The *Chicago Tribune* headline read "Woman Found Murdered in Sam West's Backyard," while the *New York Times* said "Sam West Linked to Another Murder."

"That's unfair—it's libelous!" I shouted to Camilla as we ate a small breakfast together. "It implies there was a first murder, when we all know that Sam didn't kill anyone and that Victoria is alive. This is absurd! It makes Sam seem like some kind of serial killer."

Camilla patted my hand in a comforting gesture, but her own expression was just short of murderous. "It is ridiculous. I think I will send letters to their editors, suggesting irresponsible journalism."

"Poor Sam. What must he be thinking? You know he's reading this stuff in his own house. We need to bring him over here so that he doesn't stew over it for too long."

"He said he'll be here around one thirty. He had some business to conduct before then. Many of his clients have returned since the Victoria story came out, and they will certainly not leave him over hearsay again. He's always been a good investment counselor, and now he's rather busy with his job, which is good. That will keep his mind off this *circus* of coverage."

I nodded. "Camilla, I thought it was all over. And now here we go again."

She sat up straight and put on her practical face. "And just like last time, we will soldier through. We really do need to talk about books today, Lena. You can mail out those copies to your father and friends, and you can mail some for me, as well. And then perhaps we can talk about the new book after we meet with the reporter. Which means we will have part of the morning for our investigation. Do you want to go back to the library and see what your friend found out?"

"Good idea. I don't know if she's had enough time, but it's worth checking. At this point something—anything— is better than what we've got."

"Don't look so downhearted, Lena."

"This is killing Sam."

Camilla shook her head. "Don't underestimate that man. Did you ever hear that line by Hemingway? 'The world breaks everyone, and afterward, some are strong at the broken places.' Sam has a few broken places, but they've made him stronger. He's not the type to wilt and pine. Believe in him, Lena."

I nodded, staring down at the table. "You're right. Of course you're right." I finished eating my eggs, took a final sip of tea, and stood up. "I'll just run upstairs to get some things and check on Lestrade, and then I'll go to the library."

Camilla smiled. "You don't need to look for your cat. He's right there." She pointed to the windowsill, warm with the morning sun. Lestrade lay right in the middle of the ledge, his white belly bright with sunlight. His eyes were closed, and his paws lay limp at his sides.

"Wow. He knows how to relax, doesn't he? Maybe I should take a page from his book."

Camilla nodded. "I've grown very fond of that cat. He is rather a day brightener. I might have to write him into the next book."

I laughed. "I think he would highly approve."

It was snowing when I reached the library. Blue Lake in winter was picturesque; if I hadn't been so worried, I would have marveled at the fat white flakes that fell like shredded paper on the old brick building nestled into a hill. I had again walked to the library, and thanks to a large, lined hood and a warm scarf tied snugly around it, I wasn't at all wet.

I marched up the stairs feeling energized by the cold air and long walk. Inside, I spent a moment breathing in the warm, book-scented air while I took off my winter gear and hung it on a coat tree near the door.

The tall librarian wasn't behind the main desk. Today a red-haired man with black-rimmed glasses stood there, staring down into some kind of catalog. As I approached, he said, "May I help you?"

"No, thanks. I need to speak with Belinda."

He gave me a thumbs-up. "Got it." Then he went back to perusing his catalog.

I walked to the back of the library and the desk at which I had first met Belinda Frailey. There was no sign of her, so I went behind the desk and peered into the research room where we'd discussed my search. Belinda sat there, dressed today in black pants and a pale pink turtleneck sweater that accentuated her blonde hair.

"Hey," I said. "Am I interrupting?"

She looked up and her face brightened. "Oh my gosh, have I got things to tell you!"

"That would be great. I need to hear some good news."

"Have a seat. Would you like a soda or something?"

"No, I'm fine."

"Okay." She stood up and went to one corner, where a small briefcase sat on a bench. From this she pulled a red file folder, which she carried back to the table. "I just printed a bunch of stuff out and put it in here. Check out the name."

A white label centered on the front of the folder read "The London File."

I nodded, smiling slightly.

She leaned in, a picture of enthusiasm. "You have the greatest name ever. If I ever wrote a book, I'd name the main character Lena London. It's so awesome—it could belong to some super spy or a woman on a cable cooking show or a singer. What kind of music would Lena London sing? I'm thinking something soft and bluesy. Sort of like Norah Jones or Diana Krall or something."

Normally I might have felt flattered that Belinda wanted to spend time praising my name, but my fingers were itching to open the red file, and this finally dawned on her. She swept some blonde hair behind her shoulder and pushed her glasses up on her nose.

"Okay, I get it. You want info. Well, I do have good news. First off, I have a theory about your Nikon. I think it's a man."

"A man? Is it his name, or a nickname or something?"

She lifted an article from the file and held it up; it was a printout of a story from a magazine called *Island Life*. "Wait—I recognize that picture! I saw it more than once when I was doing my searches. I remember those three men!"

"Yeah, this is potentially one of the nuggets of gold we're mining for. The guy we care about is in the middle. His name is N. Leandros Lazos."

"Yes! I've seen him before. He's some sort of shipping magnate?"

"Sort of. He's oozing money. The guy is so rich he spends money to hide how rich he is."

She held up the photo and pointed at him. "Can you guess what the N stands for?"

"Nikon!" I slapped my forehead. "Belinda, why did that never dawn on me? Not once?"

She made a stern face. "Because why would it? You were thinking, you told me, that Nikon was some sort of code or the name of a yacht. So why would you care what some guy's initials stood for in some blurry photograph?"

"Tell me about this man."

She held up a little sheaf of papers from the file. "Okay, I've got a bunch of background stuff. Normally librarians don't head straight for Wikipedia, but there's some information there that I couldn't find anywhere else. It has to be substantiated, which I'll try to do in the next few days.

Then I have a couple of *Businessweek* articles about him, as well as some gossip column junk. Oh, and a very interesting article in *National Geographic* about a project he spearheaded to help clean up the waters of the Mediterranean."

"Okay. So he's Greek?"

"Born in Greece, but brought to the U.S. when he was twelve. He has dual citizenship. Daddy, Aristotle, was a rich man, too, but our Nikon makes Daddy's money look like minimum wage."

"Lovely." I stared at the photograph that I had seen before and dismissed. Three men stood talking on a dock before a sparkling-white yacht. They all had graying hair, but they looked fit and tanned—men of leisure and privilege who plied their muscles in pursuit of pleasure rather than work. According to the caption, N. Leandros Lazos was the one with his foot planted on some sort of luggage, his elbow leaned casually on one knee. He had a square, handsome face, rugged as an adventurer's. He wore a white shirt with half of the buttons undone so that his firm chest was visible beneath, along with a sprinkling of salt and pepper hair. One of his companions had apparently said something funny, because Nikon was laughing, his head thrown back slightly, his white teeth gleaming. Above the three men was a sky of purest blue, with no cloud in sight.

"What kind of name is Nikon, anyway?"

Belinda lifted her pointer finger. "Hang on, I've got that." She rustled through her red folder. "*Nikon* has both Greek and Russian etymology. It means victory. *Leandros* is a Greek surname, the masculine version of Leander. Remember Leander from mythology? He was Hero's lover, who swam across the Hellespont each night to be with her. One night he drowned there, during a storm. Anyway, Leandros means 'lion of a man.' And Lazos, the family name, is a shortened from of the patronymic Lazarakis—a liberty old Aristotle took soon after he arrived in the United States."

"Huh. So what do we know about the Lazos clan?"

"Well, the old man died three years ago in some expensive retirement home. Nikon is the oldest son in the family, and he's basically in charge of the money, which he seems to have been spending liberally all over the world. As far as I can determine, it doesn't matter how much he spends; it seems to accumulate rather than dwindle. Either he has the Midas touch, or he just has a boatload of money."

"Does he have a yacht? We're looking for a yacht."

She grabbed my arm, her eyes wide. "He does! Or he did. He owned a yacht called *Apollo*, but apparently he sold that years ago. I found an article in *Island Life* about how he was looking for something new and better, but I haven't yet found the name of the new ship."

"Okay. Okay. This is good. This is wonderful, Belinda. I have so much to bring back now to Camilla."

She studied me with her large green eyes. "How do you feel about today's headlines? It must be hard. He's your friend, right?"

"Yes. And Camilla has known him far longer. We are disgusted by the media coverage. Sam is just as upset as anyone about the poor woman's death."

"Well, he would be, right?"

"Of course. She was found on his property. I'm sure you read the story."

"No, but I mean—because of their special connection."

I paused. "You mean his wife's connection to Taylor Brand?"

"Yes. And his. It was Taylor Brand who introduced him to his wife, did you know that?"

My stomach turned over in an unpleasant way. "No. How did that occur?"

"Well, because he dated Taylor Brand in college. I guess they both went to Columbia in New York. Here." She found a picture with a caption from a Columbia yearbook and pushed it over to me. In it was a very young Sam West with his arm slung around a younger, sweeter Taylor Brand, whose hair was short and sleek, and whose face was free of makeup. They looked to be about nineteen.

When the picture was taken, Sam West hadn't even met Victoria. His family had still been alive. He had been romantically linked to Taylor Brand.

"He dated her," I said blankly.

"Yeah. So it's got to be weird for him, having her turn up in his backyard. And funny that she never mentioned their previous relationship in her blog. I read entries going way back, and she never calls him anything but her friend's husband."

"No. And he never mentioned it, either." There was a strange ringing inside my head, as though someone had set off a giant firecracker, the noise of which had caused temporary deafness.

I stood up. "May I borrow this file?"

"Sure. I have copies. Meanwhile, I'll keep digging."

I struggled to be polite; there was still an empty, cottony feeling around my brain, but I managed to say, "You've done amazing work, Belinda. Thank you so much."

"Thank *you*! This is the most exciting job I've had since I've come to this library. My most exciting job period. Bring me work anytime." Her smile was enthusiastic and almost ingenuous.

"Yes. I will. Thanks so much." I waved, and somehow my feet led me to the exit, where I put on my coat and scarf.

At long last we knew what Nikon might mean, and it offered a possible path to finding Victoria West.

Despite the fact that I'd been longing for that very thing for two months, my mind could only process one fact as I walked home through the thickening snow: Sam West had been romantically involved with Taylor Brand; he had been given numerous opportunities to share that information, and, for whatever reason, he had remained silent.

I told Camilla that I didn't feel well and would fill her in later about the librarian's findings. She nodded with a shrewd expression and suggested I might want to lie down. I took the gift of privacy she offered and went to my room. I lay on my bed and stared at the ceiling. I didn't have to look again at the picture of Sam with Taylor, because the image was seared into my memory, and I saw it when I closed my eyes. I opened them at one point to find that Rochester and Heathcliff, Camilla's German shepherds, had nosed into my room and were standing at my bed, as if waiting to play.

"How did you get in here?" I asked blearily, scratching their big ears. But I knew; I had been so eager to fling myself on my bed that I had barely closed the door.

Eventually the dogs wandered back out, and I dragged myself to the bathroom to splash water on my face. I put on some makeup to liven up my pale skin, and tied a green scarf around my neck to add some color to my ensemble of a black sweater with blue jeans.

Finally I grabbed the file Belinda had given me and made my way downstairs. Sam was already there. I could hear his deep voice rumbling in conversation with Camilla, whose own polite and friendly tones were familiar to me.

When I reached Camilla's office I kept my eyes downcast, but I could feel Sam's gaze upon me.

"Are you feeling better, Lena?" Camilla asked.

"A bit, thank you. I'm sorry to have disappeared that way."

I ventured a glance upward and saw that both of them looked a bit surprised—perhaps by my tone or by my appearance. I was trying to act as normal as possible, but I doubted I was succeeding.

Camilla and Sam continued their conversation, but he occasionally darted worried glances in my direction. He looked surprisingly good, despite the change in his situation; he wore a navy blue shirt with a pair of khaki pants, and his often-messy hair had been combed neatly, curling slightly against his neck. I was torn between wanting to kiss that neck and wanting to wring it.

Camilla stopped talking and said, "Lena, do tell us what is wrong. You're glaring at Sam."

Sam looked surprised, whether by Camilla's words or my expression I did not know.

I stood up, still holding the article, and placed it on Camilla's desk. She glanced down at it and said, "Oh. I see."

"I don't," said Sam, looking both confused and a bit impatient. "Would you care to fill me in, Lena?"

"No," I said wearily. "I don't know what to say to you."

Sam's eyes revealed that I had hurt him, as I intended,

but it brought me no pleasure. Camilla handed the article across the desk. "Lena is distressed because you were once romantically linked to Taylor Brand, and you didn't tell any of us that information. This is a problem, Sam. Doug will find it to be a problem."

Sam took the article, his face blank, and stared down at the picture. "What? This? I—this was years ago! I was nineteen years old. What does this have to do with anything?"

My voice was pitched higher than I intended. "You don't think reporters will read anything into the fact that you once dated this woman? This woman who showed up dead in your yard? And yet somehow the fact that the two of you were an *item* has to come from someone else? How naïve can you be, Sam?"

"I barely remember that time; I never think of Taylor that way. We only dated for a few months." He set the article on Camilla's desk and held out his hands beseechingly. "Why should this make any difference? This was almost fifteen years ago! And it certainly doesn't give me any kind of motive for killing her. I just thought of her as Victoria's friend, not my girlfriend. How well do you know your boyfriends from more than ten years ago, Lena?"

I shrugged. "It's not just what the reporters will do. It's that we met last night, and we tried to find any sort of clue or link that we could, and you failed to mention a very obvious one. Why would you do that? Is your life so private that you can't share it with the people who care about you?"

Sam sat speechless, looking from me to Camilla and back again. "I'm sorry—I still don't see the point here. It was just a college fling. We both forgot about it pretty quickly. It was never—sexual. She was just Vic's friend, and so my friend by association. Those couple of months in college are irrelevant."

Camilla saw my rising anger and held up a hand. "I understand your confusion, Sam, but look at it this way. You don't think that your link with Taylor is relevant, but it's not what you think that matters here: it's what motivated someone to kill her. And in seeking out that motivation, we have to look down every possible avenue, even those in the past."

Sam sighed. "Fair enough. Lena, don't hold this against me. I didn't—it didn't dawn on me that my entire life had to become an open book. It's not that this was private, it's that it was irrelevant to me. It's history, and I never think of it."

I nodded. I believed him, but some residual anger remained, and I wasn't sure why. As always, Camilla seemed to read my mind. "I think Lena is afraid, Sam. She worries about you, and what the world will try to do to you with every little fact that they can use as a weapon. She doesn't want you giving them any ammunition."

Sam shrugged. "I have armor," he said. "And I've survived their weapons before."

I would have responded, but the doorbell rang, and we all stiffened. The reporter was here, and our interrogation was about to begin.

7

The man in the dark coat seemed impervious to the cold; indeed, he seemed to generate warmth.
    —From *Death on the Danube*

JAKE ELLIOTT CROSSED Camilla's threshold looking at home, once again, in the frigid Blue Lake climate. Camilla took his hat and coat and hung them on a hook near the door. She invited him into the dining room, where the four of us sat around a table and Elliott, after smoothing his hands over his bald head, as though to tame the hair he had once possessed, set up a small laptop computer. Rhonda had arrived just before Elliott, and she bustled in with a teapot and some scones. The table had been set when we arrived.

Elliott took two scones immediately and set them on his plate. He didn't seem shy or awkward, which I grudgingly admired. He also wanted to get right to the point. He typed a few things on his computer and then said, "Thanks for talking with me today, Mr. West. Before I ask anything, I'll need to know the truth behind certain recent allegations."

Sam's lip curled. "You mean about the latest murder I am supposed to have committed?"

Elliott looked surprised. "No, I mean about your alleged lover."

We all stared at him with blank expressions. "I'm sorry?" Sam said.

Elliott nodded. "So you haven't seen it?"

"Seen what?" asked Camilla, her voice crisp.

"An online news story broke this afternoon, after all of the murder stories. It was timed very carefully, I think, to get the most traffic. It alleges that Mr. West has a secret lover."

He turned his computer toward us, and I gasped. Under the headline "Sam West Seen Embracing Secret Woman" was a large photograph of Sam and me, locked in an embrace and staring into each other's eyes, our faces only inches apart. It was clear that it had been taken the previous evening, when I had chased Sam out into the snowy yard, and Camilla's security lights had illuminated our meeting for whomever might have been lurking in the woods nearby . . .

"This is an invasion," Camilla said.

Elliott shrugged. "It's not the only picture. You know how these guys work. They're not worried about hurting your feelings. They want to sell a story." He scrolled down and we were treated to photos of our whole meeting: my seemingly angry confrontation of Sam, our scowling faces as we argued, my hands clasping Sam's shoulders, and then, finally, several photos of our passionate kissing.

"Oh, God," I said.

Sam sat up straight, his expression resigned. "Fine. So now they know. Lena and I were trying to remain discreet until I could find out what happened to Victoria, but I have no problem telling people that I am romantically interested in Lena London. I didn't want it to happen this way, and that's exactly what Lena and I were discussing in those photos. She wanted to go public with our relationship, and I wanted the press to leave her alone. As you can see, they didn't."

Elliott tore a scone in half. "Fair enough. And is this a recent relationship?"

Sam nodded. "Yes. Lena was the woman who got me out of jail a couple of months ago. She had the audacity to believe in me when the rest of the world was content to watch me go down for a murder that hadn't actually happened. Lena kept digging, even when there was no place to dig, and she accidentally found the picture that exonerated me."

Now Elliott looked interested. "Is that so?" he said, turning to study me. "I was curious to know how all of that went down. We'll certainly want to discuss that now." He took a big bite of a scone and then moaned a little. "That is incredibly good."

"Please help yourself to as many as you like," Camilla said. "I fear we three have rather lost our appetites."

Elliott swallowed and took a sip of tea. "Don't let the Internet gossip get you down. As Mr. West has suggested, it's probably better that this is out in the open. It might even create a bit of sympathy for him. People love a romance. And it doesn't hurt that Miss London is pretty." He held up his hands at my expression. "That's not an insult; that's based on statistics and the reality of proven public response."

I held out my hand. "May I see the byline on that story?"

He pushed his computer toward me. I scrolled back up, forced to look once again at the photos of Sam and me. Now that I'd gotten over the shock, I saw that there was nothing scandalous about the photos; we looked like two people having an intense discussion, and then kissing each other. The pictures were surprisingly clear, thanks to Camilla's security light, and what they captured on our faces made me feel a burst of warmth and happiness in the midst of my displeasure. It was clear how much Sam cared. I got to the top of the article, where the byline read "Theodore Strayer."

"Who's Theodore Strayer?" I asked, pushing the computer back.

"Ah, Ted Strayer," Elliott said. "He got into town even before I did. He's good at being where the action is, but he's not as concerned about getting the story right as he is about getting the story, if you know what I mean. He's right here in town, staying at the Red Roof, or Red Door, or something like that."

I stiffened. "I met a man named Ted. He spoke to me and pretended to be a tourist taking in the sights. He looked like Ned Flanders."

Elliott laughed. "Ha! That's Ted, all right. The mustache is new, though. Maybe it's keeping his lip warm in this godforsaken, frozen town."

"It's winter everywhere," Camilla said.

"Yeah, but there's something about Blue Lake. I've been all over the world and I thought I was relatively used to every temperature. But something about this place—the cold just gets into your bones. It has a Siberian quality."

"Not to rush things, but can we start the interview?" Sam said. "I have a client call at four o'clock."

Elliott nodded. "Absolutely. Do you mind if I tape this interview, so that I can transcribe it later? I'll send you an online link to the tape."

"Fine with me," Sam said.

Camilla and I nodded. Elliott put his small recorder in the center of the table, took another sip of tea and said, "Mr. West, do you have any idea what happened to your wife?"

"No. But I am working hard to find out, both by co-operating with the New York police and other agencies looking into Victoria's disappearance, and with the help of a private detective who I hired when Victoria disappeared. I am, and have always been, concerned about my wife's welfare. Victoria and I were divorcing, but we were doing so amicably, and there was no ill feeling on either side. Not much, anyway. We had gotten beyond that."

"And are the police having any luck in finding her? It's been quite some time since the photograph proving she is alive was unearthed."

"It's been two months. I'm not sure about the police, but my private detective was pursuing a very promising lead that turned out to be false. It's frustrating and heartbreaking, and we are worried for Victoria. For the first time in a year I was contacted by her parents," Sam said. He didn't look at me, perhaps because he realized this was yet another thing he had not shared with our group. Would he dismiss this, too, as something that didn't matter?

"And why did they contact you?"

"They apologized. For a long time they believed I had

made their daughter disappear. Now they feel contrite, and they asked how they could help to find her."

"Would you mind if I reached out to them for this story?"

"Not at all. I don't know if they want to go on the record, but you can certainly try."

I was impressed with Sam's demeanor. He didn't look ill at ease, which described the way I had felt since Elliott had walked in.

Elliott turned to Camilla. "How did you happen to become friends with Sam West?"

Camilla folded her hands. "I met Sam when he came to Blue Lake more than a year ago. I knew of his story from the headlines, and I sensed from the start that he was a man of integrity. I have never wavered in that belief. Sam is my good friend." She smiled at Sam, and his eyes reflected his gratitude.

"And you, Miss London? When did you meet Sam West?"

"I met him on the day I moved here to work with Camilla, about two months ago. I was walking Camilla's dogs and Sam was smoking in front of his house. He's since stopped smoking. Another testament to Sam's willpower." I smiled at him, and he looked relieved.

"You didn't think he was guilty, either?"

"No, at no point."

"And why is it that you and Mrs. Graham were so convinced of Mr. West's innocence?"

I pointed at Sam. "You can see it. His body language doesn't reflect any artifice. He was genuinely worried about his wife and hurt that the world would think so badly of him. In fact, people seemed to take great pleasure in believing the worst of a stranger without any proof. Maybe this is the effect that Internet news has had upon people. They just want another headline, another scandal, to feed their voracious desire for gossip."

"Not all reporters have given up on the notion of coverage with integrity," Elliott assured us with a solemn expression. "And this piece will be a balanced story; I am not aiming for a Ted Strayer–style shock blog post."

I bowed my head slightly, but I still felt angry, thinking back. "Even now there are people who treated Sam abominably who have never come forward and apologized. Make no mistake about it, they owe him an apology. You can't treat a human being as a leper and then realize you were wrong and just shrug it off. Feel free to quote me on that," I said, my voice bitter.

Sam's smile was wry. "Lena has been a vocal proponent of my innocence, as you can see."

Elliott nodded. "Speaking of your innocence. There is a new reality to discuss, and that is the death of Taylor Brand, a woman who had publically blogged about your guilt, but who then acknowledged your innocence in recent weeks. Unlike the people Miss London just complained about, Miss Brand did apologize to you in writing, and she hinted that she would come out to Blue Lake to apologize in person. Did she ever contact you?"

Sam shook his head. "I've known Taylor for a long time. We actually dated briefly in college." He darted a look at me, then directed his gaze back at Elliott. "Then, as fate would have it, Taylor ended up introducing me to one of her friends, Victoria Wallace, and of course Vic and I eventually married. After that, Victoria and Taylor kept in touch, but I did not keep in touch with Taylor, or really anyone from our school days. I was focused on my career, I suppose, and building my list of clients. I became aware of Taylor's blog through Lena. It was a photo on the blog that made Lena realize that Vic was still alive." He paused and took a sip of his own tea. "About a week ago I learned that Taylor had made the statement about me on her blog. I wasn't happy about it, to be honest, because I was just starting to enjoy my life outside of the headlines, and Taylor's comment guaranteed that I would be in them again."

"But you never spoke to her in person."

"No. And I didn't think she would actually come to Blue Lake. I only knew she did because I came home yesterday to find the police had surrounded my property. Doug Heller told me that Taylor Brand had been found dead behind my house."

"This is Detective Heller of the Blue Lake Police?"

"Yes."

"Is he a friend of yours?"

"He wasn't. He's another person who has come to believe in my innocence, and he feels a certain amount of remorse for the suspicions he harbored in the past. He's been decent to me since then."

"How did Detective Heller know that it was Taylor Brand?"

Sam darted a look at Camilla, who nodded. He said, "It was actually Lena who stumbled across Taylor's body. She had come to my house to give me some mail, and after she put it in the box, she saw something in the woods. Taylor had been wearing a dark-colored coat, and it stood out against the snow. Lena thought it was an animal, and she went closer. She recognized Taylor from the blog photos. There are quite a lot of pictures of her there, I guess."

Elliott turned to me. "What did you think when you realized it was Taylor Brand?"

I shook my head. "I couldn't believe it. I had never expected to see her in person, and here she was, in this little town, and—it was cruel, what someone did. I felt very bad for her. She was trying to find her friend."

"Did you wonder why she was in Sam West's yard?"

"Yes."

"Did you ask Mr. West?"

"He wasn't home. As he told you, I was dropping off some mail, and I was heading right back to Camilla's, but I happened to see something in the snow. I guess my curiosity got the better of me. When I found her I called Doug Heller."

"Doug?"

"Yes. He's a friend. I worked with him on a previous case in Blue Lake, one you've probably heard of, involving Camilla. People were using a tunnel underneath her property for drug smuggling, and one of those people was shot and killed on the beach back here." I pointed to the spot where, months earlier, a man had died. "Doug investigated his murder and ended up arresting his killer right here in this house. He's a devoted and decorated cop, and I'm sure he'll get to the bottom of this crime, as well."

"For such a little town, there's a lot of high-profile crime and intrigue," Elliott said.

"Would that it were otherwise," Camilla commented, sipping her tea.

Elliott turned back to her. "Mrs. Graham, you are a

world-renowned writer of mystery and suspense fiction. Do you ever look at this complicated web of crimes over the last two months and see it with the eyes of an author? If this were a book, what would happen next?"

Camilla nodded. "I have occasionally marveled at the complexity of the plot in which we have all become embroiled. In the novels, of course, the perpetrator is always brought to justice, and he or she will be this time, too. There are many good minds working on this problem. They will solve it, believe me, and soon. It is like a book, though. We have a hero to root for: Sam West. He is the man implicated in something that does not involve him, the protagonist fighting against forces beyond his control. We also have a love interest: Lena London, the woman who devoted herself to Sam's exoneration and won his heart in the process."

I looked up, surprised, and was treated to Sam's slow smile. My face grew warm, and I became aware of Elliott's gaze darting between Sam and me. He was sharp, this Jake Elliott, and I wondered vaguely if it had been a mistake letting him into our house and our confidence . . .

"Of course there are enemies in the story," Camilla was saying. "Unfortunately we cannot name them yet, but they are there, just out of focus. There is Taylor Brand's murderer. There is whoever made off with Victoria West—we are not convinced that she disappeared of her own volition, after all—and there are the paparazzi who would purposely distort important details for their own ends. Perhaps there is no link between them, and perhaps there is. You could help us find that out, Mr. Elliott, with some true investigative journalism. Why not investigate Sam West's claims instead of pursuing Sam West, as all the others have chosen to do?"

Elliott smiled. "You would have made a good reporter yourself, Mrs. Graham."

Camilla shrugged and sipped her tea.

Elliott turned back to Sam. "Your wife has obviously made no attempt to contact you."

"I don't know if she's made an attempt, but she hasn't contacted me since the day of her disappearance, and she left everything behind—her phone, her credit cards, her purse. It's hard to believe she would plan to go away and not take those things with her."

"Yes." Elliott studied some notes that he was scratching on a sheet of paper. "And you have no idea why Taylor Brand was here in Blue Lake?"

"Not at all. I thought she was still in New York, as I mentioned to Lena that morning. We—happened to see each other in town, and I told her that Taylor Brand's blog post was putting my name right back in the headlines."

"Did that make you angry?"

Sam looked irritated. "Homicidal, do you mean? No, it made me depressed. I never sought out all this media attention, and if I had my way I would never be the subject of public scrutiny again. Try it some time, Mr. Elliott."

"Jake. "

"Try it, Jake. It's no fun."

"I believe that. And I also think it seems unlikely that you would kill Taylor Brand on your own property and then leave her body lying there in the open."

"It is as unlikely a scenario as it is untrue."

Elliott nodded, scratching out some more notes.

The interview went on for twenty more minutes. Jake Elliott was thorough. He asked Sam what he'd been doing in the year since Victoria's disappearance. He asked Camilla how long she had lived in Blue Lake, and why she had chosen to live here. He asked me if I had any angry ex-boyfriends who might resent Sam West. That surprised me, but I said no. I didn't even mention my ex-boyfriend Kurt, because he was from a lifetime ago, and it was he who ended our relationship.

Finally Jake Elliott gathered his things and thanked us all for the interview. "I have just one last question, Mr. West."

"Sam."

"Sam, if your wife returned today, this moment, what would you say to her?"

Sam's eyebrows rose, but he thought about the question. "If she has been kept away against her will, I would ask her if she's all right, and if there's anything I can do for her. If she left of her own volition, and was aware that I was accused of killing her—if she saw all that and still did nothing, I would ask her why she hated me so much that she could let me be prosecuted for a crime I didn't commit. How she could let me go to jail, perhaps forever, and not do something to prevent it."

"It must hurt, contemplating that second scenario."

"It does. As I said, Vic and I didn't hate each other. I didn't think so, anyway."

"Thank you. I appreciate your candor."

Elliott stood up and shook our hands, one after the other. "I think you'll find that this story is fair and balanced, and perhaps it will encourage the public to see you in a new way. You have some good friends here, Sam."

"I know. I don't deserve them, but I seem to have them anyway."

Sam walked Elliott to the door, then returned and gave Camilla a hug. She offered several comforting pats on his back, then pushed him toward me. "I must run upstairs for a moment. Sam, you're welcome to return for dinner; Lena and I have some work to do for the next few hours."

She disappeared, kindly leaving me with Sam. I moved around the table and into his arms. I leaned my head on his chest and inhaled the scent of him while I listened to his heart beating. He rested his chin on the top of my head and said, "I think it will be all right, Lena."

I sniffed, squeezing him more tightly.

"Hey," he said softly. "You know those pictures of us that some jerk with a camera decided to share with the world?"

I looked up at him.

"Now, don't get all angry again. I was just going to say that you look very pretty in all of them."

I shook my head, regretful. "You were right. I should have listened and stayed away from you."

"Except that you couldn't, because I am irresistible." He laughed at my expression, and then he kissed me. Eventually he added, "And since everyone knows about us now, because I'm sure the reputable news stations will have linked to that stupid blog, then I can see you all I want. So I will come for dinner, lovely Lena."

"Good. We still need to talk, and—oh! Oh, God. There's something I need to tell you and Camilla and Doug, but I didn't because I was distracted by the whole dating Taylor thing."

"What is it?"

"It's about Nikon. The library research lady found him for us—he's a man, Sam. Nikon is a man, and he's rich, and I think that makes him dangerous."

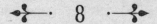

· 8 ·

Margot had long wished for some kind of clue to set her on the right path.

Now she had one, but it only made her realize how very perilous the path would be.

—From *Death on the Danube*

CAMILLA WAS JUBILANT as soon as she saw the information; she was convinced that it would be a matter of days, perhaps hours, before we found Nikon Lazos and, hopefully, Victoria West. We sat studying the files from Belinda, and Sam pointed at one of the pictures. "I think I may have seen this man once. It was one of the last times Victoria and I went out together; we did it as a favor to a friend who was hosting a charity ball. We agreed to bury the hatchet for the evening and go to support Rebecca. I think I saw Vic talking to this man!"

He turned to us, more excited than I had ever seen him. "My God, I think this is it!"

Camilla nodded. "I do, as well. It's not a coincidence that his name popped up whenever Lena searched both yachts and Nikon. It's because he *is* Nikon, and he owns a yacht, and Victoria is most likely on it."

"As what? A prisoner?" I said.

Sam shook his head. "God, I hope not. And yet how else do we explain her absence for a year? Victoria is a strong-willed woman. She wouldn't let some man keep her cooped up on the ocean all year long. She'd want to come back to the city, see her friends, see her family, work on saving her business, go shopping, for God's sake. She wouldn't just leave that behind."

"And yet in the Greek photo—she does look afraid, but not—abused. She's fit and tanned and sitting on her own. She's not in chains, or anything."

"There are all kinds of imprisonment," Camilla said. "But let's not get ahead of ourselves. Doug needs to know, and then he can notify the FBI, and Sam, you can tell your investigator. And someone will figure out where he is. This needs to happen now."

We were all in a state of near-euphoria at the idea that the long-lost Victoria might at last be found, and at first we didn't hear the knocking on the door.

Eventually Camilla tuned in, and the dogs began to bark. "Sam, would you get that?" she asked.

Sam left, and returned soon after with Doug Heller. "What's going on?" Doug said. "I only have about twenty minutes—"

"Nikon is a man!" I yelled.

His eyes grew large. "What?"

"He's a man." I held out the picture of the three men, along with the caption. "He's N. Leandros Lazos. He's a Greek tycoon, and he owns a yacht. Belinda at the library found this for me, and she's working on finding his latest yacht. He sold his yacht called *Apollo* two years ago."

Doug was still staring at the picture. "What?" he said again, this time almost joyfully.

"It is hard to believe, isn't it?" Camilla asked, smiling.

"For *so long* we have looked for a break in this damn case—" he sent an apologetic look to Camilla. "Sorry. I just—this looks promising."

"So you'll pass it on, right? To all the people who need to know. And they can go get him."

"Well, it's not quite that easy, but yes, I will."

"I feel like getting Belinda Frailey a huge bouquet of flowers," I said.

"Who?" asked Doug.

"The librarian who found this information."

"How did *we* not find it?" he asked, his face still rather shocked.

"It's not that we were bad at searching; it's that she's very good," I said.

"I think we do need to meet this prodigy," Sam said. "When it's all over, I'll throw a damn party for her."

We all stood there for a moment, entranced by Sam's words, "when it's all over." For the first time since I had come to Blue Lake and learned of the missing Victoria West, it looked as though we might actually be on the verge of finding her.

DINNER THAT NIGHT was an almost giddy affair. Knowing that we had Nikon in our sights meant that there was light beyond the darkness, and Sam was aware of that most of all.

"Once we have Victoria back, and she can tell her story to the world, then I can step back into the shadows as the man she divorced, and there won't be a clear link between me and Taylor Brand. I have no motive now, but I will have even less motive when it's established that Victoria is alive and well." He lifted his glass of wine in a toast, and Camilla and I lifted ours, as well.

"But we need to find that second yacht. It should be a matter of public record, and yet Belinda couldn't find it. That's what worries me most," I said. "What if he knew that he wanted to use this new vessel in a sort of—secret way? What if he planned for it to be under the radar, even though it's probably some huge boat?"

Camilla looked troubled. "You mean like some sort of Josef Fritzl? Planning Victoria's abduction in advance?"

Her analogy troubled me, and yet that was what I had been thinking: an orchestrated abduction. It was at least one way to explain Victoria's absence from the world for more than a year.

Sam reached out to put his hand over mine. "One step at a time, Lena. This is a victory. Let's treat it as one."

"I know, yes. And yet what about that blog post? The one with the pictures?"

Sam's smile was almost serene. "In the two hours that I left here and went home, my phone rang almost constantly. I had no problem ignoring it."

"That's odd," I said. "Ours hasn't rung at all." I looked at Camilla, who was calmly cutting her meat with knife and fork. "Has it?"

"I wouldn't know, dear. I took it off the hook."

"Camilla! You might get business calls!"

She shrugged. "My publishers, as you know, call the cell phone that they insisted I buy. Very few people have that number, and I don't need to speak to anyone who calls me on the landline. If they start knocking at the door, I'll hire a bouncer. I won't bridge the disrespect of the faux media. I have already given my story to a reporter I trust. Let's hope Jake Elliott does right by all of us."

Rhonda wandered in with a steaming gravy boat. "Let me switch this out for that other one," she said. "This one's piping hot."

"Thank you, Rhonda. This is delicious," Camilla said. "Do you know Adam wants to steal you away from me for Wheat Grass?"

Rhonda laughed as she cleared away a few dishes. "No, thanks. I love it right where I am." She turned, arms full, then turned back. "I'm going to head out now, but I'll be back for breakfast."

"Thanks again," Camilla said. "Say hello to the family."

Rhonda disappeared, but peeked in to wave good-bye a few minutes later. "Oh, I forgot to tell you. A man came over today while you and Lena were talking about books. He said he has something that you want."

"What man?" Sam asked, his voice sharp.

"He left a card—hang on." She came back in and handed a little vellum square to Camilla. "To be honest, I didn't like the look of him, so I sent him packing. I hope that's okay."

Camilla smiled. "Rhonda, I don't pay you enough for all that you do for us. Go have a good evening. You did exactly the right thing."

Rhonda waved and left through the front door.

Camilla held up the card. "Theodore Strayer," she said. "Now what could he possibly have that we want?"

"The negatives of those photos? But they were digital

photos, surely? Either way, why would it matter? Everyone has seen them now," I said.

"He's fishing for a story," Sam said. "I feel like going there and punching him in the face."

Camilla put the card down and picked up her fork. "Which of course you will not do at any point, since you would probably make that reporter's day. How pleased he would be to post on his blog that Sam West punched him—that he had seen Sam West's violent tendencies."

"Point taken," said Sam, his face grim.

"Let's go back to celebrating," I said. "We can deal with Ted Strayer tomorrow. Sam and I can go together. I have a few things I want to say to that so-called journalist."

"Me, too," Sam said.

Camilla finished eating and pushed her plate away. "In the meantime, let's concentrate on Nikon. That man is out there, and we need to find him. So what's our next plan? Doug and the other authorities will do what they do, but what can we do?"

"We can always dig further with research. I know Belinda is still hunting. We can do it, too," I suggested. Lestrade wandered into the room and began licking his paw in a casual way.

"Who's that?" Sam said.

"Oh my gosh, you've never met Lestrade! He's my special boy. I brought him here from Chicago, but he really likes Blue Lake."

"Is that so?" Sam looked pleased. "I was thinking of getting a cat once. Then I got distracted by—everything."

"You will be free of the 'everything' soon," I said.

He reached down and Lestrade gamely walked into his hand, purring loudly. Sam laughed. I had only heard his laugh on a couple of rare occasions, but I loved its youthful sound, which belied Sam's perpetually serious expression.

Sensing the attention, Camilla's dogs came loping in, and this made Sam laugh even harder. "The menagerie awakes," Camilla said with a playful smile.

In a burst of knowledge I realized that, aside from my father in Florida, my two companions at the table were my favorite people in the world.

Later I walked Sam to the door and helped him put on his coat. "Sleep tight," I said.

"You, too. Call me tomorrow when Camilla is finished with your literary inspirations, and we'll talk with Mr. Strayer in his lair."

"Okay. I'll be looking forward to it," I said, and I kissed him.

I HAD STARTED Camilla's new novel, but I needed to make some progress, so I took it to bed with me that night. Like her previous book—our previous book—it was a romantic suspense novel set in Europe, specifically Budapest, as she had mentioned. I tried to imagine a young Camilla with her husband, James, wandering through Buda's historic streets and gazing into the dark blue depths of the Danube.

I had already read the part of the book, set in the 1960s, where the heroine, Margot, learned of a plot to abduct a young woman named Sylvie, the oldest daughter in the household where Margot taught English. Margot warned Sylvie just in time for her to escape with her lover to a safe place. Now I read on to find that Margot, forced to stay in her job, hoped that the men who wanted to harm Sylvie would not realize Margot's knowledge of their plan, or realize that she was the one who communicated the plot to Sylvie.

I turned pages rapidly as it became clear that Margot had been found out. They knew what she had done, and they were determined to silence her. At this point Margot decided to go on the run, knowing not a soul in Budapest except her employers, her enemies, and a man who had claimed to love her after only a few meetings . . .

"Oh, Camilla," I sighed as I read the predictably beautiful prose. Lestrade leaped on the bed and glared at me. This usually meant that he was tired; sure enough, after a few minutes of his grumpy cat face, during which time I gently petted the ruff of his neck, he indulged in some long blinks, then curled up next to me while I read the part where Margot and the man who called himself Joe were to meet at the river under cover of night.

Despite the very exciting climax of the book, I found myself drifting away from it, worrying over the potential climax in the story I was living. Would Doug find Nikon Lazos? Would that lead to the whereabouts of Victoria, at long last? Would she need to be rescued? Who would do that? Would it be dangerous?

I shifted in bed, suddenly unable to find a comfortable position. Tomorrow, when I went into town, there was a chance that people might look at me differently. Ted Strayer was certainly going to get a piece of my mind. And perhaps Sam and I would be wise to speak to the proprietor of the Red Cottage—what had Doug said her name was? Janey Maxwell. Surely she would be able to provide some sort of concrete information about Taylor Brand.

I sighed. Lestrade was already asleep. I envied his ability to click out of consciousness and indulge in a long period of relaxed escape. I wasn't sure that I would fall asleep, after all that had happened. On a whim I reached over and grabbed my phone from a side table. I clicked it on and tapped the Internet icon, then found the story that Ted Strayer had written. Under the post, which had "like" or "dislike" buttons, I saw that the story had been "liked" by 40,471 people. "Ugh," I said.

Before I had only scrolled through the pictures; now I read the article that Strayer had posted with the pictures, and it had none of the journalistic integrity that Jake Elliott had promised his piece would contain.

Strayer began with an almost tongue-in-cheek tone:

"Those who might have thought that the much-maligned Sam West was pining away in his stylish home on a bluff in Blue Lake, Indiana, can think again. West, 35, has apparently hooked up with a local woman, originally from Chicago, named Lena London. Miss London, 27, is relatively new to Blue Lake, having embarked on a writing career as both an editorial assistant and cowriter of Camilla Graham's much-anticipated new suspense novel, *The Salzburg Train*."

"How does he know this stuff?" I asked the sleeping Lestrade, my eyes still on the article.

"It's not clear how London and West met, but clearly the sparks are flying. These photos, taken on January 10, suggest that neither member of this duo is feeling the subzero wind chills of Blue Lake."

"Unbelievable," I whispered.

"Victoria West's whereabouts are still unknown, but the fact that she is alive was actually brought to light by Lena London herself, although in news coverage back in October she was referred to only as 'a staffer in Camilla Graham's employ.' How London found Mrs. West when no one else could is anybody's guess, but these photos suggest that it might have been love spurring her desperate search.

"Police today have confirmed that another body has been found in Blue Lake, and in Sam West's backyard. Could it be that body that is causing such tension between this attractive couple?"

"Another body?" I said. There had been no first body! And why was Strayer not referring to Taylor Brand by name? But of course—when Strayer had posted this story, the police had not yet made Taylor Brand's identity public. One could only imagine what Ted Strayer would be writing tomorrow, armed with the knowledge that Sam West knew the victim.

I lingered a moment over the photographs, separating myself from the indignity of the story to realize that Sam was right—they were nice pictures of both of us, especially the one in which Sam had pulled me into a sudden passionate kiss. If I hadn't already known how he felt about me, I would have realized it from looking at these pictures. Not everyone is given the chance to see her life from an outsider's point of view . . .

This made me think of Taylor, and her blog. Blogs were strange things, because the people who wrote them might think they had a limited audience, but it was an unlimited posting. Anyone could happen across a blog post, anywhere in the world. Taylor Brand made no secret of the fact that she lived in New York, or of the fact that she planned to visit Blue Lake. Had someone been using her blog to plan a crime? Or was her death a crime of circumstance? Perhaps she surprised someone on the cliff path, doing something they shouldn't have been. But what crime could someone commit on a cold snowy cliff in January? Why would anyone be up there at all? Perhaps she had merely surprised someone, and they had pushed her without realizing what they were doing? But no: the link between Taylor and Sam, the timing of events, the friendship between Taylor and Victoria, and the location of Taylor's body meant that there was no coincidence here. Taylor had been murdered for a very specific reason.

I ran a gentle finger over a picture of Sam's face, then clicked out of the story and opened a texting window.

"Good night," I typed.

I was about to put the phone aside when I got an answering text beep.

"Good night, sweet Lena."

I put the phone back on my table and returned to Camilla's book. The man named Joe was tucking Margot into his canoe as silently as possible, because the men who sought them were just above the boat on the bridge, making their search plans.

Joe held Margot against his chest, calming her nervous trembling so that she did not cry out in fear. Somehow, in my mind's eye, Joe's face became Sam West's face, and his eyes were dark blue in the Budapest night.

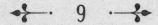

9

He had tried to warn her that the press would be cruel: that they would not care about the truth as much as they did about a story. They had her image, and they had her name, and they would do what they wanted with them.

—From *Death on the Danube*

I AWOKE EARLY the next morning, determined to do some work for Camilla before I met with Sam. I climbed out of bed, amused to hear Lestrade gently snoring near my pillow, and dashed to the shower, then dressed quickly in jeans and a warm sweater.

I went downstairs for a cup of coffee; no one was up and about yet in the quiet house, but there was a bit left in the pot from the day before. I warmed this in the microwave and took it to my upstairs space, my new and beloved home, and its beautiful wood desk, where I preferred to do my work. I sat down and began to read more of Camilla's manuscript, marking it with my green editing pencil. Lestrade, awake now, sat on the corner of the desk, taking a thorough and noisy bath. I smiled at him, then went back to work.

Camilla's story enthralled me, as usual, and when I

looked up again I saw that it was nine o'clock, and that I had been working for two hours. I got up and stretched, then texted Sam. "Are we still meeting this morning to see Ted Strayer?"

I scratched Lestrade's ears for a time, then heard an answering beep. Sam had written "Breakfast first, then Strayer. Meet you in my driveway in ten minutes."

I gave Lestrade a kiss on his fuzzy head and jogged downstairs, where Camilla sat at her own desk, flanked by a sleepy-looking Rochester and Heathcliff. "Good morning," I said. "I just finished some work on your book."

"Lovely. We're both being productive this morning."

"Yes. I'll return to it soon, but Sam and I intend to confront Ted Strayer today, and I want to do that right away."

Camilla nodded. "Yes. But proceed with caution."

"What do you mean?"

"People like that man are dangerous. Treat him as you would any snake, and be aware that he could be venomous. You don't want to make any more trouble for Sam or endanger your budding career."

"He wouldn't dare," I said.

"That's what I'm not sure of," she said. "But by all means, make that so-called journalist answer for his actions."

"We will," I said. "I'll see you soon."

"Send Sam my love," she said, and then she was back inside her work, her head bent over a sheaf of papers.

I went to the front hall, where I donned my coat and boots, and then out the door, down the porch, and to the now-familiar pebbled road that led down the bluff. The road was covered with snow, and I picked my way carefully, not wanting to wipe out on a patch of ice. Sam lived in the next house down the bluff, and I paused about twenty feet from the end of his driveway. He stood under a pine tree, in the very spot where I had first laid eyes on him.

Much had happened since that first meeting; the spot under the pine was also the first place I had kissed him. I studied him now, wondering if he was experiencing the same memories. I noted with pleasure his tallness, his messy brown hair, his jacket that gave him the aura of an adventurer, and his blue eyes, currently fixed on me. "Good morning," he said.

"We have to stop meeting like this," I joked, moving forward.

He closed the distance between us and put his warm lips on mine. "I will not stop. I intend to meet you here and many other places, and I no longer need to keep it a secret, thanks to our friend Mr. Strayer."

"No friend of mine." I took his hand and we began walking down the bluff.

A moment later Sam's hand tightened on mine. "Lena—you've said many times that you're willing to stand up to the press, but you may not realize that now you'll have to. This thing with Taylor, compounded by Strayer's photojournalism, has brought them all here like vultures. You know that, don't you?"

I opened my mouth, ready to tell him he was exaggerating, but then I heard them. Somehow they must have learned that we were headed down the hill—did they have a lookout?—and they were clamoring. "Oh, God— is that the press? Are they the ones making that weird baying noise?"

"Yes. I'm sorry. You'll have a trial by fire. The police still have the barricade up on Wentworth, and there are some officers posted. I spoke with them this morning.

The chief said that if they harass us in any way, he'll make some arrests just as a lesson to the rest of them."

"Oh, my. What should we do?"

Sam squeezed my hand and bent to kiss my ear. "I want breakfast. I'm going to offer a brief statement in exchange for them leaving us alone after that. It might work for an hour or two. Meanwhile, whatever they say to you, whatever they do to try to goad you into talking, just ignore them. Smile or say 'No Comment.'"

"Okay," I said, and then we went down a little dip in the road and there they were, straining at the barricade while two Blue Lake officers stared them down. The normally quiet street was lined with news vans.

"Lena!" a woman screamed. "Are you in love with Sam West?"

"Sam! Have you found Victoria?" A man shouted.

Another woman leaned toward me with a microphone. "Do you think Victoria West would resent your relationship?"

Then a man's voice, stern and cold. "How do you think Taylor Brand's body ended up in your backyard?"

Sam hadn't batted an eye, just kept walking, but at the barricade he stopped and held up a hand. "I intend to make a brief statement, in exchange for privacy and a quiet breakfast with my girlfriend." He pointed at me. "This is Lena London; she was loyal to me long before it was determined that Victoria was alive, and she has been my staunchest supporter ever since. Lena was the one who worked to prove, against all odds, that I was not a murderer, and she has done so. I am very grateful to her. I am also infatuated with her for reasons that are partly evident just by looking at her."

A little hum of interest from the crowd. Sam held up a hand. "As for Taylor Brand, I am extremely saddened to hear of her death. At one time she was my good friend, although I have not been in touch with her in years. I did not know she was coming to Blue Lake, and I don't know why she was here, nor do I know how she died. It's a tragic thing, and I hope they get to the bottom of it soon.

"Lastly, Victoria has not been found, but several law enforcement agencies are working on it, and I am confident and hopeful that they will find her soon. That is all; I'm sure you'll agree it was generous and that, for the most part, it's really none of anyone's business. And now I'm going to have breakfast with Lena."

He pushed past the protesting crowd and dragged me along with him. Someone hissed in my ear, "Do you trust him, Lena?"

Surprised, I turned to see who had spoken and a camera flashed in my face, blinding me momentarily. Who used a flash on a winter morning?

I turned away and followed Sam down Wentworth Street to Willoughby's, a diner where we had eaten together before. Thanks to Doug's officers, we got there without being detained by the press.

We entered the warm interior of the little restaurant and several diners turned to stare at us. Sam had long been notorious in town, and now he and I were both getting glances. Some of the faces were friendlier now than they once had been. As we were hanging up our coats, the proprietor came out from the kitchen and shook Sam's hand, saying "You're always welcome here, Mr. West," and insisting that our meal would be on the house.

Sam inclined his head and accepted with a few gracious

words, and then we followed the waitress down an aisle to a booth with a window view. We settled into our seats and I put my hands up to my hot cheeks. "What a morning!"

He shrugged, gazing down at his menu. "I've had worse."

I reached across to touch his hand. "I can only imagine. I'm sorry for all that you went through, Sam. And so are a lot of people in this town. You can tell that they're trying to make amends, if only with their eyes."

"Yes, I'm sure they're delightful."

I smiled at him. "You're funny."

"Is that why you find me so devilishly attractive?" he asked, his blue eyes meeting mine.

"Partly. But it's also because you're very handsome."

"Interesting. Go on."

I giggled. "And egotistical. I need to look at this menu. I intend to have waffles."

"I would be disappointed if you did not."

I met his gaze again; Sam and I had bonded over waffles. "I guess I'll always choose them, when we're in this particular place."

"And as tradition dictates, I will order eggs but reach across and steal some of your food."

"Fine." I closed my menu and studied him. "Are you okay? After all those questions they fired at you?"

"That was nothing. You can imagine what they asked when the world thought Victoria was dead."

"Oh, Sam."

His eyes flicked down to his menu. "Actually, none of that was as painful, in retrospect, as realizing I liked you and fearing that you might fall for Doug Heller, the Norwegian god."

I had been studying a bowl full of jam samples, and

my hand froze. "Do you know that's the first time you've called him by his name?"

He shrugged again. "Things change."

"That's for sure."

The waitress came and took our orders, and I faced Sam with a serious expression. "What exactly do we want to say to Ted Strayer?"

Sam's face closed off slightly. "Let's not ruin our breakfast. When the time comes, we'll follow our righteous indignation."

THE RED COTTAGE was actually a cluster of cottages behind one main building. They were quaint and well kept, and my friend Allison assured me that they were a tourist favorite. Sam knocked on the red wooden door, which bore an elaborate and fragrant berry and ivy wreath, and Janey Maxwell opened it quickly, pulling us inside a warm lobby filled with antiques and some over-stuffed red couches. "Come on in out of the cold and sit down, sit down," she said. "What can I do for you?"

"We're here to talk with Ted Strayer," Sam said. "We saw him earlier in the press line out there, but I understand the police have told him not to leave the area; do you know if he's in his cottage?"

She nodded. "He went back in about an hour ago and ordered a pot of coffee. I think he's writing."

"If you call it that," I mumbled.

"I'm so sorry about all you've gone through," Janey said to Sam. "You know that nice Taylor Brand was staying here before she died. I still can't believe it. Someone with so much life left to live, and suddenly she's gone."

Sam leaned forward toward her; she had settled on a chair across from our couch. "Can you tell me what you remember about her stay? Anything she said that might be relevant?"

She scratched her left arm absently. "Well, of course I told the police everything I could think of. She was a nice woman. I spoke with her a bit when she checked in, and then in the morning she sat here for a while, where we are, drinking coffee and checking her phone."

Her phone. Doug said they had found it in her purse, here at the cottage. Surely they must have found clues on it by now? "The police said her phone was in her room. Did you see her room before they did?"

She shrugged. "Sure. I make beds every morning if people are out, and she was gone that morning." She sighed. "It's funny that there was so little in her room, especially when she had told me about what she wanted to show you."

"What?" Sam said.

"She said she was excited about meeting with you. Asked where you lived and how to get there. But she was afraid you wouldn't forgive her. She asked me if I thought you had it in you to forgive, after what you'd been through. I said I was sure you would."

Sam nodded his appreciation. "But what did she say she wanted to show me?"

"Oh, she made this comment about how she needed to show you something because she wasn't sure if it was a clue or not. She said something like it was a code, and she needed you to decode it."

Sam stared at her. "But there was nothing? The police found nothing?"

"No. She just had a little suitcase, and some nice clothes

and make-up and stuff, but nothing—mysterious. I guess I was a little disappointed by that."

"Did she have any visitors?"

Janey switched her gaze to me. Her green eyes looked surprised. "It's funny you should ask that. I didn't check anyone in, and I didn't see anyone go in or out, but you can get to those cottages by just walking around this building and going down the middle path. So if cottage residents have visitors, they don't necessarily need to check in. Anyway, someone complained that morning, after she had already left for her breakfast at Wheat Grass, that she'd hosted a man the evening before and that he'd been yelling loudly. I didn't hear a thing, but I went to bed early, and I'm lucky enough to be a sound sleeper."

"Did you ever determine who this man was?"

She shook her head. "No. I never really thought about it again. She was gone by then, and I probably figured I could talk to her about it when she got back, but she never got back." She looked sad.

Sam had been thinking for a while. Now he asked, "Did the police say they found anything of significance?"

She shook her head again. "If they did, they didn't tell me."

JANEY POINTED OUT Ted Strayer's cottage, one of six that lined her little back walkway like storybook homes. Each of them had a quaint name: Gooseberry Grove, Harwood House, Caitherwood Cottage. Ted Strayer was in one called Acorn Abbey, and a little acorn wreath adorned his door.

Sam knocked, and Strayer opened the door, smiling at us as though we were friendly neighbors bringing him a freshly baked pie. "Come on in, come on in," he said. "Nice of you to stop by."

Sam glared at him. "We're not here to offer up an exclusive interview, Strayer. Or whatever you call it in your kind of journalism."

Strayer held up a hand. "Hey, there was nothing wrong with that story."

"Except that you took pictures on private property of a private event and printed them without permission," I said, indignant.

"I didn't commit libel, did I? Nothing I wrote was untrue. Just some attractive pictures with some documented background information. No harm, no foul. You both ended up looking terrific, so you're welcome."

"That's disgusting," I said.

His eyes widened. "Since you're so focused on what defines journalism, let me tell you something: element number one is called prominence." He pointed at Sam. "You're prominent." Then he pointed at me. "And you're prominent now because of your connection to him; people recognize your names and your faces, which makes you fair game for the media. People seek out stories about those that they know. That's human nature."

"It's human decency to allow people their private lives. We're not celebrities," Sam said. "We didn't seek the limelight."

Strayer smiled, like a person who doesn't get a joke. "But you are celebrities. This is a reality-TV world, and people want to know about your life. And before you complain about journalistic ethics, let me clue you in: no one cares about those anymore, including my boss. You know what those pictures of you got me? A raise, and an order to stay here until you two stopped being interesting. I've gotten other offers, too—lots of other offers. So thanks to both of you and your photogenic faces, I got a career boost. And no, I'm not sorry."

"Great," I said.

He turned to me, eager now. "Do you know how many of my colleagues at the newspaper got fired last year? Seventy-five. That includes every single one of our photographers, because they figure, who needs trained artists when we can just use cell-phone footage? I bet all those laid off photographers are glad they studied the craft for years, just so they could get kicked out and replaced by Joe Schmoe on the street, who doesn't know a wide angle lens from a hole in the ground!"

Sam moved closer; he was taller than Strayer by a head. "What's your point?"

"My point is that I still have a job, and health insurance, and a future as a journalist, thanks to you guys and the long-lost Victoria. And I will be milking this story for as long as I possibly can."

Sam said something back; I was suddenly too disgusted to listen anymore. My gaze traveled around Strayer's small and pathetic room. There was no sign of any personal possessions except for an open suitcase with a jumble of clothes dangling out, an open laptop with a screensaver of a cartoon shark swimming through curly waves, and a pile of papers on a side table.

I walked toward the windows and pretended to lean on Strayer's table so that I could "accidentally" bump the laptop and see if I could make the screensaver go away. I succeeded, and the file on the screen was a story called "The Endless Saga of Victoria West."

I scowled at it and stole a look at Strayer's smug face. Of course he had a good thing here in Blue Lake; he could simply go back over all the months that Victoria had been missing and turn it into endless exploitative stories.

Strayer was still droning on. "The news today isn't about ethics or objectivity. No one gives a crap. The news is about only one thing: ratings. And that translates into cash. And do you know how they measure ratings for my online news blog? By how many people click it. That's what it comes down to in today's journalism: the click-through."

"That's not true," I said. "People like Jake Elliott still care about the news."

Strayer sniffed. "He's a dinosaur, and he'll be the next one to get fired."

"You must be very proud," Sam said.

I leaned back, bumping into the pile of papers, and one of them fell on the floor. I bent to retrieve it and saw that it was a postcard with a lovely picture of what looked like a Greek island. Curious, I flipped it over to see that it did, in fact, have a Greek postmark.

And it was addressed to Taylor Brand.

Beyond that, there was only one thing scrawled on the card, in block letters: .R. Acie.

"Sam," I said, holding it up. My tone must have been strange, because Sam stopped arguing and looked at me, concerned. "This is addressed to Taylor Brand. And it's postmarked Athens."

The look on Sam's face as he turned to Ted Strayer was nothing short of murderous.

Strayer held up his hands, but stood his ground. "Hey, before you get any ideas, she *gave* it to me. She knew I was an investigator, and she thought maybe we could put our heads together and figure out where Victoria was."

Sam shook his head. "No, because she wanted me to solve a riddle with her." He pointed at the card. "That looks like a riddle. One word on a postcard. And somehow it ends up not in police hands, but in yours."

Strayer nodded. "Yeah. And I've been making some progress. The name Acie is relatively common, and I found fifteen of them in New York City alone. I've been working through them, trying to see if they have any connection to Miss Brand or to your wife."

Sam stared at him for a moment, then turned to me. "Call Doug," he said.

I moved to the corner and dialed Doug on my cell. He answered after two rings, and I explained briefly that we needed his help at the Red Cottage. "I'll be there in a few," he said, and hung up.

Strayer and Sam were still arguing, and this time when Sam loomed over him, Strayer did take a step back. "Listen, I'm trying to help," he said. "Why can't you see that? You two get up on your high horse and whine about ethics, but who are you to judge?" He looked at me and pointed to Sam. "*He's* married." Then he looked at Sam. "And *she's* too young for you, isn't she? Or do you just look old?"

I opened my mouth and Sam shook his head. "Don't bother, Lena. He won't hear the distinctions."

Strayer started babbling again, and we let him rant until we heard a knock at the door. Sam opened it to admit Doug, who glanced at his watch and said, "What's happening?"

I held up a card. "Might this be the evidence you should have found in Taylor Brand's room? Because Ted Strayer had it."

Doug took the card, holding it by one edge, and studied it, then put it down on the bed and glared at Strayer.

Strayer once again declared he was not responsible. "She gave it to me," he repeated.

Doug narrowed his eyes. "And when we interrogated you yesterday after a woman died tragically, you didn't think that was fit to mention? That you had evidence potentially related to her death, and to the disappearance of Victoria West?"

Strayer's mouth hung open like a hooked fish. "That didn't occur to me."

"And you touched it with your stupid hands, even though we might have been able to process it for prints?" Doug said loudly. I felt my face reddening; I hadn't considered that, either.

With a snarl, Doug took out his handcuffs and snapped them open with a satisfying sound. "You have the right to remain silent. A right I hope you intend to use." He grabbed Strayer's wrists and clapped on the cuffs.

Strayer was clearly shocked. "What exactly is the charge?" he burbled.

"Obstruction of justice," Doug yelled. "Anything you say can and will be used against you in a court of law." He took out his radio and said something unintelligible into it, then finished Mirandizing Strayer, who glared at us as though we had caused his problems.

Doug pushed him toward the door. "I have a nice squad car waiting for you. They'll process you at the station, and you can decide whether anyone likes you enough to bail you out."

Some officers appeared at the door, and Doug handed

Strayer over to them. Then he returned to the room and bent to study the card on the bed before producing an evidence bag and sliding it inside.

"It's worth a try—see if we can find any recognizable prints on it. But it's dated June, so that's a long time, and a lot of hands on it since then."

I looked at Sam. "Do you think it could be from Victoria?"

He shook his head. "I really couldn't say. It's in those block letters—she never wrote that way. But I'm guessing that if this is what Taylor wanted to show me, it was the word she wanted to ask about. Or whatever that is. This is the Nikon problem all over again."

Doug looked thoughtful. "So you think we might have to find this R. Acie the way we need to find Nikon?"

"I don't know. I have no idea. But I could kill Ted Strayer right now."

"That makes two of us," Doug said.

I pointed at the card. "If Taylor didn't bring this to you until now, it's because she thought Victoria was dead until very recently. And yet she held onto the card, so she must have known, somehow, that it was significant, and not just some prank."

The men nodded, seemingly lost in thought.

"But if Victoria wrote it," I added, "then she was under duress. Why else write only one word, coded? In case someone found it and wanted to know what it was about? This card, addressed to her best friend, was her way of giving a clue. But she couldn't risk being exposed, so she had to make it inscrutable and leave no return address. That still points to a Victoria in danger."

Doug looked at me with what seemed like grudging respect. "That's a good point. We need to add this to our list of tasks. Find R. Acie."

Sam clamped a friendly hand on Doug's shoulder. Another first. "Can you come over tonight for dinner? We owe you one for coming over so quickly."

"I, uh, actually have a dinner date this evening," Doug said, his face reddening. Then he lifted his chin with an almost defiant expression. "I'm meeting up with your librarian friend. We're going to compare research notes to see if we missed anything."

"You're going out with Belinda Frailey?" I asked, surprised. "Well, that's great! She's brilliant, and she might just be the key to this whole investigation."

Sam's look held the slightest tinge of irony. "I hear she's a lovely woman," he said.

Doug looked uncomfortable. "I need to get back. Strayer is enough like a rat that I'm afraid he'll bite through his cuffs."

We laughed and walked with him out the door. Doug waved and headed for his car.

"Well, I guess we have at least solved the mysteries behind the doors of the Red Cottage," I said, with my best guess at a Nancy Drew tone.

"Not quite," Sam said, stopping in his tracks.

"Why?"

"Because we don't know one very important thing: who was the man who yelled at Taylor in her cottage the night before she was killed?"

10

People rarely see their own lives as carefully constructed plots, but Margot had started to see hers as one, especially when that plot twisted in an unpredictable and painful way.

—From *Death on the Danube*

WE WALKED OUT the door of the Red Cottage, and I saw someone I knew hovering on the sidewalk, as though about to visit Janey Maxwell. It was the tall, leather-clad librarian I had met on the day that I had talked with Belinda Frailey. I scoured my memory for a name.

She seemed surprised to see me, and perhaps a bit unhappy to see me as well. I said, "I know you—it's Jeannette, right?"

She took a step forward and offered a handshake. "It's Janet Baskin. We met at the library, right? How are you, Mr. West?" She shook Sam's hand, as well.

"It seems we all wanted to visit the Red Cottage today," I said in an attempt to make conversation. She looked disconcerted, and then glanced down the sidewalk, as though tempted to run away.

"No, uh—I was just—did I see that reporter leaving in a police car?"

"You mean Ted Strayer? Are you familiar with him? Yes, he was just arrested," I said, not trying to keep the pleased tone out of my voice.

Janet Baskin's face seemed to grow pale. "Did—do you know what happened?"

Sam seemed to take a new interest in her. He moved closer to our conversation and said "Mr. Strayer was obstructing a police investigation."

"Oh." This seemed to disappoint her.

Sam looked as though he was about to question her further, but a black car pulled up beside us, and a tall, heavyset man emerged and began retrieving bags from the trunk with a self-important aura. He wore a gray flannel coat with a pair of dark pants and a fleece scarf.

After a moment, Sam said, "Caden."

The man looked up, focused in on Sam, and narrowed his eyes for a moment. Then he walked toward us and said, "Sam."

Sam said, "I'm so very sorry to hear about Taylor. I have no idea why she was here or what happened when she got here."

So this was Caden Brand, Taylor's brother. I watched him as he studied Sam, seeming to make a decision. I turned to see what Janet Baskin's reaction was, only to find that she was gone. I hadn't even noticed her slipping away; she was nowhere in sight.

Brand stuck out his hand, and Sam shook it. "Thank you, Sam. I'm going to take you at your word, because I always felt you were an honest person, and I've learned recently that I can't trust anything the press says about you."

Sam nodded. "True."

"Still, it's a troubling coincidence, Taylor appearing here in your backyard. Taylor dying at all." He shook his head in disbelief, and some grief flashed in his eyes. Or was that a show? For the briefest of moments he seemed surrounded by an aura of insincerity, an indefinable something.

"I agree," Sam said. "I know the police are determined to get to the bottom of things. It seems that Taylor wanted to ask me something about Victoria, and might have thought she had a clue about Victoria's whereabouts."

Brand's eyes widened. "Oh? And what was this clue?"

Sam wasn't about to divulge police information. "We have no idea," he said.

Brand nodded. "Well, I'd better park in a legal spot and go inside. I have some grim tasks awaiting me."

"Did you just come from the airport?" I asked.

Something flickered in his eyes. "Uh—no. I was actually at a conference in Indianapolis when I heard about Taylor. I just drove down."

I wondered why he hadn't arrived in Blue Lake sooner. It had been two days since I'd found poor Taylor Brand in the snow. Sam was wondering this, too, I could tell, but all he said was, "You'll want to talk to the detective in charge of this case—Doug Heller. I'm sure he has as many questions for you as you have for him."

For a moment I felt a sense of confrontation in the air. Perhaps I was just reading vibes that weren't really there, because a second later the men were shaking hands again, Caden Brand was marching his bags to the steps of the Red Cottage, then returning to his car to bring it to the lot beside the building.

Sam and I waved and began walking toward Wentworth Street. When we were a block away from the Red Cottage, Sam said, "We need to talk to Heller."

"Why?"

"This guy is suspicious."

"I felt that! But I didn't know why. In what way do you mean?"

He stopped to face me; our breath made clouds of condensation on the cold air. "He was in Indianapolis, yet he waited all this time to come here? That's a red flag. Maybe he's arriving now because he already drove out, had a fight with her the night before she died, and then left the next day. Maybe he killed her."

"You think he's the yelling man? Why would he kill his own sister?"

Sam shrugged. "Some things never change. When Taylor was in college, she always talked about her older brother. They were both rich, privileged kids, and each resented the other's existence. I don't know if things were different a decade later, but back then? They hated each other."

"Wow."

"I was glad to get away from his grieving brother act, because I wasn't buying it."

"That's so sad. She was his family."

"Yeah." Sam's eyes grew distant and melancholy, and I felt sure he was thinking of his own family, all lost to him now. "You would think that meant something, Lena, but to some people, it doesn't. Their father is still living, and now Caden will inherit everything in the will."

"Oh. Motive, then. And why isn't the father here?"

"He's old, and ill, I think. Caden will likely bring the

body back to New York, or have it shipped there when the autopsy is finished."

"The body," I said, feeling melancholy myself. Months earlier, when I had discovered Taylor Brand's blog, I had indulged in some uncharitable thoughts about her. I had assumed she was rich, sheltered, selfish, vain. But since I had found her in the forest, I had felt protective of her.

We walked back to Wentworth Street, where reporters still lingered, clearly hoping for another glance at us. I had experienced only one interaction with the press, and I was already tired of them. Sam had been right, of course, in his efforts to keep our relationship a secret.

"Oh, great," I said. "Time to run the gauntlet again."

Sam's jaw tightened, and we began to walk, but suddenly a car pulled up next to us, and a window rolled down, revealing Doug Heller in the driver's seat and Belinda Frailey in the passenger seat. She looked concerned.

"Get in," Doug said.

We did; despite the fact that the reporters took pictures and video of us climbing into Doug's car, I was relieved that we would have clear sailing up the bluff. Doug drove to the barricaded street, and when the press got too close to the car, he rolled down his window and said, "Disperse or be arrested."

They didn't disperse, but they moved back a couple of yards—enough to allow us access to the private road. I looked back to see the barricade put quickly back in place by the officers on duty. "How long will we have to put up with them?" I asked.

Sam pressed my hand. "It might be a while."

"And it might get worse," Doug said. "But we'll be on top of them."

Belinda turned around from the front seat and said, "Hello, Lena. I have some more information for the London File. That's why Doug picked me up."

"We need to talk," Doug said. "Let's wait until we get to Camilla's, so we can clue her in, too."

This was both intriguing and frightening. I looked at Sam, who shrugged. He was in the dark, as I was. He said, "Caden Brand just came to town. Or so he says."

Doug didn't miss Sam's intimation. "You think maybe he was here on a secret visit? Maybe around the time his sister died?"

"I'm not ruling it out," Sam said. "You should know they've never liked each other."

"Duly noted. I'll seek him out after we have our talk."

I felt impatient. "Doug, what's happening with Nikon? Haven't they found him yet?"

We were pulling into Camilla's pebbly driveway. Doug parked, then turned to face us. "This is the problem: Lazos is definitely out and about on a yacht, but he most likely bought it from someone else and didn't register it. Why, I don't know. He may be escaping detection by changing the flags he flies. If he's in American waters flying, let's say, Greek colors, then American ships won't detain him, unless they notice that he has an American hull number. And even that we can't be sure of."

"But he's in all these magazines and pictures," I protested. "He's a public figure."

"Yes and no," Doug said. "Belinda has actually found very few pictures of him. And they only got those because—" he pointed backward, toward the reporters—"you saw how persistent they can be. Sooner or later they get their picture. As you two have recently found out."

My cheeks grew warm, remembering the pictures that Doug had obviously seen, but Sam laughed. "True enough," he said.

"And one has a certain amount of anonymity on the water. There's so much distance to cover. Remember the missing plane in Malaysia? The one they never found? Think of how much ocean they searched, and yet that huge vehicle simply disappeared."

"But that's because it was swallowed by the ocean. Nikon is floating on top," I protested. For some reason this made everyone laugh.

"I know it's frustrating, especially for you, Sam," Doug said. "And we're about to add to your frustration. Let's go inside."

CAMILLA WAS SURPRISED to see us all, but she ushered us to our usual table, and Rhonda, who had been making lunch, brought us all coffee and biscotti.

Doug had seated himself next to Belinda, who clutched a small file. If I hadn't been studying them so closely I wouldn't have noticed the way he touched her arm, or the tiny smile that escaped her as she stared down at her folder. With surprise, I realized that the dinner they were having this evening was clearly not their first date. Had they gone out, I wondered, after our last meeting at Camilla's? I recalled that Belinda had been jealous that I knew the town policeman she and Janet Baskin called "Inspector Wonderful."

She and Doug were the perfect pair, but something about their relationship, if indeed they had one, was troubling me. I wasn't sure why.

"So what exactly are we facing now?" Camilla said, after sipping her coffee. "Clearly there's been a development."

"Yes, ma'am," said Doug. "Belinda called me this morning and said she needed to show me something. I just got around to it, since I had to arrest a certain reporter who has been a pain in my ass since he got to this town." Doug scowled. "And I have to say, you all are keeping me on my toes this week."

He did look a bit pale and tired; was it only his workload, I wondered, that had him losing sleep?

Doug pointed at Belinda. "I'm going to let Belinda explain."

She nodded. "I told Lena that I'd keep hunting for any articles or images that might be pertinent to the investigation, or that might have anything to do with Nikon Lazos or Victoria West. I kept scanning photographs from recent issues of any yachting magazines or that sort of high-life publication."

We nodded at her, waiting for the ball to drop.

"As Doug said, there are very few images of Lazos, but I did find one in an issue of *Islands* magazine. I don't know if you've heard of it—I certainly hadn't. It caters to the rich, and each issue costs almost forty dollars."

Camilla gasped and shook her head.

"Anyway, this issue had photos of a summer party thrown by some industrialist, and Lazos is mentioned in a caption. I had it blown up." She slid a photocopy of the picture to each of us. I studied mine with interest. There was Lazos, looking silver and handsome and wealthy, smiling his white-toothed smile as he held a drink in one hand and clapped a friend on the shoulder with the other. The caption read *N. Leandros Lazos, holidaying in Ithaca*

*with his friend Georgios Poulos, spent the morning at
the Monastery of Panagia Kathariotissa, saying a prayer
with his wife and enjoying a splendid view of Ithaca and
its crystal water.*

Belinda said, "It makes sense that he'd be in Ithaca,
because it's not as big a tourist destination as some of the
Greek Islands, but it's undeniably beautiful. He lives the
high life under the radar. You notice, too, that he was
'holidaying with a friend,' so that he'd be traced only to
that person's yacht, not his own."

"It says 'his wife,'" I said.

Doug nodded, darting a look at Sam. "Right. Which
means he either tells people he's married to Victoria West,
or he married her."

"Wouldn't that make him a bigamist?" I asked.

Doug shrugged. "Maybe when you're as rich as Nikon
you don't care about the pesky little rules other people have
to follow. We can't find any record of a marriage, though."

Sam sniffed. "This guy looks like a playboy. How do
we know this 'wife' is even Victoria?"

Belinda cleared her throat. "There was one other picture, and this is the one that creates a complication."

She passed out a second photocopy, and the table
erupted with gasps and shouts. In this picture Lazos, at
the same event, stood smiling with his arm wrapped pos-
sessively around a beautiful woman in a white dress who
was obviously Victoria West.

What none of us had expected was that this woman
was clearly pregnant.

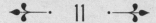

11

It was the uncertainty that she thought might kill her at the end—not the running or the fear—just the terrible, terrible waiting in the void of the unknown.

—From *Death on the Danube*

JAKE ELLIOTT'S STORY came out the next day; I read it in Camilla's copy of the *New York Times*, but it was also in both the *Indianapolis Star* and the *Chicago Tribune*, which were also on her kitchen table. I sat in the wintry light of early morning, sipping my coffee and studying the page with such intensity that I didn't notice when Rhonda arrived and started cooking breakfast, nor when Camilla left me alone, sensing that I needed to process the material individually.

The front-page picture was one of Sam standing in front of Blue Lake. It was a head and shoulders shot in which he looked human; approachable, but unsmiling. The caption read, *Sam West stands in front of Blue Lake in the Indiana town of the same name, which he has called home since his wife's disappearance.* The headline above the photograph read "The Long Persecution of an

Innocent Man." In a lengthy, many-sectioned story, Elliott
had come out strongly in Sam's defense, pointing out the
utter lack of evidence that Victoria had died, the public's
willingness to jump to immediate and dire conclusions,
the prosecutor's determination to put West behind bars
in order to serve his own career. In addition, Elliott
pointed out Sam's quiet dignity, his unwillingness to
speak badly about his wife even while he must have wondered if she had conspired against him, and the inexplicable reality of Victoria's blood, found in Sam's New York
apartment.

In a second section, subtitled "The Work to Be Done,"
Elliott suggested that the police and other officials had
real work to do. That they had done an injustice, for more
than a year, to both Sam and Victoria West, by charging
down the wrong path and leaving two people stranded,
their lives on hold, while certain figures basked in the
glory of the television cameras. The piece was a strong
indictment, especially of the New York Police Depart-
ment, the New York District Attorney, and the friends
and colleagues of Sam West who had been so willing to
turn on him when he had come under scrutiny. He mentioned Taylor Brand and the blog that she had used to
castigate West on a regular basis, her intensity fueled, it
would seem, by her grief at losing a friend.

In a final section, titled "West's True Allies," there
were two pictures: one was of Camilla Graham, sitting
at her familiar desk, looking at the camera with her
no-nonsense expression. The caption read *Novelist Camilla Graham never believed the hype about Sam West,
whom she calls her "neighbor and close friend."*

The second picture was one of Sam and me, and I had

to credit Elliott for capturing the nature of our relationship: Sam was seated, and I was behind him with my arms wrapped around him in a protective fashion. He in turn was clasping my hands against his chest and smiling contentedly. We looked utterly devoted to each other. The caption read *West's current love interest, Lena London, was the one who first determined that Victoria West was still alive. West credits her with getting him out of jail, where he had been incarcerated on a tenuous charge and with "saving my life in innumerable ways."* My face grew hot as I read the words. Then I turned my attention to Elliott's words:

"Lena London first encountered Sam West on the day she moved to Blue Lake from Chicago. Recently out of a graduate school writing program, she had snagged a job as Camilla West's assistant and collaborator. She did not like West initially, but when she learned of his reputation in town she found herself becoming his champion. She was shocked, she says, both by the intensity of feeling against West and by West's quiet acceptance of the persecution. She began to look into things on her own computer, simply Googling queries now and then. Coincidentally, she had been researching yachts for a book in progress, and eventually her two searches came together. West describes her as 'a remarkably determined person' who believed in him even after he stopped believing in his own future. London was horrified when West was incarcerated in New York; when she found the photograph of a woman she believed to be Victoria West, she sought the help of Camilla Graham and Blue Lake police detective Doug Heller. Within twenty-four hours West was once again free, and the world suddenly owed him an apology."

In a final section, titled "What Happened to Victoria West?" Elliott expanded on all of the ways that police could have followed a trail that was now cold. "Thanks to Lena London, authorities knew that West had been recently photographed on a Greek island, and were currently trying to determine her whereabouts. There was the possibility that she was being held against her will. If Sam West could ask his wife one thing, he says he would ask if she was all right. And that captures the essence of the man I met during this interview: a man of character and dignity who has no ill feeling toward the woman who disappeared so abruptly from his life, but for whom he has (along with the entire world) many, many questions."

Elliott had one last paragraph with an update that included Taylor Brand's murder. He hinted that people might jump to holding Sam responsible despite the clearly circumstantial evidence that pointed to a setup. A gray text box underneath this was titled "Full Disclosure." It said, "In the spirit of full disclosure, I must say that I knew Taylor Brand, one of the people mentioned in this article. She once applied for a job at the New York newspaper where I worked, and I had lunch with her once or twice. She was a fun and interesting woman, and while I feel sad to hear of her untimely death, neither my editor nor I considered it a conflict of interest for covering this story about Sam West."

I stared at this for a while, considering it. We had sat with Jake Elliott for hours, and he had never once mentioned that he knew Taylor Brand, had "had lunch with her once or twice." And that casual language seemed to cloak the truth. Wouldn't he, a reporter with an eye for detail, remember how many times he'd had lunch with Taylor?

I thought about this, clicking my tongue. Camilla came back in and said, "What did you think?"

"I'm relieved, and glad. It's about time someone wrote the truth about Sam, and I'm happy that Jake Elliott saw things with clear eyes."

"And good to know that there are still some reporters who care about getting to the truth."

I pointed at the full disclosure box. "What did you think of this?"

She pursed her lips, then shrugged. "It's a surprising little addition, but it doesn't change my overall gratitude. Of course Elliott hasn't even seen the biggest bombshell. Imagine what he would do with Victoria's pregnancy. Doug doesn't want it revealed to the press at this time. Hopefully no one will find out about it on their own, until we find Victoria. Poor girl. And that was months ago. Now we're looking for a woman and a child."

"Yes." A little niggling doubt came creeping into my mind, and I tried to banish it, as I had many times since I had seen the photo of Victoria. "Camilla. Do you think—is there any way the baby could be Sam's?"

Camilla turned sharply, her face surprised, and then she laughed. "Oh, Lena. Your little face! Have you not looked at the numbers? Or is your jealous heart too blinded by fear?"

"I'm not jealous," I said in a puny voice.

Camilla nodded. "Victoria disappeared in September. You located her in October of the following year. That means she had been gone for thirteen months. It is now January. Sixteen months. The picture we saw, when Victoria was clearly nine months pregnant, was taken in July."

"Yes. September to July," I said.

"Ten months," Camilla said.

"Yes—except we don't have exact dates. It could be nine months. And she could have gone a couple of weeks past her due date."

"Lena—I don't for a moment believe that is Sam's child. The timing doesn't work. But it doesn't have to be a mystery. Ask Sam. He can clarify things for you. About whether he and Victoria were . . . intimate just before she disappeared. They were divorcing, remember."

"Yes. You're right, it's not likely."

"Don't worry over it, Lena."

The phone in Camilla's office rang, and she excused herself to take it. I heard her answer, and then murmur into the phone for a while. Her tone was mainly one of surprise. I edged closer and heard her say "Yes, of course. Absolutely. I want to talk with her; Doug will want to, as well. Please encourage her to do so. Thank you, Gabby If you can set up the logistics, that would be wonderful. We're open at our end. All right. Call me back when you know."

She hung up, then saw me standing in the doorway and said, "The plot continues to twist. Gabrielle says that a woman contacted her this morning, asking if Gabby could put her in touch with me. She said she believes I have Sam West's best interests at heart, and she needs to tell us something about his missing wife. She couldn't figure out how to contact any of us except through my publicist. An enterprising woman. She was calling from Canada."

"So . . . ?"

"Gabby is going to set up a Skype session for us. She'll call back with the time. Meanwhile, we need to notify Doug and Sam, who will both want to be there."

A floating feeling overtook me then, as though reality was opening up, unfolding on itself in a way that none of us could control any longer. "It's happening now," I said to Camilla.

Because she was Camilla, she knew exactly what I meant. "Yes. And not a moment too soon."

WHEN HE ARRIVED, Doug looked a little irritated that we had called him again. I couldn't blame him; we rarely left him alone. But once he was seated in Camilla's office with the rest of us and the woman's face appeared on the screen, we all seemed to feel the urgency of the moment. It was clear from the start that she wasn't some crank caller or attention seeker. She was beautiful in a fragile way, with blonde hair turning silver at the temples, and dark green eyes. When the connection was made, she scanned the room, looking at each of us in turn.

"Thank you for meeting with me," she said. "I am so glad to be able to speak with all of you. I assume you are Douglas Heller?" she asked, and Doug nodded. "And of course Camilla Graham—what an honor. I've read many of your books. And I am so glad to see you, Mr. West, and Lena London. I read the article by Jake Elliott and I knew that I had to speak to all of you regarding Victoria West. I'm afraid you might not believe what I am telling you at first, and perhaps I am entirely off the beam. After all this time, I can't always be sure myself. My life has some surreal elements . . ." She looked into the distance, seemingly uncertain. She was sitting in a small room with comfortable-looking furnishings. In the background I saw a window that revealed sun and trees, and perhaps the hint of a mountain in the distance.

Sam spoke first. "What made you want to contact us, Miss . . . ?"

She looked back into the camera. "Oh—I'm sorry. My name is Grace Palmer. I had been following your story, Mr. West, and a few months ago something occurred to me and I thought I must be going crazy. But then when I read the article in the *Times*, I thought again that it might be true, especially when they couldn't find Mrs. West. I don't think they will, not without help."

Doug leaned forward. "Why is that, Miss Palmer?"

"I fear that Mrs. West might be, uh—detained—by a man named Nikon Lazos."

All four of us gasped, and Sam stood up, then sat down.

Grace Palmer's face was equally surprised. "You've heard of Nikon?"

Camilla gathered her wits first. "Mr. Lazos's name has come up in this group, as we pursued our own research. Actually a local librarian found him for us. And we believe that Mrs. West is with him, yes. Can you tell us what you know about him?"

She looked down at her hands. "I was married to Nikon almost twenty-five years ago."

Again we reacted loudly, shocked and somehow jubilant to have our suspicions confirmed.

Sam made eye contact with the woman on the screen. "Miss—Can I call you Grace?"

"Yes, please. And may I call you Sam?"

"Of course. Grace, would you be willing to tell us your story?"

She nodded and took a sip of water from a bottle on the table beside her. "In a way, you might be the only people in the world who would understand what I'm about to tell you. If you've been investigating this, then some of it might sound familiar." She brushed back her hair in an unconscious gesture and said "I was twenty-five when I met Nikon. We were both in Vienna for an art festival, and he was older and, to me, very worldly, and sophisticated. Oh, and he was rich and handsome, and I fell in love very quickly. And he fell in love with me. I do believe he fell in love."

I realized I was holding my breath, and I forced myself to relax. Sam seemed to realize this, and he took my hand in his.

"We were married one month later. What you call a whirlwind romance," she said with a small smile. "We flew to Paris for our honeymoon, and then we traveled to Italy, where we went to the coast and boarded his yacht. It was blissful. It was heaven. I sent letters to everyone in my family with gorgeous pictures and romantic tales. We all believed that I was about to experience happily-ever-after."

She paused again, and I sensed the tension of everyone in the room. We were like coiled springs, and I wanted to scream at her to get on with it. She sipped her water again, and I saw that she was struggling with some emotion. There might have been tears in her eyes.

"From the start he was possessive, which I, in my naïveté, found wildly exciting. Nikon wanted to keep me from the press, so there was no formal announcement of our wedding. First we lived in Italy, in a little room we rented there. Very sweet. But then we moved onto his yacht, which was really larger than I could have imagined, and was absolutely a lovely place to live. We went from Italy to the Greek Islands, and for a year we were moored off Corfu. It was a wonderful, exciting time, but I found myself growing lonely and wanting to make friends with the locals. Nikon discouraged this, saying we wouldn't be staying long, and I would just end up missing my new friends. When I would feel disappointed, he would make some grand gesture, or buy me an amazing gift to distract me. I was sad not to meet women my age on Corfu, so Nikon bought me a puppy. A delightful dog that I named Dassia, after a town we visited. She was my special girl, and I was lucky enough to have her for a long time. She learned to live on the ship; she was a born sailor." She looked up and sensed our tension. I spared a glance at Camilla's beautiful German shepherds, who leaned against her as she sat in her chair. Rochester, catching my glance, walked over to me and butted his head against my leg. I scratched his ears and hugged him against me. Grace continued, her voice almost hypnotic.

"This became a pattern; we would stay only until he saw I was getting restless, and then we would lift anchor and go somewhere else. Sometimes we were on the yacht, other times we were in foreign cities—rarely in the States. If Nikon was off on business, he would assign his friend Mike to 'protect me,' but I eventually realized that this meant Mike must watch me. Oh, he was always friendly— I'd like to believe we were friends, in a way—but he had to do what Nikon said. So if I went to town, Mike went too, and followed me everywhere. After years of this, I felt the oppression so strongly it made me depressed. I felt I had to get away or die."

"That's terrible," I said, feeling angry on her behalf.

She looked up at me with her lovely green eyes. "You should know he was never unkind. He was so attentive, so loving. Every woman's dream lover. That's what confused me—I told myself I was ungrateful, I was terrible. I told myself it was all my fault. Boo hoo, poor little rich girl, and she finds problems for herself. But I rarely had a chance to consult anyone for advice. It was hard to contact my family without someone there. They were always listening, and if I asked for privacy, my husband would hug me and kiss me and say, 'We're married! There's no need for secrets.' Except he had them; I knew he did. He made late-night phone calls on the deck, and he told me it was business. Perhaps it was. I found myself growing envious of those calls. I wanted to wander up on the deck, under the moon, and call someone, anyone, and have them listen to me. I wanted them to tell me to meet them somewhere away from the yacht, where I could walk and walk and know I would never have to return."

"You left him at some point?" Sam said.

"I really didn't think I ever could. And then once, late in summer, after we had been together seven years, Nikon went away. He said it might be a week. And of course he asked Mike to 'protect me' as always. I'd been feeling sad, because Nikon wanted a son, and I had been unable to get pregnant. We had argued about it; he wanted me to try insemination, and I was reluctant; I don't know why. Maybe I knew, deep down, that I would leave him.

"We were moored at Kavala, which is a large port, and I convinced Mike to let me go into the city and visit some shops. I couldn't take much with me, but I packed as much as I could into my largest bag—money, a change of clothes, my passport, some food. I put a leash on Dassia and persuaded Mike that the poor dog never got to stand on solid ground, and she should be allowed to go with us. He agreed, and we set off down the gangplank."

Sam's hand tightened on mine; Doug kept changing position in his chair. Camilla sat still and serene, as though her soul had left her body, but her eyes were locked on the screen. Grace smiled ruefully.

"Poor Mike never guessed I would betray him. We laughed and talked as we walked down a main street, and then I saw an alley full of outdoor vendors; I asked if I could buy a shawl, and he said yes, he would have a cigarette and wait for me. I walked into the alley at a leisurely pace, but by midway through I was running, with Dassia at my side, running as hard as I could, and then I was out the other side and twisting through the streets until I was sure I had lost him. But I knew I had very little time. I found an outdoor bar where it seemed many of the sailors were gathering. I sat at a table and ordered some ouzo and some bread for my dog, and I listened. I picked out a couple of voices that were American, and one of them spoke of getting back to his ship, which was ready to sail. He said he would be back in New York, and back to his wife and children, by morning. I waited until his friends left, and then I went to his table. I still remember the surprised look on his face. I asked him how much money it would take for me to get a ride to New York for my dog and me, no questions asked. The saddest thing is, I could tell he felt sorry for me. And it was that compassion that made me want to cry.

"He had no idea how rich I was. I had twenty thousand dollars in my bag, but he asked me for two hundred. He said he wanted to buy something nice for his wife and his daughters. I said I'd give him that and more when we got there safely. He agreed. I followed him to his boat, which was just a cargo ship, but it was more beautiful to me than the yacht had ever been. He made a makeshift seat for Dassia and me against some pallets, and we sat together and waited to start our new life."

"You were very brave, Grace," Doug said.

She shook her head, her expression mystified. "To this day, I don't know exactly what motivated me, or how I felt. I called my parents when I got to New York and said I wanted a divorce. They were relieved. They had been troubled by the lack of communication, and they'd missed me, as had my siblings and friends. I had many joyful reunions."

"Did Lazos contest it?"

"Oh, Nikon." She wiped at her eyes. "You have to understand. He is a collector. He had many beautiful art collections on his yacht and in his various homes. He liked to keep things to himself, and that was true of me, as well. He loves all of his collections passionately. But once I was gone, he saw that I had been tainted, I suppose, by the outside world. I think it was that which made him more willing to let me go. He granted the divorce. I never spoke to him again."

"What happened to Mike?" Camilla asked.

"Yes, I was worried about that. I feared Nikon might

punish him in some way. But I followed stories about him in the news, when they were there, and I saw Mike in the pictures at his side, as always. The two of them still seem to be the great confidants they always were. And there is a part of me that wonders if Mike knew I was trying to get away. If he let me do so."

"Why would he let you get away?" Doug said.

"Because I couldn't bear a child," she said. "I wonder if Nikon was willing to give me up for a—more improved model. But as far as I knew he never married again. He had women, many women, but Victoria is the first one who reminds me of me." She drank water again; her voice had become a bit husky with the telling of her story.

"Did you marry again?" I asked.

Her face brightened and softened into affection. "I did. My husband and our sons kindly took a walk so that I could make this phone call. And in case you are wondering, no, I did not need a fertility specialist to conceive my boys. I asked my doctor about this, and she said that women under extreme stress can have trouble conceiving. For a long time I didn't know I was living under stress, but I think my body did."

"I'm glad to hear about your family," I said. "I hope you're happy."

She smiled. "I am."

"Why do you think Victoria is with Nikon?" Doug said.

She nodded. "So many things seem to fit the pattern. Her sudden and inexplicable disappearance. Nikon was big on passionate, spontaneous gestures. Her photograph on a Greek island, but their inability to trace it. I looked that photo up online, and her face reminded me so much of the way mine once looked in the mirror. Happy on the surface, but so very sad and lonely in the eyes. And of course there is the unexplained fact of her blood in Mr. West's apartment. That has Nikon written all over it."

"Explain," Sam said, his jaw tight.

"Nikon went to great lengths to preserve his illusions. Or in this case, an illusion he might want the world to believe, assuming Victoria West is his newest collector's item."

"Will he hurt her?" Doug asked.

She looked surprised. "Oh, no, he would never hurt her. He probably loves her very much. Nikon is full of emotion."

Her eyes wandered the room, and she lingered on each of our faces in turn, making sure she had our attention. "But here is a testament to the power of his charisma: I left Nikon eighteen years ago, and I never looked back. But there is a part of me that is still in love with him, and always will be."

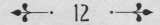

12

*Margot had never been more aware of her family,
and her love for them, now that they were utterly
out of reach. She could hear her mother's soft voice
in her head, her father's hearty laugh. At night,
when she climbed into her lonely bed, she sighed
over all the moments she had taken for granted.*
　　　　　　　　　　—From *Death on the Danube*

BEFORE GRACE SIGNED off, Doug asked her if she knew
anyone named Acie, and she frowned. "Is that a first name
or a last?"

"Last, we think."

She shook her head. "Either way, I don't know the
name. It doesn't even sound like a real name. More like
a made-up one."

It was a name, though. Sam and I had looked in the
white pages and found many Acies across the United
States and beyond.

"Thank you so much for your call," Sam told her. "And
for reaching out to help Victoria."

She sent him an intense, green-eyed stare. "If Victoria
is with Nikon, my wish for her is that she gets away as
soon as possible. It's been more than a year now, yes? The
first few months, she probably didn't realize that she was

essentially a prisoner. He is wonderful at distractions. She probably didn't even question his refusal to let her use the Internet on the yacht. He probably told her they had no access. I'm guessing now, because there was no Internet when I was with him. But I assume he has his own office with working Wi-Fi, and that his lovely Victoria is forced to do without, like a woman in another time. And she would accept this, because he would make it seem natural. That is his gift. He can sell anything and make it look beautiful."

Doug was staring at her with an intense expression and occasionally texting notes into his phone. Now he said, "What was the name of the yacht you boarded, back when you married him?"

"It was called the *Cassandra*. Then later he bought a larger one called the *Apollo*. Is that helpful at all?"

We looked at Doug, who shook his head. "He sold that ship five years ago. We think he has purchased another one, perhaps secondhand, and that it may be registered in someone else's name. Do you know of any friends who might have made this arrangement with him?"

She sighed. "I can't help you, I'm afraid. Nikon had so many friends, and I got to know very few of them. But I wasn't the only one under his spell. So many people who would do anything for him. The power of personality."

Doug scowled at this, and Sam sniffed his disapproval.

Camilla lifted a hand. "Is there a chance that we're looking in the wrong place, and that they're not on the water at all?"

Grace didn't even think about this. She shook her head. "Nikon can never be far away from the sea. He must have captained a ship in some past life, because he yearns for the water. Once in a while, when we would dock and find ourselves a house for a time, I'd beg Nikon to let us stay there, to live on land because I liked it so much better. He would get this look in his eyes—half disbelieving and half fearful—and then launch into his favorite speech about how ships were meant to be sailed, and he hadn't spent millions on his yacht just to let it rust in harbor."

Doug typed a couple more things into his phone and then stood up. "Grace, might I ask you to remain available for the foreseeable future?"

"Of course," she said graciously.

"You have Camilla's contact information—let me give you mine," Doug said. He gave her his number, and then she said good-bye to all of us and ended the call.

Doug was still standing. He turned to us, his expression hard. "We know we're right, and Grace has proven that we're right. I've been feeling that our friends in the CIA have not been making this a priority. Maybe they figured they'd leave it to the NYPD, who obviously don't have the resources to catch someone like Lazos. I need to make some calls. Camilla, thanks for contacting me. Someday I would like to come here just to eat Rhonda's cooking and not to have to worry about crime."

Camilla patted his arm. "Thank goodness you're on the job, Doug. Let me walk you to the door."

Sam and I sat together, thinking our thoughts, and his phone buzzed. He looked down at it, read a text message, and laughed. Then he clicked it off and put his arm around me. "Doug seems disturbed, but you know what? I feel good. They'll find Lazos soon, I can feel it. I could be in jail right now, and instead I'm with you." He squeezed me hard and kissed my cheek. "And thanks to

Jake Elliott's story, I am getting the most interesting calls and text messages—literally from all over the world. I have to say it is refreshing to have people praising me instead of sending me death threats."

"They sent you death threats?"

He patted my hair. "This is the twenty-first century, Lena. People send death threats even when you don't agree with their politics, never mind when they think you've killed your wife. It's a strange world."

"Yes." I sighed, not really feeling Sam's euphoria.

"Hey." He waited until I looked into his eyes. "I want to throw a little party. At my house. Invite some people who have been supportive. My social instincts are returning at long last. Will you help me?"

"Um—of course I will. Aren't you afraid of what people will say—since Taylor was so recently found, and since Victoria hasn't been? Aren't you afraid you'll get more death threats?"

Sam sat up straighter. "No. I really want to do this. I'm sick of being depressed. It's time to let people in again. And you can wear a pretty dress and stand by my side, and we'll share some good wine and good food with our friends. Doesn't that sound nice?"

Now his mood was rubbing off on me, just a little. "Yes, okay."

"Great. We'll plan it soon. What do you have to do now?"

I glanced at the doorway. "I have to work. Camilla is always so accommodating of these other things in our lives, but she pays me generously, and I haven't made much progress on her new book. I need to get up to my computer."

He leaned in and kissed me softly. "Okay. I'll work, too. Since we're being industrious."

He stood up. "I'll go say my good-byes, too. Call me if you get lonely." He flashed me one of his surprising smiles; it made him look dangerous and sexy.

I waved and watched him walk away.

UPSTAIRS I WORKED for two hours, reading Camilla's book and making my notes, then typing reports. Her story was as suspenseful as always, but I felt that some scenes were slightly too long, and I had ideas for ways to keep the pace more rapid.

When my eyes grew tired, I leaned back in my chair. My head was immediately invaded by some of the worries I had been keeping to the background. I had forgotten to ask Doug about Ted Strayer. Was he in jail? Or would his paper, supposedly so enraptured with his nosy reporting, have bailed him out so that he could continue with his muckraking? And what about Taylor's brother, Caden? He had put on quite an act at the Red Cottage, managing to suggest he was a grieving brother who half suspected that Sam had something to do with his sister's death. And yet, the more I thought about it, the less I believed in the performance. Caden Brand had struck me as insincere and rather obnoxious, and if, as Sam had suggested, he hated his sister, might he himself have had something to do with her murder?

And then there had been Janet Baskin. She had appeared outside the Red Cottage, but had frozen there while all the chaos went on—Doug had taken Ted Strayer away and Caden Brand had arrived with his bluster and bellow. Something about her expression had been strange. Had she seen something that bothered her? Had she felt frightened? Guilty? Whatever the case, she had disappeared quickly rather than staying to talk to any of us.

My thoughts disturbed me enough to propel me out of my chair, seeking a view out my window, where the white, snowy world and the cold expanse of Blue Lake calmed my mind. Lestrade jumped on the windowsill and started purring. I picked him up and cuddled him for a while. It's true that animals make you feel better. It was impossible to hug my fuzzy cat and not experience a lifting of the spirits. "Thanks," I said into his fur. He wiggled, and I let him go. He hopped back onto the windowsill, his eyes intent on some creature I could not see. Did mice ever hop along the snow, or did they hibernate? This was a question I had never contemplated.

My phone rang, interrupting my racing thoughts. I clicked it without looking, assuming it was Sam. "Did you give up on working?" I said.

"I'm retired, but I think you've been pretty busy," said a familiar voice.

"Dad!"

"Hey, sweetie. I thought I should check in."

"I'm so sorry I haven't called in a while. Things have been crazy here. I suppose you've . . . seen some stuff in the paper."

"I saw that there's been another murder. And that you discovered the body."

"Yes." For the thousandth time, I tried not to picture Taylor Brand.

"Are you all right?"

"Yes. In and out. I try not to think about the bad stuff. There are good things, too, and I distract myself with them."

"I saw some pictures of that, as well. Your stepmother happened to find them online."

"Sorry about that."

"Why? They're very nice photographs. That's a dashing young man that you've found for yourself."

"He's a good man, Dad. Did you read the piece in the *New York Times* today? Or maybe it was in your Florida paper? It was a profile by a writer named Jake Elliott."

"Yes, we read it. Tabitha Googles your name each day, just looking for updates on our girl."

I had never gotten to know Tabitha very well, but I was flattered by her devotion to me. She had no children of her own, so I think she found it exciting to have earned a daughter late in life, even if I was not authentically hers.

My eyes were back on the snow outside. "I want you both to know that Sam is a good man, and if he had his way he would not be the center of this media circus."

My father took a sip of something—perhaps a cup of coffee. "Honey, we trust that anyone you choose as a friend is a person of value."

"I love you, Dad."

"However, we do not plan to wait much longer before we meet this gentleman for ourselves. We've been waiting since October, as you may recall."

"I know. If you can just hold off until it's not quite so cold—then hopefully they'll have found Victoria, and solved the murder of Taylor Brand, and cleared Sam's name once and for all. We'll be so ready to celebrate!"

"Or maybe you two would like to come down to Florida. It's nice and warm here, honey. We can't even imagine snow. It's a distant memory."

"That sounds great, Dad." I had a sudden image of a

sandy beach and a blue sky beyond it, dotted with white scudding clouds. In the forefront of this fantasy stood a new and different Sam West: bare-chested, carefree, smiling like a boy. "It really sounds wonderful. But it will have to wait until spring. I'm sure I can work it out with Camilla."

"Bring her along," said my ever-amiable father. "I'd love to meet her. Tabby and I have been reading her books—they're really something. Oh, and Tab blew up that cover you sent us to poster size and we had it framed. It's in the office. It's gorgeous, hon. I always knew I'd see your name on the cover of a book, but I didn't think you'd shoot to fame this fast, I must say."

For some reason my eyes were spiked with tears. I had needed my father's voice, but I hadn't known that until right now. And despite the congratulations of some acquaintances in Blue Lake, I felt I had not really been acknowledged until this very moment. "I miss you, Dad."

"I miss you, too, angel. I want you to call me within the week, calendar in hand, to make these arrangements we're speaking about. It's no good to just say someday. Tabby and I aren't getting younger."

I laughed; my father didn't normally deal in clichés. "I know. I promise."

We talked some more, mostly about lighthearted things like the dogs he and Tabby had been looking at in the humane society. "She's pushing me to get one, but I don't know. You can't go anywhere once you have a dog at home. It's like having a baby."

"But you don't go anywhere. And a dog is a good companion and good protection."

"That's what Tabby says. And we all know she'll win. I'm thinking I like the German shepherds."

"Well, now you really have to come and visit. Camilla has two of them, and they're gorgeous."

"That's a promise. Whether you want me or not. I want to give my girl a big hug."

"I want that, too, Dad. Love you."

We finally ended our call, but the feeling of comfort stayed with me, and I was smiling when I left my room.

I GAVE MY notes to Camilla, who thanked me. "These are lovely, and quite timely, because I'm just finishing with the previous corrections. I'll have to look at them later, though, because I'm going out for dinner."

She had changed her clothes, I realized now, and donned an attractive knit dress of deep purple, which she wore with black boots and a long jet necklace. Her hair, normally in a demure bun, was gathered into an elegant clasp. "Wow. Camilla, you look beautiful."

The slight blush on her face could have been a trick of the light, but I thought she was pleased with the compliment. "You are kind to say so. Adam is picking me up early so that we can make the drive."

"Oh—you're not going to Wheat Grass?"

"No, no. He'd be too distracted there. The proprietor can't relax in his own domain. No, he's taking me to some sort of surprise destination. Adam loves surprises."

I had a feeling Camilla was starting to like them, too. "I hope you have a wonderful time. It's been so crazy around here—you probably wish you could have your quiet house back, and that you could go back in time to last fall, before so many crazy things happened."

She stood in front of me and held my arms—a rare moment of physical contact. "I would not go back. If I did, I would not have you in my life, or Adam, or this new, happier Sam. This is the time that I like best."

"Good. I wouldn't go back, either." I hugged her before she could resist. When we first met, Camilla had been surprised by my huggy affection, but she seemed to be growing to like that, too. "Okay, I know you have to get ready. I can't wait to hear where he takes you."

"Yes. I'll be happy to fill in the details later. Let me just go comb my hair."

"It looks perfect. I love that silver clasp."

"What time is it?"

I looked at my watch. "It's four thirty."

"Oh, goodness. He'll be here any moment."

With a start, I realized that Camilla was nervous. I wondered why. She had been dating Adam for a couple of months now, and it seemed like an easygoing and serene relationship. What would make her anxious today?

The doorbell rang, and Camilla's eyes widened. "That will be Adam."

"I'll get it, if you'd like."

"Thank you, dear."

I went to the front door, accompanied by a frisky Rochester and Heathcliff, and opened it to find Adam, looking more handsome than I had ever seen him. His glasses were gone, and his eyes, I noted for the first time, were green. He held flowers, as he so often did. "Hello, Adam. You look so nice! This must be a great place that you're taking Camilla to."

"Oh, yes. I did a fair amount of online research to find it. I hope she'll like it." He was gazing over my head at Camilla, who had appeared with her coat on. "Hello, Cammy."

"Adam, dear, did you want to come in, or—?"

"No, no, we should be on our way. The reservation is at six, and we have to drive for a bit." He held up the flowers. "Something to put in water."

"Oh! A little touch of spring," Camilla said. "Lena, would you . . . ?"

"Yes, of course. You two go and have a lovely time."

Camilla waved, and Adam took her elbow and escorted her out the door into the frigid air.

I went into the kitchen with the flowers. While I was filling a vase with water, I thought about what Camilla had said about Adam loving surprises. What a sweet thing to do while he was courting Camilla—going out of his way to surprise her with lovely things and events.

I tucked the flowers into the water and set them on the kitchen table. Then, on a whim, I dialed a familiar number. I had a surprise of my own brewing.

SAM'S HOUSE WAS illuminated by blue and white landscaping lights when I drove up. I left my car on the gravel road and crunched through the snow to his doorway. I rang his bell, suddenly nervous. Now I knew how Camilla felt.

The door opened and Sam stood there. "Hey. Come on in," he said with a smile.

"Actually, I'd like you to come out," I said.

"Oh? And why is that?"

"I'm whisking you away."

"Where to?"

"It's a surprise."

He studied me for a moment with an amused expression, then shrugged. "As long as I'm with you, fair Lena, I don't much care where you take me."

"Good. Get your coat."

He returned in two minutes, wrapped in a brown coat and a flannel scarf. "Take me away from it all," he said, and I giggled. By the time we were seated in my car we were both in a jubilant mood, prompted perhaps by the invigorating air or the thought of spending time together.

Sam slid over on the seat and gave me a warm kiss on the mouth, then slid back to his spot and buckled in. "So do I get to ask questions?"

"Yes, that will be fun."

"Are we going to a restaurant?"

"No."

"A movie?"

"No, although we could watch one there, if we wanted."

"Are we meeting at your friend Allison's house again for a lover's tryst?"

"Yes and no," I said, pulling onto Green Glass Highway. I turned to him. "We are going to Allison's, because she's my best friend. And I realized that you and she have never really properly met, except at Camilla's little reception. And since I hope you and I will be—together in the future, and Allison and John are married, there's a chance we'll spend lots of time hanging out, just the four of us. And I'd really like you to have some friend time. I know it's been a solitary existence, alone in your house on the hill."

He nodded and studied me in his assessing way. "I think you really planned this just because you thought it would make me happy, didn't you? You want to give me friends on a silver platter."

"Well, not exactly, but yes. I want you to have your old life back, and I know it can never be the same, and this is not New York, but—it can be fun. Allison and John are great, and they really like you."

"*Now*."

"Yes, now that they know you. All they heard before was rumor and innuendo, like everyone else. Allison feels very bad about ever believing it."

"Good. Is she feeding us? I was going to order food for you and me."

"Oh, yes. She's a wonderful cook. She said she's making enchiladas. And John fancies himself a beer and wine expert, so you'll be taken care of in that respect."

"All right, Lena London. I would like to go on a double date with you. Thank you for whisking me away."

We were nearing Allison's subdivision. "You're welcome, Sam West."

"WHAT'S A FULL house?" Allison asked, peering at her cards. "And does it beat a flush?"

A whispered conference with her husband, and then, "Okay, full house. Read 'em and weep." She laid out her cards, and we all moaned. She had won three games in a row after claiming to not know how to play poker.

We recovered quickly, thanks to some mellow red wine and bellies full of inspired homemade Mexican food. Allison, John, and Sam may as well have been friends forever, because they had been laughing and joking together the whole evening. I had watched carefully for any undertones of suspicion or resentment, but there were none. Then again, Allison would be hard for anyone to resist. She's a blonde, pretty ray of sun.

"How about a different game?" John said. "We've got board games galore out there in the porch."

"But it's so cold out there," Allison said, feigning a shiver. "Let's do something warm by the fireplace. We can play charades or something."

"Why don't we just talk?" Sam said. "I have all sorts of questions."

Allison loved this idea. "Okay. We can all get to know each other better." She had already cleared away dishes; now John gathered up the cards, and we stood up, ready to adjourn to their big, comfy main room and its crackling fire.

"Will there be pie in this scenario?" I asked. Allison was a pie genius, and I hated to miss out.

My best friend giggled. "Yes, there is pie. Apple cream cheese."

"Nice," I said. "Do you want me to make coffee?"

Allison waved a hand. "John's already got that brewing. Now go sit down."

Sam took my hand and his wineglass, and we moved into the living room, where he dropped onto the couch and pulled me against him. "How did you and John meet, Allison?"

She flounced in and settled in a chair, her face rosy with excitement. Allison loved entertaining. "It's very romantic. John had just gotten his master's degree and was living in the city, sending out resumes and working part-time as a waiter. A certain *Lena* had dared me to go to one of those online dating sites and make a date, which

I did, at John's restaurant. Except that the guy never showed up. John was my waiter, and he was just infuriated that someone would do that to me."

John's face was indignant with memory. "I still can't believe it. You can see how beautiful Allison is. What sort of moron would send her to some place to sit alone? And yet I'm very grateful to the guy." He smiled, and I saw why Allison had fallen in love. He had a sexy, sincere smile.

Allison flashed him a lover's glance and then said, "John had been talking to me when he brought my water and a free appetizer and stuff. Then he got someone to cover his shift and he took off his waiter apron and sat down with me. He said, 'That guy loses out, because I'm your date now.' And we had the best time! I found out that he was a finance major, and he learned that I was about to finish the nursing program."

"And after that night you kept seeing each other?" Sam asked.

"Yes." Allison hugged a pillow against her. "My romantic John didn't want me to sit alone, and he won my heart."

"Did you ever contact the guy who stood you up? I can't remember," I said.

"No. Why bother?"

"I did," John said, his brown eyes twinkling.

We all turned to him. "What?" Allison said.

He shrugged. "Remember how you took that selfie of us, and posted it with the message *My sweet waiter had dinner with me when my date stood me up*? Or something like that?"

"Yes."

"You told me the guy's username on the dating site. It

was EagleEye. So I joined the site and sent him the picture with a note."

"What note?" Allison's eyes were huge. "Jonathan Branch, you tell me right now."

John looked ever so slightly like a chastened puppy. "It said 'You snooze, you lose, jackass. Some people know how to treat a lady.'"

To my surprise, Sam laughed out loud. "An appropriate response. Did he write back?"

John shrugged. "I think he said something like 'Tell her I'm sorry, I was sick.' Really lame."

Allison shook her head, half annoyed and half pleased. "Now I have a question. Sam, what made you come to Blue Lake? I mean, I can understand why you wanted to get out of New York, but we're not exactly a prime tourist location."

Sam took a sip of wine and nodded. "There is a reason, actually. I had a memory, from back when I was a kid, when my family traveled to Michigan to stay at some budget-friendly resort on the lake. On the way there we stopped in Blue Lake to stretch our legs, and we ended up having a meal at a restaurant on the water. It's not here anymore, sad to say. I think it was called Luna's Place. It was a fun day: my parents were flirting with each other, and we had a hilarious meal, all of us in high spirits. In my memory there is sun shining on us all the time. My little sister saved the bread from our basket and fed it to the ducks that swam around the dock. I took a lot of pictures on a camera my parents had given me for my birthday. When I wanted to get out of the city, I remembered this place, and I did some searching online and found my house. It looked perfect."

"So Blue Lake is just a happy memory," Allison said, and then her face grew sad. "And we ruined it for you. I'm so sorry, Sam."

"You're making it up to me. I have no idea whether I would suspect someone in the position I was in. People are trying to make amends. And Blue Lake will always be the place where I met Lena."

He turned to me with a warm expression. I squeezed his hand, but I was trying to send messages to Allison with my eyes; I didn't want her to ask about Sam's family.

She didn't get the message. She turned in her chair with her puppyish, eager expression, and said, "So where is your family living now?"

Sam must have expected it, but I could tell it hurt. His eyes flicked downward, and he studied his wine as he swirled it. "They were killed in a plane crash when I was in college. My parents were taking my sister to look at colleges herself. She was eighteen."

He may as well have slapped Allison's face. She looked so crestfallen that John came to stand behind her. "Oh my God, I'm so sorry—what you must have gone through! Oh, Sam."

"You have nothing to be sorry for. It was a very long time ago. I have had the nicest evening here in your warm house, and I won't forget your generosity in letting Lena and me meet here recently. Seems like a year now, but it was just a few days ago."

Allison hadn't recovered from Sam's news. "I just—I wish there was something I could do."

I put an arm around Sam. "Allison's a healer. She doesn't like to see pain she can't help."

Sam leaned back against my arm. "You are helping.

All of you. Soon enough they'll find Victoria and the baby, and my life will be my own again."

Now Allison and John were both leaning forward. "What baby?" they said in unison.

THE REST OF the evening was spent explaining the latest in the Victoria West saga, with some sidebars about journalists like Ted Strayer, and Doug's arrest of him earlier in the day.

Allison had told Sam that she wanted him to try some pie, and then, Allison-like, kept feeding him until he was moaning.

Finally, after coffee and endless conversation and too much dessert, we stood up to leave. "Oh, do you really want to go out in this weather?" Allison asked. "We have a guest room."

I looked out the window. "The weather is fine, Allie. We'll be okay. And next time we'll invite you over."

Sam held my coat while I got into it. "Yes, I meant to tell you. I'm going to be throwing a little party. A belated New Year's thing; you're both invited. I'll contact you soon."

Allison clapped. "Oh, that sounds lovely. I've always wanted to see inside that great house of yours."

Sam pulled her into a casual hug. "I'll give you a special tour."

"Thanks for coming out, both of you," Allison said.

"Thanks for having us," I told her.

She and John waved to us from the doorway as we got into the car. I let it warm up for a moment in the cold night. "Sam."

"Hmm?"

"I was just wondering—if you ever thought Victoria's baby might be yours." It was out now, and I couldn't un-say it. I stared at some ice on the windshield, afraid to look at him, but his laughter made me turn in surprise.

"No, Lena. Because that would be absolutely impossible. We hadn't been together for months before she disappeared. We were estranged, in every sense of the word. I haven't been sure of much lately, but I am sure of that." He smiled at me, his face reassuring.

"Okay. I just—I had wondered. And now I want to say one other thing that's personal, if you don't mind. We've never talked about your family, because I never wanted to intrude on what was private. But if you ever want to talk—you know you can talk to me."

"I know. And I will. After the Victoria thing is over."

"Yes, all right." I touched his hand and then started driving toward home. We sat in companionable silence, thinking our thoughts, and I was surprised when I eventually pulled into Sam's driveway, not remembering much about the journey back.

"Come in with me," Sam said. "I want to show you something."

I followed him inside his house, and he flipped on some lights that illuminated the warm wood of his flooring. He led me to a long hallway where a selection of tastefully framed photographs hung on the rust-colored walls. I had seen them before, but had never really studied them.

"This is us," he said. "The complete family."

His father, I realized, looked very much like Sam, with dark hair and broad shoulders, while Sam had clearly gotten his blue eyes from his mother. His sister had similar features, but blondish-red hair and braces. "They're beautiful," I said. "What was her name? Your sister."

"Wendy."

"Wendy West."

"Yeah. She got teased about it," he said lightly.

"I know I would have loved her. All of them."

He turned me to face him. "And for that reason, I know that I love you."

"Sam," I said, intending to say more, but he silenced me with a kiss, and by the time we were finished I knew that I wouldn't be going home.

"Have I ever shown you the upstairs?" Sam asked, his lips on my cheek.

"No. But I would like to see it."

"Maybe you should send a text to Camilla. Tell her you're in good hands."

"I'll tell her I'm in roaming hands," I joked as he stroked my back.

"Mmm. Come up and keep me warm. It's kind of cold up there."

"I feel like I will raise the temperature of your entire house if you keep kissing me like that."

"I most certainly will," Sam said.

I sent a quick text to Camilla, and then Sam West took my hand and led me toward his elegant staircase.

My last thought before ascending, strangely enough, was the first thing Camilla told me about him, months earlier. "They call him the Murderer," she had said with a mysterious expression.

From that point to this, I had never believed it.

"I'll race you," I said, and I bolted past him on the stairs to the sound of his laughter.

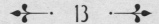

13

Margot felt that she and Joe may have solved one mystery, but it brought no consolation in the wake of a much larger puzzle: the whereabouts of the man who wanted to kill them both.

—From *Death on the Danube*

IN THE MORNING I lay against Sam West and gazed at the frost on his bedroom window while he ran a lazy hand through my hair. The day was cold and beautiful, and I was warm. "I might never leave this spot," I said.

He nuzzled my neck. "Good idea. We'll stay here, like the Lennon and Ono of Blue Lake."

"I know John Lennon, but I don't totally get that reference," I said.

He sighed. "There was that whole thing about the Bed-In? It's an old story, even before my time. That's what I get for dating a younger woman."

"You're eight years older than I am. That's barely an age difference at all. You're not ancient, Sam."

He flopped back onto his pillow and stared at the ceiling. "I just feel that way."

"But not with *me*?" I prompted.

He grinned and looked impossibly handsome. "No, not with you. I was feeling energetic as a teenager well into the early hours."

I rubbed his chest, lightly furred with hair and silky to the touch. "I can help you plan your party today, if you'd like."

"I would like. I like every minute I spend with you. And I need a woman's advice."

"It will be fun."

"Yeah." His smile disappeared, and he seemed to be concentrating on something.

"Are you okay?"

"Yeah, I'm great." He touched my nose. "It's funny— I haven't talked with anyone about my family in so long, and then last night you talked about them, and I thought about them, and something came back to me."

"What's that?"

He sighed. "This goes back a long way. Almost fifteen years. And after a while, I just put it out of my mind."

"Okay."

"My dad called me at school, before he and Mom and Wendy made their trip. Just a casual call, asking me how things were going, did I need money—regular Dad stuff."

"He sounds like a good dad."

"He was." He still looked distracted. "He said a few things at the end of the call—I thought nothing of them. But then when they died, I thought about it more and more, and I felt like—maybe there was something there that I needed to investigate."

"But you never did?"

"No. I was a kid, and I was grieving, and I didn't know

how I might look into something so vague. And then after a while I just put it away."

We both thought about that for a moment. Sam stared up at the ceiling. "Then last night I was looking at you while you slept, and thinking about what you said about Wendy, and it all just came flowing back. What he said to me on the phone, the sound of his voice, Wendy talking nonstop in the background, my mom occasionally calling things out that she wanted him to tell me. All the chaos of home."

My eyes felt warm. "Sam. You've been like Odysseus. Away from home and loved ones for so long . . ."

"And you are my Penelope," he said.

"Tell me what your father said."

"Weeks later I tried to remember. I wrote down as much as I could recall in a little notebook. I've always kept it, but after a while it just seemed like scribbled nonsense. Now I feel like I've come full circle, and I'm back to wondering about it."

"Is the notebook here?"

"Look in the top drawer of that nightstand next to you."

I moved to the edge of the bed and opened the drawer of an ornately carved mahogany nightstand. A small leather notebook sat inside, along with a scattering of papers and a few official-looking envelopes. "I think I found it." I rolled back toward Sam and handed him the book.

"Yeah, this is it." He flipped through it and showed me a page half filled with scrawled statements, written by Sam at eighteen. I felt a moment of ridiculous sentiment, picturing him as a boy.

I leaned against him, and we read it together.

"When we get back, we need to talk about some family stuff."

I asked him if it was bad family stuff, and he said no, just complicated.

"Sometimes life hands you the unexpected."

I told him he sounded like a fortune cookie, and he said the older he got, the more he felt like one.

I asked him what had suddenly brought this up, and he said "Your mother received a letter."

I told him now I was getting worried, and he laughed, and said, "No, no—nothing like that. We'll talk when we get back. It will probably make you happy."

Sam's writing ended there. I turned to look at him. "Family stuff?"

"Yeah. Does that seem like a significant exchange?"

I sat up straight. "Of course it does! He had news, and it was important enough that he didn't want to tell you over the phone—he wanted to wait for a face-to-face meeting!"

Sam looked encouraged. "That's what I had thought at the time. That maybe Wendy already knew, but that my dad wanted to tell me in person. Dad and Mom both."

"He says it's unexpected, and that the news came in a letter. Did you find the letter?"

He shook his head. "The executor never knew anything about it, and it wasn't in the house. I'm thinking—maybe it was on them. Probably in my mom's purse."

I had a sudden idea. "Sam—you know what a genius Belinda Frailey is. Can I show this to her?"

Sam West thought about this, rubbing at his stubbled jaw. "I don't know. I don't know. I guess I feel like I want to keep it private. I haven't shared it with anyone until you. And you earned it."

My face warmed, and I attempted to make light of it. "Do you mean with my sexual prowess?"

One side of his mouth lifted in lazy amusement. "You know what I mean. I owe you everything, including my confidences."

"Sam." I climbed on him and kissed him all over his face until he laughed, and then he kissed me back, and then neither of us was laughing, and when I next thought to look at the clock it was an hour later. I realized a bit sadly that I would have to get out of Sam's bed, but only because I was hungry.

WE SAT TOGETHER over breakfast and planned Sam's party We made an invitation list, which grew to an impressive fifty people. We thought about food options and decided to ask if Camilla would let us borrow Rhonda on the day of the event, with the idea that Sam would hire whatever assistants she needed. Sam had excellent taste in food and wine, and he even thought about what music he might want to play in the background of the festivities.

"This will be a fun night," I said. "Just what everyone needs after all the tension around here. And the reporters just make it worse."

"They are horrible," he agreed, biting into a piece of toast. "But hopefully we can make them go away soon. I've considered getting a Doberman, or a dire wolf, or something terrifying that I can put on a leash."

"Borrow Camilla's hounds. I was deathly afraid of them on the first day I got here."

"That's how I first saw you. Walking those two giant

beasts and looking too small to control them." He smiled at the memory.

I finished my eggs and wrote the last of my notes for Sam's party, then pushed the pad over to him. "Okay, that's what we came up with. Now I have to return to Camilla's and do some work. Much as I would like to stay." I touched his hand. "You made me feel like a princess, but my coach is about to turn back into a pumpkin."

"Then I'll keep one of your shoes," he said, his voice light.

We were both very aware of something in the room— something serious that we weren't ready to confront.

I got up, put my dish in Sam's sink, and returned to kiss his head. "I must go. You look very sexy in your robe, but duty calls. I'll be back later, maybe." I went to the door, turning back only once to smile at him. He waved, his eyes warm and locked on mine, and then I made myself turn away and head to his front door, where my coat hung on a little wooden tree. I bundled up, walked out, and saw a burst of light one second before a voice yelled, "Lena! Did you spend the night at Sam's house?"

"Lena, are you in love with Sam West?"

"Are there any leads in Taylor Brand's death?"

"Lena! Where's Sam this morning?"

"Miss London, did Sam tell you anything about Victoria?"

"What does Camilla Graham think of your relationship with Sam West?"

"Lena!"

"Lena!"

"Lena!"

The reporters had made it past the barricade at the foot of the hill, and our quiet bluff was under attack. A quick glance at my car showed me that they essentially had it surrounded, but there was a small opening to the right of Sam's driveway, and I instinctively ran there. I could pick up the car later.

Hands jammed in my pockets, I pushed through the small crowd working hard to keep my face blank. After a while I was able to tune out their questions, but their voices followed me as I walked, then jogged, up the bluff toward Camilla's.

Her door was open when I got there, and she was standing in it. She waved me in, and I ran up the stairs and past her. I heard her say a few cold words to the reporters who had bothered to follow me instead of clinging like burrs to Sam's house.

I took off my coat and hung it up, then tried to smooth my hair and gather my thoughts. Camilla came back in, but her stern expression was gone, and she was smiling at me.

"Did you have a nice evening?"

I sniffed. "You're teasing me."

"Not at all. I'm happy for you and Sam. What a wonderful couple you are."

"And what about you? How was your date?"

"It was lovely. Adam took me to a restaurant and pub in the basement of a charming little inn. We actually stayed there last night. We returned early this morning."

"Oh." This was a surprise, but it explained why Camilla had been so nervous the evening before. Perhaps she and Adam, too, had reached a new stage in their relationship.

I think we were both blushing as we contemplated each other across the room. Then I started laughing, and Camilla joined in. I dropped onto the couch; she walked over to sit next to me, and we laughed some more, until the giggles left us. She patted my arm. "I do hope the reporters didn't bother you."

"I can handle them. Sam had to put up with far worse. That's all I have to tell myself."

"You admire Sam."

I turned to look into her wise brown eyes. "I'm in love with him, Camilla."

She nodded.

"I feel like one of the heroines in your books. Young and sort of silly in contrast to this older, beautiful, tragic man. He's not that much older, but this whole experience has aged him, somehow."

"There's nothing silly about you. You are remarkable, and Sam knows it."

"Do you love Adam?"

She looked down at her hands. "It's still very new, but I'm coming to depend upon him a great deal. I miss him when he's not there, and I find him so impossibly sweet, it almost brings me to tears sometimes. I must be half mad in my old age."

"You're not mad, and you're not old," I said.

"I will say I feel younger with him. I'm not sure how he does it, but he always has that effect on me."

"Well. How unexpected. I come to Blue Lake to work with you, and a few months later we're both embroiled in romances."

"I suppose if this were a book we were writing, it would be inevitable."

"True. Oh, Sam's going to have a party; he wants to be more sociable. He feels a bit less reclusive now that people are being kinder to him."

"Good. The boy needs to live a little. Being with you is the best start."

"Speaking of books, did you get to look at my notes?"

"Yes. We should talk about those today because I have some ideas to run past you. I hate to ask you this, because those reporters are horrible, but would you consider going to town and picking up something from my editor at the post office?"

"Sure. But I'll drive, I think. It's easier to ignore them when I'm in a car."

"Maybe we can ask Sam to step outside for his mail or something, get them all looking at him, and then you can sneak past in your vehicle."

"It's worth a try. Now I know how celebrities feel. If I never see a reporter again, I'd be fine with it."

She nodded. "I agree. Although Jake Elliott was a life-saver. He changed perceptions about Sam, and his article made Grace Palmer reach out to us."

"And has that brought us any news?" I asked hopefully.

"Not yet," said Camilla. Her dogs loped in and rested their faces on our laps, as though comforting us.

BICK'S HARDWARE WAS having a sale on firewood, and there was a line at the front of the store. I moved past the flannel-clad patrons and went to the back of the store, where Marge Bick presided over the stamps, letters, and packages in the ancient and tiny post office. "Hey, Marge," I said.

"Hello, Lena." Her eyes were sharp as an eagle's as she looked me over. "You look pretty as can be. Did you get a new hairstyle?"

"No. Everything's the same." It wasn't, but I didn't intend to give Marge the satisfaction of knowing that she had correctly identified the glow of love. I had seen it in Sam West's bathroom mirror early that morning. "Camilla wonders if her agent sent her a package from New York? She needs it desperately."

"I know I saw something. Hang on one sec; let me run to the back."

She disappeared briefly, leaving a trace of perfume that smelled like the past. I turned to study the store and saw two men speaking in the kitchen utensils aisle, their voices quiet, their heads close together. They looked almost like conspirators. One of them glanced up and I saw, to my displeasure, that it was Ted Strayer. I narrowed my eyes, and then the other man followed Strayer's gaze and made eye contact with me. It was Jake Elliott. I stared, my mouth open, disappointed and almost angry to see the two of them together. Elliott walked toward me, but Strayer walked away and began a conversation with a woman at the end of the aisle; I recognized her as a bartender from the Big Bar on Kelter Street. Her name was Carly or Carrie or something. My eyes flicked away from Strayer's hated face and back to Jake Elliott.

"Hello, Jake," I said. I didn't smile.

"Lena. Did you read the story?"

"Of course. We all read it. It was a terrific piece—thank you very much."

"You don't look happy."

"I guess I don't like the company you keep."

Elliott shrugged. "I just ran into him. We were sharing some intel, I guess you'd say."

"Why are you still in town?"

He looked surprised; then he laughed. "You are surprisingly strict, Miss London."

"It seems to me that you were granted a story by Sam West, and that he quite generously let you into his life and his confidence. What more could you possibly want in this frigid place?"

"I'll tell you the truth, Lena." He stretched and stifled a yawn. "The word is that something is about to happen in the Victoria West investigation. For that reason alone I need to hang on for a few more days. I would be a fool to miss out on what will clearly be the story of the year."

"And who is giving you this 'intel'? If it's Ted Strayer, then my respect for you will shrivel and die."

Elliott nodded. "Ted Strayer has heard some things to that effect, but he's not the only one. Reporters, over the years, build up a sort of second sense. They can feel it when a story is imminent. Then they flock to it."

"Like birds of prey."

"Hey, you know that I would do justice to the story. What does a person have to do to earn a smile from you?" His own smile was flirtatious.

"A person would have to cut ties with Ted Strayer. Why isn't he still in jail, anyway?"

Elliott's face went blank. "He was in jail?"

"Doug arrested him yesterday for obstructing justice. He had evidence which had belonged to Taylor Brand, yet somehow he failed to mention that to the police."

"What evidence?" Now he looked a bit pale.

"I can't go into that. You'll have to ask Doug Heller. It's in his hands now."

He sighed. "Fine. I will do that." He gave me an assessing look. "You're looking good, Lena."

"Thanks." I turned slightly to see that Marge Bick had returned, and was avidly listening to our conversation. "Did you find it, Marge?"

"Oh, yes. Right here, along with a few letters for the both of you."

"Great. What do I owe you?"

I took the mail, well aware that Jake Elliott continued to stand there, apparently waiting for me. I did not want Marge, the town gossip, to get the wrong idea. "Marge, have you met Jake Elliott? He wrote that big piece about Sam in yesterday's paper."

"Oh, did you? We all read it. It was the talk of the town yesterday, I can tell you. Mr. West certainly has a new reputation."

Elliott nodded, looking distracted. Marge honed in on him. "So are you from around here?"

"I live in Boston," he said.

"My, my. We get people here from all over the U.S." Marge looked pleased about this, as though she were a cruise director. "From other countries, too. Some of those reporters out there at the barricade are speaking other languages."

I hadn't noticed this; I looked at Elliott for confirmation, and he shrugged. I said good-bye to Marge and started walking toward the front. Elliott followed me. He was wearing the same navy pea coat that made him look like a sailor on shore leave.

"What are you doing now?" Elliott asked. "Would you like to join me for a drink?"

We were walking through the front door of Bick's and passing the giant grizzly bear statue that told us Bick's was best. I had stowed the mail in my messenger bag, and now I turned to him with my hands on my hips. "Are you hitting on me?"

Elliott smirked. "No, I'm not hitting on you. I wouldn't have the courage. But I am looking for companionship, and you amuse me. To be honest, this is a boring town."

I had only been in Blue Lake for a few months, but this statement made me feel defensive. "It's not boring, it's quiet. And we like it that way."

"It's priceless, the way you get that stern teacher look. Your disapproval couldn't be more obvious."

"Good," I said, and began to walk again.

Elliott walked alongside me, undeterred. "Lena. Can I ask you one question? Do you have any idea where Victoria West is right now? Or any information about Taylor Brand?"

I stopped and looked at him in surprise. "Why would I? Are you saying you think Sam knows something? Because he doesn't. He's as much in the dark as anyone." I sensed a presence behind us, and I turned to find Ted Strayer smiling at us.

"Hey, kids. Are you saying anything I should know?"

"No," I said. "Stay away from me."

"Come on, Lena. Give me a break. How about you give me a nice little one-on-one, the way you did for Jake here? You would be the star of my blog."

I turned to glare at him; he was about to raise his camera, but Jake Elliott put a hand on his shoulder and said, "The lady said no, Strayer."

"Not to the second question, she didn't," Strayer said, persistent as a virus.

"No," I said again. "You'll have to get your *clicks* without me."

Strayer, as usual, was unflappable. He smiled. "I do, Lena. Every day. That's why I stick around here, don't you know that? Ask your friend Jake here. Blue Lake has been a gold mine. No one's going anywhere."

I stomped away from him and unlocked my car, where I stowed my bag. Elliott waved at me and wished me a good day.

Even after I drove away I could hear Strayer's voice in my head, taunting me with his popularity. No matter how much good Jake Elliott's article had done, there would always be people who liked sensational news, whether it was true or not. And Ted Strayer was one of many who would feed that insatiable desire for garbage.

I accelerated onto the rutted road that led up the bluff, hoping a reporter didn't jump in front of my car. In my mood at that moment, though, I couldn't have predicted the results if one of them did.

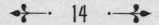

14

One could fall into complacency, Joe had warned her, and that was the time that danger could strike. Danger, he said, was the snake in the high grass. Danger was the cold dark water beneath the seemingly solid ice.

—From *Death on the Danube*

SAM'S PARTY HAPPENED the following Saturday. Doug had put the barricade back in place with an increased police presence, so Sam's guests would be free from media harassment. Sam's place looked beautiful; the wood floors gleamed, a fire crackled in his large stone hearth, and some artfully placed Italian lights added a festive air. The smell of Rhonda's cooking permeated the house, and every time a guest walked in I saw a visible reaction as they sniffed the air and smiled. Sam seemed calm on the outside, but I could tell he was a bit anxious about letting people back into his life, his home, after so long an enforced solitude.

I hadn't spoken to Doug since our conversation with Grace, nor had Camilla, but he had promised to show up, and to bring Belinda Frailey with him. This had bothered me at first, but the more I thought about it, the more I realized they would be a perfect couple, if in fact that was what they were becoming.

I looked around the living room as it began to fill up, and my heart warmed for Sam. Camilla was there with her Adam, looking radiant in a pale pink sweater and gray slacks. Allison and John were there, too, holding hands and studying Sam's wall of pictures. Allison had brought a peach pie, which Sam had immediately hidden in his pantry. This simple gesture won him Allison's heart forever.

Jake Elliott was there because Sam felt grateful about his article. I tried to avoid his eye, which seemed to amuse him. Marge and Horace Bick were there; it had been brilliant of Sam to invite them, because even though Marge was a terrible gossip, she was also surprisingly loyal, and if she considered Sam a friend he would never need to worry about being the topic of the day again.

There were other townspeople there; Frank Attenborough, who owned Willoughby's Café, had been kind to Sam, and he was there with his wife Deana. Some of the architects who had helped with the renovation of Sam's house were there, talking about weatherproofing and knocking on wood panels. I had asked Sam to invite Lane Waldrop and her husband Clayton. Lane and I had struck up a friendship when I first came to town, and though it had been briefly strained by what I felt was a conflict of interest, we had patched things up, and met for lunch now and then. She and her husband were inspecting the hors d'oeuvres with great enthusiasm. She caught my eye and said, "You know I'm always hungry, Lena."

"And yet you stay so slim," I said, smiling.

Her husband nodded and slid a possessive arm around

her waist. I hadn't really ever spoken to him, but I wasn't entirely sure how he had won Lane's heart. I tucked this uncharitable thought away and vowed inwardly to make a point of talking with Clay Waldrop before the day was out.

Doug arrived, looking handsome in his Viking way. Belinda Frailey arrived one minute later, making me wonder if they had come together but were pretending that they hadn't. Belinda made a beeline for me. She wore jeans and a black sweater, and her blonde hair was gathered into an elegant twist. "Hi, Lena."

"Hey, Belinda. You look pretty. Those glasses really accentuate your eyes. You actually look kind of sexy with the specs."

She giggled. "People keep complimenting me, which is weird, because before this month I was really just a wallflower."

"You're no wallflower. You were just hidden away in that moldy library where no one could see you."

She blinked at me. "We don't have any mold in the library. It's quite dry, and our patronage has actually risen this year."

"I was not being literal, Belinda."

"Oh, I get it. Sorry. I think I'm a little nervous to be here. You're really the only person I know. I mean, I met some of the others last week, but that was a solemn occasion, and—"

I nodded. "Let's get you a drink, and you can say hi to Sam."

"He looks surrounded."

"He has been, yeah. I'm so glad. These people should have surrounded him with support a long time ago, and they know it. But better late than never."

Sam had been in the hallway between the main room and the kitchen, and we saw him greeting Doug Heller as we approached. The men did that hearty man-handshake and clapped each other on the shoulders, then disappeared into the kitchen. We followed them and found that Sam was bent on finding Doug just the right beer from his little fridge of foreign labels. They looked, I realized with a start, like friends, which I supposed they were these days. It was hard to believe they had once despised each other.

By the time we reached them Doug had already taken a sip of his Carlsberg, and Sam was saying ". . . any updates at all?"

Doug shook his head, looking irritated. "No, but I spoke personally to a representative at the Bureau, and I made my displeasure known. They assured me that it's not on the back burner, and that they are actively on the case." He spoke quietly, so that he was practically drowned out by party chatter. "I think our revelation of her pregnancy might light a fire under them."

Sam shook his head, then saw us and smiled. "Lena and Belinda will cheer us up. What's the good news from the library?" he joked.

Belinda blushed slightly; she was clearly an introvert who enjoyed attention but was perpetually surprised by it. "Oh, not much. We got some new shelving, and I'm a little busier because Janet took a leave of absence."

I turned to her. "She did? Why is that?"

"She didn't say. Something just came up, and she needed to take some personal time. I'm a little concerned, but it's none of my business. I've sent her a couple of texts, but she hasn't returned them."

I caught Sam's eye. "She was there outside the Red Cottage when we saw Caden Brand. She seemed disturbed about something."

Doug leaned in so that he could be heard over the party's hubbub. "Brand has been paying me regular visits, demanding that I charge someone in his sister's death."

Sam sniffed. "Let me guess whose name he's offering you as the prime suspect."

"Yeah. Methinks Caden Brand doth protest too much." Doug studied his beer with a wise expression.

"As I mentioned the other day, he and his sister fought all their lives. Not much love lost there," Sam said, sipping his wine.

"We're looking into Brand. He's not swaying me with his rhetoric."

Sam pointed at Belinda. "You don't have anything to drink. What can I get you?"

She blushed again. "That wine you have looks good."

Sam took her arm. "Come with me, Miss Frailey." Belinda giggled as they walked away.

I looked at Doug Heller; his brown-gold eyes were perceptive, as always. "She's cute," I said.

"I think so," he said, sipping his beer. "You have a problem with that?"

"With the two of you? No, of course not."

His face said he didn't believe me.

"Okay, at first I was a little jealous. I guess because at one time I thought you and I were going somewhere."

"Me too." He stepped a little closer. "You made your choice, Lena."

"I know. And it's the only choice I could ever make.

But I guess it's still a little weird to see you with someone. Although if you hadn't honed in on her, I probably would have tried to match you up with each other."

He smiled and nodded. "One way or the other. It's early days yet, anyway. But I like her."

"And I'm guessing she more than likes you. When I met her she called you "Inspector Wonderful.""

Doug threw his head back and laughed. "She didn't even know me then."

"No, but she had seen you in the paper and on television. You're photogenic."

"Huh."

"Anyway. I'm glad we talked about it; now it won't be weird anymore."

"It might be. It's still hard sometimes for me to see you with Sam. But we'll both adapt. And it helps to know that Sam's a good man."

I searched his eyes. "Will people say it's a conflict of interest, you treating Sam as a friend?"

He shrugged. "Maybe. But he's not currently a suspect, so there's no reason not to come to his party."

"Do you—have a suspect?"

"A few, but no evidence yet. We're on it."

"I know you are—you always are. I really respect you, Doug. We all know how hard you work."

Sam and Belinda were back. She now sipped white wine out of a beautiful crystal glass with a dark blue stem. "Mmm, you're right, Sam—a sweet and delicate aftertaste."

"Like you," Doug said. "Sweet and delicate."

Belinda blushed and pushed her glasses up on her nose.

Sam cleared his throat. "I don't think I've ever mentioned this to anyone here, but my dad was a cop."

Doug started, and if he had possessed antennae, they would have been vibrating. "A cop? Really? Was this in New York City?"

"No, we lived upstate. But he loved being a police officer, and he was really into police history. I inherited some volumes he has about early police forces. I thought you might want to look at them, so I put them out in my library." He turned to Belinda. "One of them is a first edition."

"Oooh," she said, in the same way I would have responded if someone said that Rhonda had made chocolate cupcakes.

"If you'd like to see them, the library is down that hall and on the right."

"Thanks," Doug said. His eyes were alight with interest. "I think we'll check it out."

He took a couple of Belinda's fingers in his hand and began to lead her out of the room. She turned back to me and smiled a blissful smile. I gave her a thumbs-up.

Sam slid an arm around me. "You're jealous of your boyfriend's new girl."

I pursed my lips. "*You* are my boyfriend, but yes, it did feel weird for a while. Doug and I just talked it out, and now it's fine."

"Good."

I reached up to smooth his slightly disheveled hair. "What I'm jealous of now is that you never showed me the library. I didn't even know you had one. And now Doug and Belinda are seeing it first."

"I will give you a thorough tour tonight. I intend to make out with you in every room."

"I support that plan."

He sipped his wine, looked out at his snowy backyard, and said, "Do you think it's significant that the Baskin woman stopped coming to work?"

"Yeah, kind of."

"Maybe we should pay her a visit."

"Would that be stepping on Doug's toes?"

"We can clear it with him first."

I was drinking a Diet Coke, but Sam's wine was starting to look appealing. "Anything that feels like progress would help at this point. We're spinning our wheels in a big ol' Blue Lake snowdrift. Can I taste that?" Sam smiled and handed me his glass. I sipped it and was immediately warmed by the alcohol.

He stared. "Your cheeks just turned pink!"

"I don't have much of a tolerance."

"We'll build you up slowly," Sam said, grinning at me. "Now give me that glass back."

Jake Elliott entered the room and studied the food on the buffet table. I narrowed my eyes at him and said, "He was in Bick's yesterday with Ted Strayer. Did you know Strayer was out of jail?"

"No," Sam said. "That is not good news. In fact, I think I would like to speak to Doug about that."

"Me, too."

Sam waved and smiled at some people as we left the room and moved down a cool dim hallway to a doorway that opened into a sunny, wide-windowed room lined with books. At one window was a large oaken desk, and in the center, grouped around a dark blue rag rug, were three brown leather chairs and a little coffee table. Doug sat in one of the chairs, studying a book, and Belinda sat on the chair arm, reading with him.

"Doug," Sam said.

Doug looked up, his face bright with interest. "This book is awesome! I may have to come over here a lot to drink your beer and study your dad's collection."

"Always welcome," Sam said. "But I have a question about Ted Strayer."

With a sigh, Doug put the book on the table and held up his hands. "His boss paid his bail. I've got a tail on him, though."

Sam moved closer and sat across from Doug; suddenly I didn't want to hear any more about stupid Ted Strayer. Sam's splendid desk was calling to me. I crossed the room and sat in front of it, running my hand across the smooth wood and looking at some notes Sam had made and stuck into his blotter. He had neat, masculine handwriting. It made me think of what he had written in his little book when he was eighteen and had just lost his whole family . . .

"Isn't it beautiful?" Belinda asked, approaching me. "I would love a desk like this. What am I saying? I would love a *house* like this. This desk wouldn't fit into my apartment."

"Yeah, it's gorgeous."

We exchanged a glance that only lovers of books and stationery would understand. "I wonder if Sam would care if I opened a drawer. I just want to see how deep they are."

Belinda leaned in with a confidential expression. "The way he looks at you? You could set this desk on fire and he would probably say it was okay."

I accepted this with a warm little feeling in my mid-section, but I shrugged. "I am not going to set his desk on fire, but I am going to just peek into one drawer. Okay, two." I opened the top middle drawer to find an assortment of intriguing pens and pencils and highlighters, along with an attractive spicy scent. "Ooh. He's got a sachet in here somewhere. I'll bet his cleaning lady put it in."

"Nice," Belinda said. "Hey, I want you to know that I'm still working on the London File. My top-secret, James Bond–lady assignment. It's always on my mind, Lena."

"Join the club," I said as I opened the bottom right drawer and saw Victoria West smiling at me. I jumped slightly, then pulled out the framed picture. It was one I had never seen before—a younger and more relaxed look-ing Victoria, with her reddish-brown hair tumbling on her shoulders. It was a summer shot, and she wore a sleeveless white button-down blouse and small silver ear-rings. Out-of-focus flowers added a touch of color in the background. It was a lovely photo, and the first picture I'd seen where Victoria West looked affectionate and warm—like someone's friend.

Sam had put it away, but not far. This thought pleased me rather than bothered me, because it seemed appropri-ate. He still cared about her and wanted her found. But she wasn't his anymore. I set the picture on the desk. "This is the lady we're working for," I said. "And I don't see in this face the sort of woman who would betray Sam the way it seems like she did."

Belinda nodded. "She's so pretty. Sort of vulnerable, though."

Now we had Sam and Doug's attention. "What's going on over there?" Sam said.

"I apologize, because I was being nosy and looking in your desk drawers while I sort of made love to your gorgeous desk. I found this picture of Victoria, and it's so beautiful. It makes me wish all the harder that we could find her soon and make sure she's all right."

The men stood up and moved toward us. Doug reached for the picture and I handed it to him. Sam said, "It's my favorite shot of her. It was taken maybe three years after we were married. She's probably about twenty-six."

We sat for a moment while Doug studied the picture. "The eyes are different here, Camilla's right. These eyes belong to a serene woman."

Sam looked upward, as though at a memory. "The funny thing is, we were staying with Taylor for the weekend. Her dad had a summer house in Maine, and we had driven there and spent a few days swimming and eating lobster and goofing around. I remember—they had this old board game in the house, a crumbly old Password game that was probably from the seventies, and Taylor and Vic played against me and Taylor's boyfriend. We were complaining because the women kept winning, and we were sure that they were cheating, because they would always guess on the first clue. No one can do that.

"We guys got kind of mad about it. We accused them of looking at the words in advance, and they were insulted. Vic said that she and Taylor had always had kind of a psychic thing, and they could just read each other's minds with very little encouragement. Like one signal word was all it took."

I sat up straight. "Like one signal word on a postcard?"

Doug's eyes widened. "What if the postcard had just

one word on it?" He set the picture down on Sam's desk. "What if it's not 'R.Acie,' but 'Racie'?"

"But racy isn't spelled that way," Belinda said, her brows furrowed.

Sam nodded. "And yet it seems that if the card was from Victoria—and now I really think that it was—then a word would have been enough. But Taylor thought Victoria was dead, so she didn't pay enough attention. She probably thought it was a crank thing from a reader of her blog."

"But she finally brought it to you, and even tried to get Ted Strayer to use his investigative skills to help determine what her old friend was trying to say."

Doug sighed. "We tried to run it for prints, but there was nothing useable, except for Taylor's own prints, and Ted Strayer's."

"Knock knock," said a voice at the door. We turned to see Jake Elliott, looking apologetic yet curious. "I just came to say thanks for the invitation, Sam. I have to get going. I got an assignment this morning and I need to hole myself up and write. Unless you would like to give me another interview?"

Sam went to the door to shake Elliott's hand. "Not now. But when the time comes, and if you're still around, then yes—I'd like to tell you some things about the search for Victoria. Or at least Doug might. Right now only he knows it all, and that's as it should be."

Elliott nodded. "Fair enough. You all enjoy the party. Sam, I am stealing some cookies for the road, so don't let that lady setting things out slap my hand."

Sam laughed and waved, waited until Elliott had disappeared down the hall, and then turned to us. "How much do you think he heard?"

"I'm sure he wasn't there until the last moment. I was sort of watching the door," I said. "But I'm so paranoid, I have visions of him putting a bug in your house. Maybe Doug should search for one before he leaves."

"You are paranoid," Sam said, but he sounded worried.

"You're both paranoid," Doug said. "It's not like you sit in here by yourself talking out loud about Victoria. Even if you talk to Lena, there's not much you can do but speculate."

"True. But did he touch anything in here?" I asked.

They laughed. Then Belinda held up a finger. "I keep thinking back to the baby. I can't imagine that this rich, rich man would make his wife or girlfriend have a child all by herself, without medical attention. Which means someone out there delivered that child. That's what we should find, isn't it?"

SAM'S GUESTS LEFT on a wave of good feeling that had him smiling, but tired. "It's exhausting, throwing a party," he said to the few of us who were left. Camilla, Adam, Doug, Belinda, and me.

"Let us help you clean up, Sam," Camilla said.

"You already did. The place looks okay, and I have someone coming in to vacuum and dust in the morning. I'll be fine."

"It was a terrific gathering," Adam said. "Lots of great people in the community—even a couple I hadn't met yet. Thanks for inviting me."

"You'll always be invited because Camilla will always be invited," Sam said. "And you two seem inseparable these days."

"We're going steady," Camilla joked, and Adam put a courtly arm around her waist. "But now I have to go home and write. Lena, I know you'll want to stay here and help Sam, so perhaps the two of us can work on that next chapter in the morning?"

"Absolutely. Thanks, Camilla."

Sam walked her and Adam to the door, then returned with a bottle of wine. "Anyone want to drink this last one? Or Doug, maybe you and Belinda would like to take it?"

Doug took out his phone and scrolled through some texts. "I think I have to take Belinda home and go in to work for a while." Belinda looked disappointed, and he said, "Not *that* long a while."

"Anything new?" I asked, because hope, the thing with feathers, was perching in my soul. How right Emily Dickinson was about so many things.

"Not really. Just Caden Brand, wanting to bend my ear."

This irritated Sam. "Trying to implicate me again? Be sure you ask him who will get all of his sister's money, along with her inheritance, when their father dies. And ask why he happened to be in Indianapolis the day before Taylor died. Oh, and Lena and I learned that someone was yelling at Taylor on the night before her fall."

Doug nodded. "Yeah, Janey told us that. We don't have an eye witness account, but it looks like it could have been Brand. And I might just detain him on all this information."

"Arrest him?" I asked.

"Nope. No evidence. But detain, yes. Maybe make him

miserable for a while. I've had just about enough of that man."

This satisfied Sam. The two men shook hands, and Sam gave Belinda a casual hug, and then they, too, headed for the door.

Finally Sam's big house was empty of everyone except him and me. "That was a nice party," I said. "Thanks for inviting me."

"Thanks for helping me plan it, Lena my love."

"Should we go sit on your couch and put up our feet?"

"Yes."

We strolled to his living room, which seemed oddly silent now without a crowd, and Sam stoked the fire. Then he dropped onto his brown leather couch and pulled me into his lap. I rested my head on his and looked at the flames. "I heard Marge Bick tell someone that she never suspected you of anything."

"She remembers incorrectly."

I laughed and played with his collar. "What would you like to do? Watch a movie?"

"I'm afraid I can't. I have an appointment."

I turned to look into his face. "Aw, Sam, I was hoping we could spend the evening together. Camilla just gave me permission to sleep over, didn't you hear her?"

He shook his head, looking rueful. "I made a promise earlier, at the party, and I really have to keep it."

"What promise?"

"I told my girlfriend I would make out with her in every room of my house."

Laughter bubbled out of me, along with some very real excitement. "Oh, *that* appointment. I'm okay with that. How about if we start right here?"

"That will work," Sam said. "And how about if we keep track of our progress by leaving a souvenir in every room?"

"A souvenir? Like a coin, or one of your nice books?"

Sam's mouth was on my neck, and his hand slid to the collar of my blouse. "I was thinking clothing, Lena," he said against my skin.

I giggled like a fool, then broke away. "Give me one minute. My Diet Coke went through me, and I need to run to the washroom." I got up and began to hurry toward the door, then heard glass shattering behind me. I thought perhaps Sam had dropped his wine glass, but I turned to see him lunging at me, his eyes wide.

"Get down, *down*, Lena! That was gunfire."

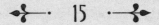

15

The good and the bad, she thought one night as she gazed up into dark heaven. The starlight shone down upon them both, and in that ambiguous illumination one might be mistaken for the other.

—From *Death on the Danube*

SAM'S HOUSE WAS illuminated by red and blue lights, eerie in the night and the snowy landscape. The strobe effect made the home's interior seem like a strange disco, and I found it discomfiting.

The police had secured the scene and searched thoroughly; Doug stood before us, looking concerned. "We know where the shooter was standing, but whoever it was is gone. We tracked the footprints to the road, where he got into a car and took off."

Sam was pacing. "The question is, who were they trying to shoot? Were they aiming at Lena, or was it just a coincidence that they shot when she stood up?"

"Don't jump to conclusions. You had a lot of supporters in your house tonight, but you still have some detractors in town. One of them could have just taken a pot shot at the Sam West house. It could have been a drunken teenager on a dare. I'm not saying we're not taking this seriously. We take shooters very seriously, Sam. But give us time to figure out intent."

"I hear what you're saying, but I'm not buying it. Whoever it was waited until my guests were gone, waited until it was just Lena and me. That smacks of intention," Sam said.

"*Or* it could be coincidence. You can't let emotion get in the way here," Doug said. "I know you're worried, but we have to let logic rule. Let us do our job. We'll keep you both safe, don't worry about that. And I'll find out who did this—that is a guarantee."

This didn't please Sam. "Excuse us if we're emotional. Someone shot a bullet through the window and almost hit Lena. A distinct possibility is that it happened when the guests left because it *was* one of the guests," Sam said.

Doug put a hand on his arm. "We've got a good impression of the footprint and the tire print. We got the bullet out of your wall. I think we'll have this guy pretty darn soon, and then we can get a lot of questions answered. I also had a message to call my contact at the CIA, but I rushed back here. Maybe they've made some progress, and everything will fall together this very night."

I pointed at Doug. "You are really good at talking people down from the heights of anxiety."

"Just doin' my job," Doug said, tipping a pretend hat. Even Sam laughed.

"Okay, fine. Go find this person. Meanwhile, should I take Lena to a hotel or somewhere?"

"No place safer than right here. I've got people on your

place and on Camilla's, just in case. No one's getting in or out without being swarmed by cops. Oh, and just a heads up. We will make a brief statement to the press with a warning that they'd better stay the hell away from you both."

We thanked Doug and he went back outside; Sam took my hand. "Doug thinks I overreacted."

"Of course you didn't overreact. Someone *shot* at us, Sam!" My hands were still shaking slightly.

"Yes. And in that moment, I just thought, *you would really take Lena, too*? I guess I was talking to God. It was terrifying, the thought of losing you."

"You won't lose me. Doug promised us we'd be safe. And it looks like you're stuck with me tonight, because I am *not* walking home in the dark."

"Are you afraid?"

"Equal parts fear and anger. And the anger is starting to win."

Sam hugged me against him. "Not to be ungrateful, but when do you think all these guys will be gone? We never finished our business."

"Business? That's an interesting euphemism."

His blue eyes twinkled at me. "For what will prove to be an interesting activity. And a good way to distract us from our thoughts."

I laughed and ruffled his hair. Even in the midst of uncertainty and imminent threat, Sam West made me feel good.

That night I peered out of Sam's bedroom window and saw the dark shapes of police cars on the gravel road, and a little distant light that seemed to be in Camilla Graham's house. Both images were comforting, and I wasn't even afraid as I climbed into the large flannel-sheeted bed and watched the fairy-light snowfall outside. The snow looked cold but lovely, and Sam's arms were warm, providing the final bit of security that I required.

I woke up feeling far happier than one might expect in a woman who had been traumatized by gunfire. Sam was gone, but I could hear him puttering in his kitchen below. I lay in his bed for a few minutes, reminiscing about some of the "business" we had accomplished after the police had left for good. Sam appeared in the doorway.

"Hello. I caught you smiling. Are you thinking about me?"

"Yes, you vain man. Do I smell waffles?"

"Yes, you pampered woman."

We gazed at each other for a while, thinking our thoughts. I finally stretched and said, "Can a person become addicted to a bed?"

"It's understandable. I'm far fonder of it now that you've spent two nights in it."

"Mmm. Do I have time for a shower?"

"Only if I don't join you in it."

"That's a real catch-22," I said, letting my eyes move slowly over him.

"Uh-oh! Do I smell something burning?" he said, and ran back down the stairs.

"Darn," I said to the ceiling. I got up and took a quick shower, then dressed and found Sam in his bright kitchen.

Sam placed a plate of waffles in front of me, which I began to eat without ceremony. I really was pampered. "Have you talked with any cops this morning?"

"It was a quiet night—no activity, no calls from anyone in town."

"Huh."

He waited until I met his gaze. "It could drive us crazy, wondering about that bullet. Wondering when the next one might come."

I nodded and sighed a quavering sigh.

"So we might want to assume that it was a random thing. A one-time pot shot to harass the guy the townspeople love to hate."

"I don't know if I can do that. I think I might want to lie low for a while."

"Whatever you'd like. But I think we're better off feeling angry than afraid."

I sighed again.

He poured me some coffee, then sat down across from me with his own plate. "We're in the papers again. Adam Rayburn dropped these off this morning." He plopped some newspapers down on the table. The headline of the *Blue Lake Piper* read "Gunman Fires into Sam West's House." The *New York Times* headline said "Unknown Gunman Fires on West's Indiana Home."

"Suddenly you're the victim."

"Interesting, huh? For a real treat, check out Ted Strayer's blog."

"Oh, no. I need more waffles for this one." I shoved a bite into my mouth and enjoyed it for a moment before facing the inevitable. Sam's laptop was still open on the table, so I Googled Strayer's name and found his latest posting, titled "The Sam West Saga Continues—With Gunfire."

"He's a real word artist," I said, my voice dry.

"It gets better. He may as well be writing a hard boiled mystery—it's full of guns and dames and hard men."

"Seriously?"

"I may be exaggerating. But believe me, so does he."

"And the guy gets paid for that gutter journalism."

"Eat up. What do you think about calling that librarian today? Or asking Belinda to do it?"

I nodded. "God, anything to get some information. I'll text Belinda right now to ask for Janet's number." I shoved another piece of waffle in my mouth and smiled at Sam while I dug for my phone. I sent a quick text to Belinda and then returned to my food.

Five minutes later the phone buzzed and I had Baskin's number, along with a note from Belinda that said, "Let me know what's going on!"

I powered through my food and said, "I am truly spoiled. Thank you."

"You're welcome. I like watching you eat. A cross between delicate gentlewoman and starving orphan."

I giggled. "Who should call—you or me?"

"You. No woman wants to get a call from a strange man. She'll remember you."

"Okay. Let me go in the next room so that I won't be distracted."

"I'll miss you," he said.

I ignored his last comment and jogged into Sam's sunny living room to make my call on his landline. I wasn't sure exactly what I'd say, but I hoped I could summon up some charm despite the awkward situation.

"Hello?" A voice said. It seemed familiar.

"Is this Janet?"

"Yes. May I ask who's calling?"

"Janet, my name is Lena London. I met you at the library back when—"

"I remember, Lena. You and Belinda are working on a research project, right?"

"Uh, yes. Anyway, I was going to ask you a question at the library, but they told me you took a sort of leave of absence. Is everything okay?"

There was a moment of silence, in which Janet Baskin must have wondered why a virtual stranger was asking after her welfare. That had been a wrong move.

When she did speak, her voice was smooth and slightly amused. "Everything's fine. I took off because my mom had knee replacement surgery, and I had to drive out to her place and stay with her a couple of days until another caregiver could tag in."

"Oh, well—that's good to know."

"Yeah. So what can I do for you, Lena? You said this was about the library?"

"No, not exactly. That's just where I would have gone to ask you this. Actually it's about the other day. I happened to see you over by the Red Cottage Guest House."

There was another silence. Then, "Yes. I saw you, too."

"The thing is Sam West and I have been working closely with the police in hopes of solving Taylor Brand's murder."

"Oh, wow."

"And we happened to notice that you seemed . . . uncomfortable when we saw you."

"I see. Are the police going to come and talk to me about this?"

It was an odd question to ask. "They don't even know that we saw you. We didn't think it was significant, but then we thought about it, and we wondered what you were reacting to. It might be important."

"I did tell the police, back when they found the body, that I have a friend staying at the Red Cottage, and I happened to be there visiting when the Brand woman was there. And I told them about some yelling I heard on the night before she died."

"Okay." I hadn't known that Janet Baskin was one of the sources of this information, but of course all the residents of the cottages would have heard loud yelling. "But is that what made you uncomfortable?"

"No. I also told the cops that the next day I saw her talking to a guy in the morning—I don't know if it was the same guy—but they seemed to be having a disagreement. In retrospect it seems kind of sinister."

"And who was this man?"

"I didn't know. I still don't know. Except that I saw him talking to you when you were at the cottages."

"Caden Brand?"

"If you say so. I don't know the man from Adam, but it made me uncomfortable because I had wondered about him, and if he was the last person to see her alive."

"Janet, you need to go back to the police. This is crucial information!"

"Uh. The thing is—if they want me to make some kind of statement—I can't."

"I'm sorry?"

"Listen, Lena. I was visiting an old friend at the cottages. An old girlfriend, to be honest. And I have a current girlfriend. You see my dilemma. I don't want to be very visible in this whole thing. If you can just pass on the information that would be great."

I filled my mouth with air and then blew it out, noisily, while I thought about this. "I can pass the information on to Doug Heller, but I can't promise that he won't have additional questions."

"Okay. I guess that's the best I can hope for. And I'm ending it. We were just sort of—reconnecting for old times' sake. It made me appreciate what I have and realize that I don't want to lose it, even though I risked losing it. I hope you'll be discreet."

I sighed. "I have no business prying into your private life. I know what it feels like to have your secrets exposed."

"Yeah, I saw that online. Sorry about that."

"But if need be—if the police contacted you about identifying Caden Brand—you'd be willing to do that? It's very important. As you said, he might be the last person who saw her alive. Maybe even the person who caused her death."

"This is heavy stuff. But yeah, I would look at a line-up or whatever they do. Hopefully they could contact me discreetly—maybe at the library—and I could come down to the station."

A gust of sadness went through me; I wasn't sure if it was because of Janet Baskin's duplicity or because of Taylor Brand's murder or some combination of the two, but suddenly I wanted to be off the phone. "All right. Thanks, Janet. I'm sure Doug Heller will be in touch."

We said good-bye and ended the call. Sam came in, his brows raised, and I told him as much as I could remember, some of it verbatim.

"Ah. Does every person in this town have secrets?"

"I'm guessing every person in *every* town has secrets.

But it's still depressing. It would be nice to know that some people are exactly what they seem to be."

Sam leaned against the couch. "Do you think I am what I seem?"

"For the most part. When you surprise me, it's usually in a good way."

"Okay." He thought about this for a moment. Then he said, "We should probably tell this to Doug."

"Yeah. What if Caden tries to leave town?"

Sam nodded. "I'm on it. Hand me that phone." I gave it to him and then leaned back, trying to relax and not think about the shooting, the murder, the number of times we'd had to call the police in the last few weeks.

Before he could dial a number, the phone rang in his hand. He clicked it on, brows raised, and said, "Hello."

Then he listened, and his face remained surprised, with a touch of anger. "I don't see why that would be necessary, Caden. It seems to me you've done plenty of talking to the police about me."

He was quiet, listening again, and then he shrugged. "Fine. I'm here with Lena London, and I'm sure she'd like to be a witness to our conversation."

He said a few more words, then clicked off the phone. "Caden Brand wants to know if he can come by to talk with me. He says he regrets going to Doug—that he was acting on emotion."

"Which suddenly he doesn't feel anymore? This sounds fishy to me."

"And to me, but I'm far too curious to send him away."

"Doug should be here."

"No. But I think I'll take the liberty of taping it for Doug. Hang on while I get my iPhone." He left the room briefly and I leaned my head back on the couch, studying Sam's ceiling and wondering at how many things had changed in a few months' time. How much would be different in another three?

Sam returned, tucking his phone behind a flower arrangement on the side table. When Caden Brand knocked at the door a few minutes later, Sam asked me to answer it, and when I ushered Brand into the room, Sam seemed to be putting the last minute touches on a flower arrangement. Then he turned around and stared at Brand.

"Caden," he said, without offering his hand.

"Sam. Thanks for seeing me. I know you've probably heard an earful from your pal Doug Heller."

"What makes you think we're friends?"

"People gossip, even to strangers."

Sam shrugged. "Very recently Doug Heller was convinced I killed my wife, just as you seem convinced I am guilty of a different crime."

Brand, still in his coat, looked over at the furniture, but Sam did not invite him to sit, or to hand over his outerwear. "Listen. You have to know where I was coming from. I was just told my sister, my only sibling, was dead. You'd go a little nuts, too." He ran a hand through his hair. I noticed that he still looked well-fed, despite his supposed trauma. Sam had grown quite thin in the midst of his.

Sam put his hands on his hips. "Why don't we tell it like it is, Caden? You and Taylor hated each other. That goes way back, and it lasted up until she was killed, didn't it?"

Brand narrowed his eyes. "You shouldn't make assumptions, Sam."

"Okay. Then what were you screaming at her about on the night before she died?"

He paled slightly. "What are you talking about?"

"We know it was you. There's a witness."

"The police didn't mention it," he said, his mouth twitching slightly.

"They will."

He sighed, then shrugged. "Whatever. Yes, Taylor and I fought all the time. A lot of siblings do. It didn't mean I didn't love her. And I needed to know why she was here—what she wanted. It was complicated. She told me she was here to talk to you and only you. So I need to ask you, Sam. What did Taylor tell you?"

Sam blinked. "As you know, Taylor never made it to a meeting with me."

"But she must have contacted you. She said she was going to, in order to make an appointment and to be sure you'd receive her. She said she had to apologize first, then meet with you later. So you must have heard from her. She was going to do it right after I left."

"And that's why you suspected me of killing her?"

"I don't know." He looked at the furniture again, as though he were tired of standing. Sam refused to get the hint. "Listen—if she contacted you, I need to know what she said. You don't have to tell the cops if you don't want to, but I need to know if she mentioned anything . . . sensitive. Confidential."

"Like what?" Sam said. He was clearly trying to gather evidence for Doug.

"Nothing that concerns you."

"And yet here you are."

"Just—Taylor had some issues with me over some financial things related to our dad. She and I did tend to bicker over money, and him."

"I'm guessing she wanted you to stop stealing it."

Caden Brand's face was so surprised and horrified, his body language so over-acted, that it was clear Sam had hit a nerve. "Don't be ridiculous. We just had disagreements about certain accounts of Dad's that he had given us control over."

"And why, Caden, do you think your sister would come all the way to Blue Lake, Indiana, to talk to *me* about some of your father's finances?"

Brand's eyes darted around. He was hiding something. "I don't know. Who knows why Taylor did what she did? But as you pointed out, we had just experienced a blowout fight, and she might have wanted to vent to you."

"And even if she did, who cares? What would it matter now?"

To my surprise, Brand looked relieved. Perhaps he realized, by Sam's ignorance of whatever he feared he had learned, that he would not be in trouble. This was going to interest Doug.

Brand made a big show of sighing and drooping his shoulders. "I guess you're right. I guess it doesn't matter now."

"What does matter is that you've been demanding my arrest, and yet you were the last one seen with your sister, in a towering rage, from what the witness says."

"And who exactly is this witness?" Brand said, his face red.

"The person prefers to remain anonymous," Sam said. "But I'm guessing there must be at least about six of them, since you were yelling so very loudly."

Brand was back to his sneering self. "You've got it all wrong, Sam, and I'll tell the police that if they ask. I would never hurt my sister."

Perhaps I was overreacting, but it bothered me that Brand didn't look Sam in the eye when he said that. The men said their good-byes soon afterward, and Sam ushered him out, then went to his phone and stopped the recording. "Doug will most likely be at the station. I'm going to drive this over," he said.

"Drop me off at Camilla's? I don't want to risk any gunman shooting or reporters stalking."

"You've got it. Don't worry—we've still got a cop out there. And if the paparazzi try to take a picture, I'll be sure to give you a really wet kiss."

CAMILLA AND I worked for the rest of the day, and between my notes and her editor's, she felt she had made some valuable progress. We ate a quiet dinner, served by Rhonda, who was still glowing with the compliments she had received after Sam's party. It was nice to sit with Camilla in her quiet, warm kitchen, enjoying good food and good company and contemplating the book that would be sent to New York in a matter of months.

We talked about *The Salzburg Train*, which was to hit shelves in a few weeks, and about some appearances Camilla and I were committed to make. It was fascinating to contemplate—like the promise of entering a far-off, glittering world. "Hopefully all our work here will be done," Camilla said. "Victoria will be found, and there will be nothing to distract us from our publicity obligations."

"I do hope so. It's very hard to concentrate with so many unknowns."

"Poor Lena. Little did you know, when you came to this town, what all awaited you. I'll bet you thought it would be boring here."

"I did!"

She smiled and patted my hand. "Life will fool you that way."

After dinner we shared some coffee and Camilla said she would go back to her office for an hour or so. "Go ahead and watch television or whatever you'd like to do," she said.

"You know what? I'm really tired. I think I'll turn in early. Good night, Camilla."

"Good night, dear." She smiled and wandered off toward her office, her dogs at her heels.

Up in my room, I hunted down my long-lost friend Lestrade, who seemed a bit cool to me now that I'd spent a couple of nights away from him. I lay on the bed and tucked him against me; eventually, with some petting and persuading, he was purring as loudly as usual, and he watched while I rolled over on my stomach, grabbed my laptop, and logged on to check my e-mail and various social media accounts. After I answered all the necessary correspondence, I typed in the address of Ted Strayer's blog. Surely he would have posted more obnoxious things by now, and I wanted to keep track of them.

I gasped when I read the headline: "*Sam West Visited by Dead Woman's Brother.*"

Mouth agape, I read the ridiculous article, which said nothing of note, but insinuated plenty, both about Sam and Caden Brand. As usual, Strayer was relying on the idea that a tantalizing headline would be enough to justify a non-story.

"Unbelievable," I said to Lestrade. He purred and licked his paw.

I clicked out of the offensive blog, but grabbed my phone and sent a quick text to both Doug and Sam with a link to the story.

Before I turned out the light, I Googled "Nikon Lazos has child" and "Nikon Lazos becomes a father." The only things that turned up were in Greek, and when I asked Google to translate them, they were unrelated to the man I searched for. Disappointed but not surprised, I set my computer aside and went to my little bathroom to get ready for bed.

As I brushed my teeth I contemplated the idea that every person in my circle of friends was focused, for one reason or another, on finding Victoria West. I wondered if Victoria, wherever she was, ever sensed that so many people were looking for her. Was she so isolated in her own Nikon-fashioned world that she really had no sense of the outside? Was she too distracted by her child to think much about what was happening away from her yacht?

I wondered who had shot at Sam and me, and if Doug was any closer to finding them.

I wondered where Nikon Lazos was.

I wondered who had killed Taylor Brand, and why.

And I wondered if Taylor, before she died, had figured out the meaning of that postcard on her own. If she had, was it that knowledge that had gotten her killed?

16

Margot had never before believed in Fate, but she did now.

—From *Death on the Danube*

THE NEXT MORNING, I spoke to Sam on the phone, but told him I would work with Camilla for as long as she needed. "Then maybe I can sneak out and see you," I said.

"Good. Call me when you're finished; I'll come and get you."

"Okay. So you'll be around?"

"Just waiting for you."

"Your voice is sexy," I said.

Sam said something very intimate in response to that, and I blushed in the privacy of my own bedroom. Lestrade was unimpressed; he looked at me briefly from his windowsill, then went back to studying a bird.

"You are very good at that," I said to Sam, my voice breathless. "I'll call you soon."

* * *

AFTER BREAKFAST I joined Camilla in her office, and we worked. We had developed a graceful style of interaction that involved very little talking—just some pointed questions and then, depending on our task, some shared reading, writing, or jotting of notes. At the end, we compared and discussed.

Today Camilla seemed less able to concentrate, and her eyes kept straying to the window, where a tentative snowfall had begun. "It's supposed to turn into quite a blizzard," she said. "I'm so glad none of you has to travel far—you, Sam, Adam, Doug. All my little chickens safe in the coop." She smiled at me. "You must think I sound silly."

"Not at all. I know how hazardous those Blue Lake roads can be. I watch the news. And even though I've only lived here for a few months, I kind of feel like a townie."

"You are one. It doesn't take long to feel at home in this place. And I came from much farther away than you did."

"Camilla," I started, but her desk phone rang and she picked it up, holding up her pointer finger.

"This is Camilla Graham," she said. She listened, and then her eyes widened and she gestured to me to pay attention. "Just a moment, please. I want to put you on speaker phone so that Lena can listen, too."

She covered the receiver and said, "It's Grace Palmer. She said she thought of something she wanted to tell me."

My heart was beating rapidly by the time Grace's voice greeted me. "Hello, Lena. I'm sorry if I'm disturbing you two. It's just that I thought of something else about Nikon. I really probably should have made arrangements to come out there and answer the questions the police might have, but—well, I have a family, and I don't really feel equipped to leave them right now."

"Do you think Nikon knows you have a husband and—you said you have children?"

"Yes. Two sons. There's no way that he could know, and yet I think he does."

"Why?" Camilla asked, her voice sharp.

"When my oldest was born, I received a huge sheaf of flowers at the hospital—just giant. It must have cost hundreds of dollars. The card said, "Best wishes always." But there was no signature. My husband thought it might be from one of his coworkers, but I always sensed it was from Nikon. And since it seemed to be a blessing and not a warning, I was content to let it go."

Camilla was thinking hard. She visibly pulled herself out of a reverie and said, "But what was it you wanted to tell us?"

There was a small sigh. "I feel that I made you all think Nikon was some sort of terrible criminal. Maybe he is. Maybe I have something like Stockholm syndrome. But I wanted to tell you that wherever he has Victoria, he's not hurting her. I doubt she has ever felt more loved. It's just—he loves things too hard."

"And she is not a *thing*," Camilla said crisply. "Nor were you."

"No. No, you are right about that. Nikon is at best old-fashioned and patriarchal. And at worst—well, you know."

"Grace, when you were with him, did he ever mention some of his favorite places to go with his yacht? Out-of-the-way mooring spots?" I asked.

"Maybe. Nikon didn't tend to confide his routes to me, or even the next place we were headed. Once in a while I probably overheard the names of places—islands, ports.

But I confess I never really paid attention. It didn't seem important, back then." She sighed again, but then made a startled sound in her throat. "Oh—oh. Wait. I do remember that when we talked about having a child—so many years ago—he told me that not all of the Greek Islands had good medical care, but that we would be fine if we went to Athens or Thessaloniki. Yes, those were the two."

"That's terrific! We can definitely work with that," I said, feeling excited for the first time in a while.

Camilla asked a follow-up question, but my mind was racing away, trying to remember what I knew of those two cities from the research we had already done. Athens was easy, of course—a capital city and the oldest in existence, filled with art and culture and history. Certainly Athens would be a likely place to have the child. It was the most populated area in all of Greece.

But Thessaloniki—that I knew less about. It was large, I knew, and culturally important. It had a bustling commercial port, named for Thessalonike, the half sister of Alexander the Great. I vaguely remembered pictures I had seen of Thessaloniki at night—glittering gold and reflected in the water of the bay under a large round moon.

". . . do you think?" Camilla was asking me.

"Oh? I'm sorry, I didn't hear you."

"I was asking if you think that Nikon would take her off the yacht when it was time to deliver the baby."

"I don't know—Grace, what do you think?"

Grace Palmer was silent, and for a moment I thought the connection had been broken. Then she said, "If his relationship with Victoria is anything like his marriage to me, he would be reluctant to let her off the yacht for any reason, unless he or someone else could watch her very closely. And don't forget Nikon has vast amounts of money. If he wanted a whole hospital unit to set up shop on board, he has the resources to do so."

We talked some more, asking after her family and about her plans for spring. Eventually Camilla thanked her for calling and promised to let her know if we had any more questions, or any updates, for that matter. Then we said our good-byes.

Camilla studied her blotter for a moment, making mysterious notations with a ballpoint pen. She was a bit of a doodler. Finally, she said, "What kind of a man has all the money in the world and yet has not enough confidence to let his wife live her own life? What does he fear would happen if he let poor Victoria walk around or live on land? How do these odd notions become culturally embedded in oppressive men?"

"Someday I would like to meet Nikon Lazos face-to-face and tell him what I think of him."

Camilla's pen was busy in the corner of her blotter. "Be careful what you wish for," she said, and when she looked at me her eyes were troubled.

By the afternoon the snow was coming down in earnest. I stood in the front room and contemplated the growing drifts, wondering how difficult it would be to walk to Sam's house.

The scene just outside the living room window was peaceful and, for once, blessedly devoid of people. How nice it would be when Blue Lake returned to its natural serenity, with no press, no curious visitors, no murders, no Sam West stalkers, no manipulative bloggers . . . As if in response to my final thought, Ted Strayer appeared on the road in front of Camilla's house, bundled in a winter coat, but bare-headed; he was walking north. The only thing in that direction was the road to the bluff path—the path from which Taylor Brand had fallen to her death.

Strayer wasn't in a hurry, but he was leaning slightly against the growing wind and marching determinedly upward. What could he possibly want up there, especially in this weather? I moved closer to the window, studying Strayer and his slouched posture. I pulled out my cell phone and called Sam. It rang four times and went to his answering machine; the same thing happened when I tried his cell. He was probably in conference with a client. Meanwhile Strayer disappeared from my line of sight.

While I considered my options, another figure materialized on the gravel road, walking with a determined stride. It was Jake Elliott; I recognized his blue pea coat. Without further ado I grabbed my coat and a brimmed hat and donned them quickly. I tucked my phone into my pocket; if need be, I would have photographic evidence—of what, I didn't know. I needed to see what would bring these two reporters out in what was fast becoming a blizzard. I knew the bluff better than they did, and thanks to Camilla's curious dogs, that meant some side paths and hiding places from which I could observe the men.

Camilla was still napping; I didn't want to disturb or worry her. I waited until Jake Elliott disappeared on the path, and then I went out, moving down Camilla's front porch on careful, booted feet. I pulled down my hat brim to help preserve my vision in the blowing snow. Testing for ice with careful footsteps, I moved through the yard and out to the gravel road, now swathed in white. I thought about trying Sam again or Doug, but I needed to know what this was first. If it was just another sharing of notes in an out-of-the-way place, then there was no point in dragging poor Doug Heller away from his office yet again. I feared I might somehow lose the men in the snow, and I really wanted to witness their confrontation, if it came. What did Jake Elliott want to see? What was Ted Strayer looking for?

It was a steep climb up the bluff path, but it normally wasn't much trouble for people used to taking it. Today, though, it was slick and treacherous, and as it wound around, providing a slightly obscured view of Blue Lake on one side and a steeply sloping bluff on the other, I found it intimidating for the first time. I couldn't escape the reality that this was where Taylor Brand had walked, for reasons unknown, before she plunged to her death very near the house of the man she was seeking. Why, *why* had Taylor come up on the bluff? Why hadn't she just stopped at Sam's place and knocked on his door?

A sharp breeze buffeted me and pushed me slightly to the left. I balanced myself against the trunk of a white birch. I was heading for a stand of pines where I knew I could observe without being seen; in addition, they would shelter me from the storm. Even if the men were in the pines, I could stay in the shaded protection of the low-hanging branches on the outskirts of the stand, while maintaining a view of the clearing at the center of the trees. The pines were ancient, and they towered like wintry giants, their tops invisible in the snowfall. People down in the town could see the tall trees from the road—one of the landmarks that showed them how to reach the bluff path.

I pushed forward again, the snow needling into my face, and was rendered breathless by the wind, which blew into my throat. My feet seemed unconnected to me, cold and silent as they plodded through the snow, lurching me forward until I touched the first pine and inhaled its lovely fragrance. I moved into the shadow of what the locals called "The Big Three," the first three pines that formed part of the stand. Instantly the pressure of the storm lessened and the noise did, as well. The pines, like three protectors, had brought me relief from nature's onslaught. They had also brought me the view I sought. Tucked against the trunk of the second tree, I spied Strayer as he hesitated to leave the shelter of the evergreens and enter the blizzard once again. On our right was the best view of the town—a broad and spectacular vista of winter over the lake. On our left, the pines disappeared into nothingness as the bluff plunged steeply downward, revealing the stark beauty of rock and haphazard trees that grew sideways out of the hill. I spied a large bird's nest in one of these happenstance growths, and I wondered if eagles had made it.

Strayer spun suddenly around in the small clearing, which was its own silent, white world, and pointed at Elliott. "What's up, Jake? You don't like my journalism, but you're following me for ideas?"

Elliott stopped and folded his arms against his blue coat. "I don't need ideas from you, Strayer. Some of us have authentic talent and real thoughts that don't come from viewer comments."

Strayer shrugged, rubbing his gloved hands together. "So you came up here to insult me?" His teeth were chattering slightly.

"I came here to find out why you were climbing up during a storm. What a strange thing to do. And being a good reporter, I thought I sensed a story there." He moved forward slightly, putting only a few feet between him and Strayer. "You were talking weird in the bar last night; it got me thinking, so I figured I'd follow you. And just now, as I watched, I noticed a funny thing. It seemed like you were looking for something, Ted. At first I thought you might just be hunting for pinecones or some crazy thing like that, but then I realized that you were only looking back and forth in the last few yards. Right around the place that Taylor Brand fell over. So let's have it—what do you know about her death?"

Strayer frowned. "You're making a lot of assumptions there, Jake. That's not good journalism, at least not by your definition. Crap, it's cold up here!"

Elliott's posture changed then; he straightened, and it reminded me of uncoiling, the way a snake would do. "You're deflecting. What is it you don't want me to know?"

"Write your own story! Just leave me alone, Elliott. I'm sick of people talking down to me, telling me what scum I am. I provide for my family. You wouldn't know what that's like, having to provide for people."

"Sure I do. I have an ex-wife who likes expensive things. What were you looking for, Strayer?"

Strayer's face was hard to see at that distance, but he used broad enough body language that I could tell he was overcompensating, acting out a role of a man who is tired. "Not that this isn't a super fun conversation, but I'm headed back down to a warm room and some hot coffee."

Elliott stuck out a hand, as though to bar his way. "You know what just dawned on me? You could be the one who pushed Taylor off the bluff. That would explain how you knew so much about the story and how you got details so quickly! You knew to hang out at West's house before any of the rest of us did! What happened, Strayer? Did she talk down to you, too? Did she call you scum? Did she tell you to stop stalking her and—oh my God."

Strayer's body was still as death; he had stopped acting now, but his voice had some forced and brittle amusement in it when he said, "What now? You should write fiction."

"You were wearing that stupid orange press lanyard when I got to town, and then you stopped wearing it, but not before I saw that the ID was gone."

There was a short silence, and then Elliott said, "Did she rip off your ID, Strayer? Maybe when she fell?"

The two men stared at each other for what seemed like twenty minutes in the charged and snowy silence. The moment felt so long that I started to wonder if I had imagined the whole exchange, and if the three of us were up here at all, in this dreamlike landscape where the wind buffeted the snowflakes all around the giant pines. I tucked more closely into my pine tree, suddenly fearful that they would both turn and point at me, like men in a horror story.

Instead, in total silence and without warning, Ted Strayer rushed forward at remarkable speed and barreled into Jake Elliott, pushing him backward and over the bluff before Elliott could say a word or raise a hand in his own defense. In an instant Elliott was simply gone, and Strayer stood alone, panting and clenching his gloved fists. He only turned because of the sound that pierced the air, high-pitched and horrified. At first I thought it was the eagle, returning to her nest and finding human intruders, but when Strayer turned with a murderous expression I realized that the screaming was coming from me, and that this was a horror story after all.

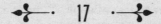

17

*She had only one lucid thought as she faced a man
whose eyes were hard with malice and whose gun
was pointed at her chest: I never said good-bye.*
—From *Death on the Danube*

MY MIND WAS completely blank, and for a moment, I
think Strayer's was, too. He regarded me from fifteen feet
away, panting with exertion and adrenaline, and the moment seemed to hang suspended. Then he was in motion,
rushing toward me, and my feet responded, pumping back
down the path the way I had come, convincing me that
in that direction lay safety. I would have screamed if I
had not needed all of my breath for the exertion of running at top speed. I didn't dare glance down the bluff to
see its steep decline, or to glimpse the roof of Sam's house
far below.

Sam. If only he had been home when I called. Instead,
I was in a white, swirling maelstrom with a madman.
Occasionally I could hear his muffled footfalls behind me
and I had the terrible sense that he was closing the distance
between us. I rounded a bend and saw a giant elm that

Camilla's dogs liked to sniff; they often paused in its shade to cool themselves before continuing up the bluff. With some primordial instinct, I dove at the tree and began to climb it. Strayer had no weapon; if I were above him, my brain told me, I would have an advantage. He could try to pull me down, but I could kick him from a height.

I had not climbed a tree since my childhood, but even in my winter gear I moved nimbly up through the branches, spurred by terror. There was always the hope that Strayer wouldn't see me and run right past.

He stopped, though, right at the foot of the tree, and said, "Come down, Lena. I'll come up and get you if I have to, but I'd prefer that you just come down so we can talk."

"Talk about what?" I almost screamed. "How you murdered Taylor Brand? How you just killed Jake Elliott in front of my eyes?"

Strayer shrugged. If my eyes didn't deceive me, he looked merely regretful, as one does when his library book is overdue. "What could I do? He accused me of murdering Taylor. He was wrong, of course. I did no such thing."

"Of course," I said. I felt oddly detached from our conversation, as though I were wrapped in cotton, or talking to him through a thick door. "You are innocent, so you had to kill Jake to prove that. I'm sure the jury will agree with you, Strayer."

He ran a hand over his sopping wet hair, dislodging some snowflakes. "Okay, fine. He figured out the truth. I did walk up here with Taylor, okay? I told her she had to see the view. We had argued that morning, because she suspected me of stealing her postcard, and I finally convinced her that I didn't. I said, "Let's bury the hatchet; I'll show you a view like you've never seen before.""

"But why kill her?" I said. "Even if she found out you stole the postcard, so what? You could just give it back."

Strayer nodded, still with that fake regret. "Yes, I could. The problem was that Taylor was here, with a giant clue, and she intended to solve the Victoria West disappearance with the help of Sam West. And then in an instant my two most lucrative stories would simply dry up. I've built a career on Victoria West alone; Sam West's miseries were icing on the cake. And without her little clue, this could potentially drag on for months, years. I can't have someone marching into town and shutting down the gravy train. It's a dog-eat-dog world, Lena."

From my high branch, he looked weirdly truncated, planted there in the snow, his glasses wet with condensation. It was then I realized he wasn't a man at all. He was without conscience—a weird by-product of a greedy and shallow society. He was a monster of the modern age, and he had killed two people without apparent remorse.

Something dawned on me then, as I faced the fact that Strayer was without morals. "You shot Sam's window out. You did it yourself, to create your own story. You're evil."

He shrugged. "It got me a lot of readers. It was news."

"Yellow journalism."

"Come down, Lena," he said. It was terrifying, how normal his voice sounded. It implied that he didn't feel the weight of his sins, but also that he was ready to wait all day if necessary.

"I won't."

"Then I'll climb up. But if I do, I won't be gentle. I'm going to drag you out of that tree, and I'm going to hurt you, Lena. It would be better for you if you came down of your own accord. Taylor never had a moment's fear—

well, a couple of moments. She did scream when I pushed her, but it was such a short scream. Seconds only, and then it was over. I spared her a terrible death."

And in that surreal moment I was transformed. It was not fear coursing through me, but anger—perhaps even hatred. Ted Strayer had ruined lives—Taylor's, Jake Elliott's, Sam West's, and he was taking responsibility for none of it. Again, my feet seemed to be working independently of me as they found the right branches and led me out of the tree. Strayer waited, his face patient and pleased.

When I reached the bottom he started to say something— a mundane comment with a touch of condescension, and I slid off my gloves, tossing them aside an instant before I dove at him, channeled my anger, and launched a right-handed punch at his face, which made satisfying contact with his cheekbone. His glasses flew into the snow near the edge of the path, and he turned slightly blind eyes to me, clearly surprised and, for the first time, angry. "That was unnecessary!" he yelled, holding his face with one hand.

I put up my fists, ready to hit him again. The snow burned my eyes and made me blink at Strayer, who was trying to find his glasses with one eye while keeping the other on me.

This seemed to be my opportunity to get away; he probably wouldn't chase me until he could restore his sight. I backed away, testing my theory, and I saw that he was torn between chasing me and finding the security of his vision. He squinted at me with his myopic eyes and I saw that he would never make it back down the path without his glasses.

Feeling a spurt of triumph amidst my terror, I ran.

At the bottom of the path I ran toward the trees behind Sam's house while I dialed my phone. This time I called Doug. "Doug Heller."

"Ted Strayer just killed Jake Elliott and he's chasing me!" I yelled.

"Where are you, Lena?" His voice was clipped and a bit frightened.

"Sam's house. Right behind. Oh God, I see Elliott now. He's moving. He's alive! But he'll need an ambulance. I don't know where Strayer is. We were up on the path."

"Look now. Tell me if you see him."

I turned and studied the cliff path. "I don't see him. He was behind me, but he lost his glasses. No, wait. There he is."

"Can he see you?"

I ducked behind a tree and lowered my voice, studying Strayer as he staggered down the path. "No. He's not even looking over here. He's moving down the pebbled road. He's past Sam's now and still walking."

"Wait there. Be sure he's gone."

"He's out of sight now. You can get him, Doug. He killed Taylor and shot Sam's house. He admitted them both to me. He's crazy."

"Hang up. I'll be right there. See what you can do for Elliott and get Sam to help you."

I clicked off the phone and stumbled through the snow to Elliott, who was gray with pain but still managed to smile at me. "Lena. The goddess emerges from the storm."

"Are you badly hurt?"

"This big-ass snow drift probably saved my life, but my leg—" he winced in pain. "Pretty badly broken. Distract me, or I'll go insane."

I knelt next to him and poked and prodded the rest of

his limbs while trying not to look at his left leg, which was twisted in a way it shouldn't have been. "I'm so glad you're alive, Jake. I was there—I saw what he did. I didn't have even a second to help you."

"God. Listen, if I pass out, you should know—to tell the police. Strayer and I had a drink last night at the bar on Kelter Street. He was talking weird, going on and on about how these Blue Lake stories were a gold mine, and how lucky he was to have 'hit the Sam West vein' because it was setting him up for years to come. He's always been a braggart—oh God, that hurts—but this was something different. He was talking about Taylor Brand without even a gleam of regret. I said that he was feeding off of human misery, and he looked at me with total incomprehension.

"It was then I realized he wasn't quite right; maybe the endless pursuit of the story has just twisted him. But I determined that I would keep an eye on him, which is why I followed him this morning."

"I hear the sirens, Jake. Stay with me—they're almost here. They'll stabilize that leg and get you on an IV. Hopefully the worst of the pain will end right here in the snow."

"Where Taylor died. God, that poor kid. Tricked by a jackal like Ted Strayer, when she just wanted to find her friend. Ah, shoot." He was close to fainting.

I turned in desperation to see Sam West, holding a paper grocery bag, walking up the steps to his house.

"Sam!" I cried.

He looked up, dropped the bag, and ran to us. In a moment he was kneeling in the snow at my side, taking in Elliott's injuries. "What happened?" he asked.

Elliott closed his eyes, so I answered. "Strayer pushed

him off the bluff. He pushed Taylor, too. Strayer's insane, Sam."

Sam looked at Elliott's white face. "He's going into shock, and I wouldn't be surprised if he's bleeding internally. That leg—"

Jake Elliott opened his eyes. "Ted Strayer is dangerous," he said, "And he's still at large. Focus on him."

"We will. Jake, hold on. Here's the ambulance. You're going to be okay."

"Good to know," Elliott said with a sickly smile, and then he fainted.

THE AMBULANCE LEFT quickly, lights flashing, after the attendants carefully stabilized Elliott on a stretcher. I felt grateful that he was unconscious, because the pain of being moved would have been horrifying. Doug appeared and spoke briefly with the EMTs before they left with Elliott. Then he walked over to us.

"I've got men looking for Strayer, including two officers combing the bluff path. What happened, Lena?"

I told them, as succinctly as I could, why I had followed the two men. "It was surreal, the whole experience. This weird white world, and Strayer's blank eyes. He's lost all sense of morality. He said that he fought with Taylor because she accused him of stealing her postcard. She didn't give it to him; they didn't consult over it. He just took it, and she suspected it, and so I'm guessing he returned it and offered then and there to make it up to her by showing her this amazing view. Or maybe he convinced her that someone else took it. I don't know why Taylor agreed; I think Strayer is a good actor, and probably pretended to be all sorry and regretful, and she fell for his 'aw shucks, I'm a struggling reporter' act. Then he pushed her off the bluff. If he had given back the postcard, he must have taken it just before or . . . after." This last option seemed so ghoulish I couldn't even imagine Strayer doing it. And yet . . .

Sam touched my arm. "Lena, I can't believe I chose this time to get a few groceries. I'm so sorry I wasn't there when you called."

"It was scary," I said. "But I got angry—so angry for Taylor and Jake and all of his victims that he's destroyed for the sake of a story. I punched him in the face."

Both men turned to study me, surprised. "As in, you made contact?"

"I knocked his glasses off, which is how I was able to get away from him. Otherwise I might be lying there where Jake was."

This thought seemed to horrify all of us, and we avoided each other's eyes for a while. "Lena, do you have any idea where Strayer would go?"

I shook my head. "I have no clue. I just wanted to get away from him. Oh—Jake Elliott accused him of looking for something. That's how he figured out what Strayer had done. He asked Ted what he had dropped, and then he remembered that Ted had worn a press ID on an orange lanyard. I saw that lanyard, too, when we were in his room. It was sitting by his computer. But Elliott realized that the ID was gone, and he asked if that's what Strayer was looking for. He asked if Taylor ripped it off as she was falling."

Doug's eyes grew wide, and he said, "Excuse me. I need to tell my guys up there to hunt for that ID." He took out his phone and walked away from us, speaking rapidly.

A fair distance from Sam's house, emerging like weird zombies from the white wall of snow, were a few dark-clad members of the press, staggering forward to find the story. For once I wasn't angry to see them. They would talk to Doug, and eventually to Jake Elliott; they would learn the truth about Taylor's death and Sam's innocence, and at least one problem would finally be solved.

Sam took my hand. "I'm sorry I wasn't there. I wish I had been."

I held his glove against my face. "You were there in spirit. I was thinking of you up there, and all that you've been through because of people like Strayer. And it worked out for the best, because I got to punch him right in the face. I was afraid, and then my fear turned inside out and I was so angry I couldn't resist doing him violence. Now I know how men feel, with all their testosterone."

Sam laughed; for an instant he looked like a teenager, and all the stress of his life was wiped away by relief and amusement.

Doug waved to us from the road. "I'll check in later," he called, and then he got in his car and drove away, speaking tersely to the reporters before he left.

"Quick. Into my house before they accost us," Sam said. We moved swiftly to his porch and up the stairs to his door.

"Mr. West," they were calling. "Lena!"

Sam waved a vague hand. "Another time," he said. We closed his door and collapsed, weary, on his couch.

"Just think," I said. "We thought we just hated Strayer because he was a slimy reporter. Now I'm wondering if our instincts were trying to tell us something."

"Now if only our instincts would tell us one last se-cret," he said. "Come on—we need to call Camilla and get you into some warm clothes."

I changed into a pair of his sweats and he poured me some hot coffee. Sam called Camilla and filled her in, saying that I would stay with him for the present. He ended the call and said, "She sounded grim, but satisfied. Lena? Are you okay?"

"Something's not fitting. Janet Baskin said that Taylor fought with Caden Brand on the morning she died. But Strayer just said that it was him, and they fought because he stole her postcard."

Sam leaned back on his couch and looked up at the ceiling while he thought. "What did Janet say? Something like, 'She was fighting with the guy I saw you with.' But if Janet was staying with someone in one of the cabins, then she could have seen us with Strayer when we went to his place. She was probably talking about Strayer all along, and we just assumed she meant Brand."

"This is all so confusing, like a tangled thread. How did we get caught up in all of this, Sam?"

He pulled me against him and said, "We just got one of the knots untangled. Things are looking up." I leaned back on his chest and we looked at the snow which came down soft as lace now, filling in the footprints made by recent visitors, and effacing all evidence of conflict on the cliff path above us.

18

*Later she would look back in awe at the events of
that part of her life and wonder anew at the things
she had been willing to do for the sake of love.*
                            —From *Death on the Danube*

BY MORNING THE whole world knew the truth about Ted
Strayer, and he was perhaps the most wanted man in the
country. Caden Brand appeared on the news, his face
looking as pompous as ever, talking about how much he
loved his sister and how much Ted Strayer had taken away
from him. He even worked up some insincere tears, which
made Camilla sniff and turn off the television.

"Let's walk the dogs," she said with a bright expression.

"Doug said not to walk around until Strayer is caught."

Camilla gave me her regal look. "I do not intend to be
a prisoner in my own home; my dogs know what to do to
anyone who threatens us."

It was true; Heathcliff and Rochester, though gentle
as lambs with the people who loved them, were particularly ferocious to those who might be perceived as a threat
to Camilla. "All right. I'd like that. And then I suppose

we should take a stab at chapter eleven. I have some questions about the scene by the cathedral."

"Yes, good idea. This book has made halting progress at best, thanks to all of our distractions, but I do think it will end up being good."

"I know it will. You have such an amazing talent, Camilla."

"You are sweet to say so. I have a remarkable collaborator."

We donned our winter gear and went outside, each of us holding a dog on a leash. The pups were pleased to be in the snow, and eventually we let them run back and forth to work off some of their winter doldrums.

I told Camilla the story of Ted Strayer in a bit more detail, and she gasped at the end. "Lena. It was brave of you to follow them. You're like me, and you need answers above all else. You like writing mysteries, not living them."

"So true."

"I am not happy with the risks you took—confronting Strayer, staring down a madman like that." Her voice wobbled slightly.

"Camilla? Are you all right?"

"I just don't know what I'd do, Lena, if you weren't in my life. You've become a part of my daily reality, and I don't want to be without you ever again."

This was the most emotional thing I had ever heard Camilla say. I stopped in my tracks, turned to her, and pulled her into an embrace. "You know I feel the same way. But I didn't know I was taking a risk at the time. I thought I was just spying from a safe location. Things went—a bit haywire."

Camilla, more composed now and smiling at me, shook

her head. "Perhaps I'm an egotist, and I only love you because you remind me so much of myself. But I do love you, Lena."

I hoped that she would think my hot cheeks were red from the cold, and not from the intense joy of hearing those words from my lifelong idol. "I love you, too, Camilla."

We walked for a while in silence; I occasionally took her arm to help her over an icy patch, but Camilla was generally a sturdier walker than I was.

"Does Adam know about everything?" I asked.

She paused and studied the sky, which was a gentle blue today and filled with fluffy clouds, seemingly unconnected to the bitter gray sky that had spit out a blizzard with nearly deadly results. "He knows the basics. He's coming by today for coffee; he wants to hear your harrowing tale; Lord knows he'll be able to process it better than I could."

"I like Adam. He's very sweet, and he's handsome."

"I agree."

"How long have you known him?"

She snapped for the dogs, who returned to us, panting and playful. We picked up their leashes and resumed our walk. "James and Adam were actually childhood friends here in Blue Lake. When we lived in London, we would get the occasional letter or Christmas card from Adam, but he was just a name to me. When we moved to Blue Lake, Adam simply became a part of our lives. We would all do things together—James and I, Adam and his wife. Her name was Vera. He lost her years before I lost James, to cancer."

"The most evil disease."

"Yes. And then Adam and I remained friends; he was

very comforting after James died, and we would get together now and again to share our memories. He truly loved James like a brother."

"So did you avoid his advances at first because it felt like a betrayal of James?"

"Not really. As you know, I didn't pick up on the fact that Adam was making advances. That seemed like something from another life—the whole notion of romance and wooing."

"Wooing!" I said, giggling. "There's a word you don't hear too often."

Camilla lifted her chin. "Adam is very good at wooing. I'll bet Sam is, too."

I nodded. "He woos with waffles."

Camilla laughed, sounding like a girl. "We'd better get back. If Doug catches a glimpse of us out here, we'll get a long sermon. But I am convinced Ted Strayer is as far from Blue Lake as he can possibly get."

CAMILLA WAS WRONG about that—perhaps for the first time. We tucked back into her house and did a bit of work while drinking hot tea, the dogs sleeping practically on our feet. I was reading a line about an evil man in Camilla's book and the secret lover who hides him, temporarily, from the police, and an image popped into my head. The more I studied it, the more I couldn't sit still. The dogs rustled below me.

"Camilla."

"Hmm?"

"A few days ago I saw Jake Elliott and Ted Strayer talking in Bick's Hardware."

"How is Elliott today, do you know?"

"Sam said he's stable after surgery, and high on pain medication."

"Oh, good. I feel so bad for that man, when I think—"

"Camilla!"

"Yes?"

"I saw them in Bick's Hardware, and then I talked to Elliott, and Strayer started talking to some local woman, who I think tends bar on Kelter Street. The more I think back—the more I feel like her expression was kind of—familiar."

"As in you'd seen it before, or as in she was familiar with Strayer?"

"B."

"Call Doug."

I did, using Camilla's speakerphone. "Doug Heller," he said, and I blessed him for always, always answering his phone.

"Doug, it's Lena."

"Are you okay?"

I blessed him for that, too. "Yes, thanks. I might have a link to Strayer."

"What is it?" I could tell he was sitting up straight now, wearing his alert cop face.

I told him about Carrie from the bar.

"It's Carla," he said. "And thank you for the tip."

He said good-bye and hung up, and I stared at my lap for a while, knowing that Camilla's sharp gaze was on me. "He confuses me sometimes," I said. "I know I love Sam, but . . ." I met her eyes. "You must think I'm crazy. But when Doug showed up with Belinda the other day, I was jealous. What is that all about?"

"I wonder," Camilla said. "This is a theory—tell me what you think. She's taking away his time, and you want to know that he'll still be in your life. You don't recognize these feelings because you've never had a sibling. From the start you have loved him like one—like a big, handsome, protective older brother. Sometimes that's a bit like hero worship, and sometimes we can be sort of in love, platonically, with our siblings, or any members of our families."

"A brother," I said. "That makes sense. Doug *is* like my brother. And I do love him. He's always there when I need him."

"He always will be. For the same reason."

"You should charge me money for all the wisdom you've doled out."

She laughed and sipped her tea. "I have enough money," she said.

THAT NIGHT SAM and I visited Allison and John Branch again; Allison had almost recovered from the news about Sam's family, but she was still trying to compensate by overfeeding him, and Sam was moaning when we left their house. He looked woefully at me in the car. "She is such a good cook," he said. "But I think she's trying to kill me."

We were driving through town, on our way to the bluff road. "Pull over here," I said. "We'll walk up and down the streets and breathe some crisp winter air, and it will help you digest your food."

"Good. Maybe we can get some coffee somewhere, too."

We got out and began walking down Wentworth Street, hand in hand. Blue Lake is always pretty at night, with the water sparkling dark blue in the distance and store lights dotting the darkness with various cozy hues. A scent of wood smoke permeated the cold air, adding to the lonely loveliness of the night. "I can see why Camilla stayed here, even though it's not a glamorous place," I said. "It has its own special allure." I squeezed his hand. "I can even see why you stayed here."

He nodded. "Yes, despite my status as a pariah, I always liked the view, and my house. It's a great house."

"It is. Can you imagine ever finding something like it in New York?"

"No. Especially not at that price."

We turned onto Sabre Street, heading for Yeats. Suddenly a car screeched up next to us, blue and red lights flashing. Another pulled up behind that one, and for a terrible moment I feared they were there to arrest Sam once again. My hand tightened on his, ready to hold on at all costs.

But the police officers leaped out and ran right past us, their guns drawn and held low.

"That was scary," Sam said, his voice shaking slightly. I touched his face.

"Never again," I said.

We had only moved forward about three yards when I saw a figure running toward us on the dark sidewalk. He materialized into Ted Strayer, moving at top speed. He had managed to find his glasses on the bluff, but they looked a bit mangled, and they added to his overall unbalanced look.

I had no time to wonder why he was heading our way; he looked to his right to see that police cars barred his passage. He was clearly going to try to pass on the left, where the storefronts met the sidewalk. As he approached he said, "Out of my way!" and started to fly past us.

Sam put out a casual arm at the level of Strayer's neck and effectively clotheslined him. Strayer landed on his back, the wind knocked totally out of him. Another figure pelted toward us; we eventually recognized him as Doug Heller. He looked from Strayer to Sam to me and smiled. "Good tip, Lena. We've been watching Carla all day, and she managed to lead us to Ted there."

Sam's foot was resting lightly on Strayer's chest. Now Doug bent over and hoisted him up so that he could put on the cuffs. "Ted Strayer, you are under arrest. I am charging you with the murder of Taylor Brand and the attempted murder of Jake Elliott. You have the right to remain silent . . ."

Strayer looked defiant. "I didn't do anything! You can't prove it!" He paused for a minute, then said, "What do you mean, 'attempted murder'?"

Doug looked pleased. "Jake Elliott is alive and well, and has been kind enough to explain everything that happened up on the bluff."

Strayer's mouth stayed open; apparently he hadn't realized that Elliott had survived his fall. "I want my lawyer," Strayer bellowed, sounding petulant. "I won't go anywhere with you until I get my lawyer." Doug started dragging him toward one of the police cars, and Strayer yelled louder. "I want my lawyer!"

"Yeah, and I want you to shut up. We'll probably both have to wait longer than we'd like," Doug said, almost cheerfully. He stowed Strayer into the police car and turned to give Sam a thumbs up. "You ever think about law enforcement as a career?" Doug asked.

Sam laughed. "Not once," he said.

"You should. I could use you on the force."

Sam nodded. "Maybe just deputize me as needed."

Doug waved to the cops who were coming back to their cars. "Get this guy to the station and I'll meet you there," he said. "Tobias, ride in back with him. He's slimy enough to slip through the crack in the door."

"That's for sure," I said under my breath.

Doug waved to us and said, "We'll talk soon." Then he was walking away, presumably toward his own vehicle, and the police cars pulled away from the curb, escorting Strayer to the Blue Lake PD and his temporary jail cell.

WE FINISHED OUR walk and then had our coffee at Sam's place. "I hope you'll stay tonight," Sam said. "I find the house unbearably quiet when you're not here."

"Am I loud?"

"You know what I mean."

"I'll call Camilla and give her a heads up."

"And I'll lend you some pajamas. Maybe you should— you know leave a few clothes here, and toiletries and things. I can give you a whole room of your own to keep your things in."

"Like some grand hotel," I joked.

"I'll even put a mint on your pillow."

I kissed him. "We should talk soon about those notes you made after your dad's phone call. We need to make a plan of investigation."

He leaned his elbow on the table and rested his chin on his hand. "We're always making plans of investigation. I'm getting a little tired of mysteries."

I covered his other hand with mine. "We're getting there, Sam. We've made so much progress. We just need a little more—we're on the verge of something. Even the reporters know it."

"What?"

"Jake Elliott and Ted Strayer were talking about it in Bick's Hardware. They said reporters have a second sense, and that they all know Victoria's case will break open soon. They're gathering in the water, waiting to feed."

"Creepy, but somehow promising."

"That's what I thought."

"Can I tell you something? I'm a little scared."

"Why?"

"It's been so long since I've seen or talked to Vic. I don't know her anymore; she's like a woman from a dream. If somehow she materializes again, it will be more than disconcerting. I'll be relieved, of course, knowing that she's okay, but—who am I supposed to be to her? I don't feel like anything but a widower. That's what everyone assumed I was, for a year. What if she wants to be in my life?"

This was a fear I had harbored myself. A year with Nikon Lazos might certainly have made Victoria West more conscious of how good Sam West had been. What if she wanted him back? I wasn't about to relinquish him, no matter how much I pitied Victoria and her baby. Did that make me a bad person? "I've had some similar qualms. But I think we should take things one step at a time. We have to make sure she's safe. Everything else comes later."

Sam nodded. "You're right, of course."

"But there is a complication."

"Oh?"

"No matter what happens, you're not going to be able to get rid of me."

This made him smile. "Come on, princess. You can choose your favorite room upstairs, and you can fill it with all your choicest possessions."

"Hurrah!"

He stood and held out his hand. "But you do not have a choice about which bed you sleep in. I'm afraid that's nonnegotiable."

I slid into his arms. "I'm a terrible negotiator anyway." Over his shoulder I could see the dark blue sky and a glimmering of stars, and I wondered if Victoria, wherever she was, could view the same sky and could sense that those visible constellations, like a glittering path, connected her to us.

19

*Truth can come in an instant, and when one looks
into Her eyes, one's vision is forever altered.*
—From *Death on the Danube*

FOR A COUPLE of days, life was as quiet as the snow that
fell on Blue Lake. Later Camilla would refer to it as "the
calm before the chaos." Sam and I spent some peaceful
times together, enjoying our new romance. Two days after Strayer was arrested, we had lunch with Doug and
Belinda at Wheat Grass, compliments of Sam, who told
Doug he far preferred him as a friend than as an enemy.
Doug wryly agreed, and then, man-like, they made plans
to watch a football game together the following Sunday.

Belinda and I sat to the side and talked about her research. She had continued to hunt out things for the
London File, and had found some interesting biographical
pieces on Victoria, Taylor, even Sam, but nothing that
seemed advantageous to our quest. She had been looking
at hospital birth records in hopes of finding a baby for
Nikon Lazos, but so far she had not been successful.

The *New York Times* printed a front-page story written by Jake Elliott, who continued to convalesce in the hospital but had clearly been slaving away at his laptop. Camilla knocked on my door before I had even fully dressed, and came into my room to show me the paper. She lifted Lestrade and petted his fuzzy head while I read the article, my mouth hanging open in disbelief. The headline read "Hero, Not Villain: Sam West Saved My Life."

Jake Elliott, in a surprisingly moving article, described his fall and his pain and torment in the snow. He described the way I looked when I ran to him, "like an angel of mercy in a white and uncertain world," and how soon after Sam West had dropped his bag of groceries and run to his side, gauging his injuries and waiting for help while trying to soothe and distract him. The article was no less than a glowing tribute to both Sam and me. The last paragraph, however, castigated the society that was so willing to condemn Sam, and who treated him like an outcast when, in fact, there had been no evidence to do so. He wrote,

"Sam West lost his wife to an uncertain fate; soon after, he lost his friends, his home, and his reputation, thanks to the people who turned a cold shoulder to him in his time of need. This crime—which had many accomplices—was committed without any threat of punishment. Sometimes justice is not served. The miracle is that people like Sam West retain their strength of character no matter what the world throws at them."

I finished reading and set the paper down on my bed. "Wow."

Camilla nodded. "I had to run up here. What a good man Jake Elliott turned out to be."

"Yes. Quite the opposite of Ted Strayer. God, when I think that poor Taylor spent her last moments with that horrible man . . ."

"Try not to think about it. One could go mad, obsessing over things like this. Focus on the good being done now—by Elliott, by Doug, by Belinda with her research."

"Yes. You're right." I went to my closet and found a sweater to slip on over my shirt. In Blue Lake, one was best off dressing in layers. "I need to call Sam and ask if he's seen this."

"All right." Camilla was looking at Lestrade, who was practically dozing in her arms. "I might sit here with your kitty for a moment. We have bonded over this good news."

I smiled and patted her arm, then moved swiftly down the stairs and into the kitchen. I poured myself a cup of coffee and called Sam.

"Hello?" His voice rumbled in my ear in a warm and familiar way.

"Good morning. Have you seen the paper today?"

"The *New York Times*, you mean?"

"Yes! What did you think?"

When Sam finally spoke, I could tell he was smiling. "It felt damn good, Lena. Come celebrate with me."

"I will, soon. Camilla and I have some work to do."

He sighed. "Me, too, I guess. Nowadays I just want to hang around with you and not do my job. And I've been distracted by the letters, the e-mails, the phone calls—all from well-wishers."

"There will be others. You'll be drowning in acclaim."

We let that irony sink in for a while. Then Sam said, "God, Lena. If we could just find her. I could have a normal life back. Do you know that once I was a relatively carefree guy? I did my job, came home at night, ate my dinner, watched TV, just like the average American. When Vic and I were breaking up, I was trying to reinvent myself. I had a new apartment lined up—it's hard to find something good in New York City—and I was thinking of getting a dog or a cat. Some new companion to start my new life."

"And it ended up being me."

"Life can be kind sometimes."

I looked out the window into Camilla's snow-covered backyard. Blue Lake, pale and cold, twinkled icily in the distance. "What can we do? There must be a way. I mean, I found Victoria just by using search terms online. Then Belinda found Nikon the same way. This is just a big puzzle, and thanks to the Internet, that puzzle should be much easier to solve. This time we just have to find . . . a baby."

"How does one search for a nameless baby?" asked Sam.

Even after we said our good-byes and promised to meet up later in the day, his question echoed in my mind. How could we search for the child? For certainly he or she was the key to this whole thing. If there was no record of Nikon marrying or fathering a child, then he had reason to keep those two things a secret. But could anything be kept secret in this new world of exposure? Did privacy really exist?

Normally that question would have depressed me, but now it excited me. I ran to the stairs, where Camilla was just descending, still holding a drowsy and very content Lestrade. "Lena, I think this is the first time I've spent time with your cat, and he is simply delightful. He reminds me of a cat I knew in London, long ago. He wasn't mine, but he visited me every morning and we would have tea together. He even knocked on the door, if I wasn't quick enough to let him in. Such a character. He belonged to a neighbor, I found out, but really he also belonged to me. His name was Biscuit."

"That's very sweet. Might I leave you two to your bonding and do a bit of Internet research? I'm feeling inspired."

"Of course. Doug has received no updates, as I recall, and it doesn't seem anyone has come close to solving our mystery. Go do what you can, Sherlock."

I grinned and ran up the stairs to my room. Even after months with Camilla, I always took a moment to appreciate my space, my big comfortable bed flanked by large windows, and my beautiful dark wood desk, smooth and inviting as always. I ran to it and opened my laptop, almost falling off my chair in my haste to begin.

Belinda was searching databases, hospitals, public records, all for the mention of a child who might be linked to the name Victoria West or Nikon Lazos. She was the expert at doing that, and I would have no idea how to go about it. Instead, I wanted to pursue what Sam had said—that if I could just find mention of the baby, I might have the link I needed.

I began by Googling things like "Victoria West baby" and "Nikon Lazos baby."

That didn't turn up anything besides a few gossip sites which speculated, not about a baby but about where Nikon had been. One of them spoke of various big names, and devoted a paragraph to Lazos, which said, "Nikon Leandros Lazos, the handsome and eligible bachelor who had once been so prominent in the Mediterranean social scene, has kept a lower profile for the last few years. Rumor has it he has found the love of his life, although few people have spotted this red-haired beauty. Lazos seems to be lying low, occasionally vacationing with friends or taking jaunts on their yachts."

Their yachts. Yes, that would explain the difficulty in finding him.

I tried searching "Lazos child, West child, Greek island child." As I expected, they turned up nothing but seemingly unrelated results. I remembered what Belinda had said: "Someone out there delivered that baby."

This gave me another idea. I searched "I delivered a baby for Nikon Lazos." The results were disappointing; just a lot of pediatric sites and the occasional doctor's personal experience blog, along with some of those harrowing "I delivered my wife's baby on the expressway" types of news stories.

With a sigh, I stood up and paced my room for a while, appreciating the radiated heat and the plush Persian rug under my feet. I had a craving for some of Camilla's tea, so I ran downstairs and poured myself a cup, then headed back. Camilla called, "Solved it yet?" and I laughed.

Then back I went, braced by a sip of sugared Earl Grey. I tried to imagine that I was the doctor, telling my story. I typed "I delivered a baby on a yacht moored off a Greek island." I laughed at the ridiculous search term, but I clicked enter and scrolled through the results, which were again useless. Most seemed to be about doctors or hospitals, and some seemed to be from Greek travel sites, many of which used alluring language to try to earn a clickthrough. I scrolled through pages and pages—perhaps a hundred entries—and then decided to give up. One last title caught my eye, though. It was another medical page, what seemed like a professional blog, called *Obstetrics*

Today. The search had brought up an interview on the site titled "Dr. Ian Foster Discusses His New Practice, His Favorite Deliveries, and the One That Got Away."

I clicked on this and saw a picture of a fiftysomething man in a white coat, smiling charmingly at a camera for his professional photo. The interview, in a Q and A format, asked him about his life, his schooling, his first practice, his most difficult times. I scrolled toward the bottom of the interview, to the question "You recently had an interesting experience while on vacation in Greece. Can you tell us about that?"

Foster's response followed, and it was long. I took another sip of tea, then began to read.

Yes, it was interesting. I was vacationing in Crete, taking some much-needed family time. One night we were sitting outside a café with a view of the ocean. It was spectacular, with just candlelight and a stunning view of the stars. I was sipping ouzo and looking at my wife, and she said that the Greeks believed strongly in presentiments, and she was having one. Something was about to happen.

I laughed and reached out to muss her hair, and moments later someone was touching my arm. It was a local man who had been asked to seek me out; he said that a gentleman's wife was having a baby, and he heard that a specialist was staying at the hotel. This wasn't surprising, since the town seemed to run on gossip, but there were medical facilities available on the island, which I told the young man. He said that the man had been most insistent, and that he was willing to pay any price to have the American look at his wife. My own wife began to feel urgent, telling me that I had to go, because what if there was a woman in distress?

I agreed to go with the young man, promising my wife I would text her when I got to my location. To my great surprise, I wasn't led to one of the whitewashed cottages that dotted the coast, but to a giant yacht in the harbor. The thing was massive, and I felt like I was stepping into a fairy tale when I walked up the gangplank with my anonymous guide. I made sure to text my wife my location before I climbed aboard, although I never felt that I was in any danger.

My heart started beating rapidly, and I felt a bead of sweat run down the back of my neck. I reached for my teacup and realized that my hands were shaking. I put it down without drinking and continued to read.

Once I got to the room where the woman was in labor, I almost laughed aloud. They didn't need my services at all. The man had paid for every modern medical convenience, and he had created an entirely sterile room, complete with ultrasound machine and all medical necessities for his wife, who looked comfortable enough, even after several hours of labor. There were several paid nurses on hand who were quite competent, and the young woman had already been administered an epidural. I said as much to those assembled—that they clearly didn't need my services and that everything looked excellent. But the woman asked them all to leave and then clutched my arm with a frightened expression and begged me not to go.

The article ended there, with a note that said "Like this sample and want to read more? Subscribe to *Obstetrics Today!*"

"Agh! I screamed. I jumped out of the chair and dove for my purse, which sat on a table by my bed. My hands were shaking as I fumbled for my credit card and ran back to the desk. "Please be her, please be her," I murmured. I went through the tedious process of entering my name, my address, my credit information, and committed to paying fifty dollars for a year's subscription to a magazine I would never read.

I clicked "no" under the question "Are you a physician?" and submitted my information, ready to scream with anticipation. Finally a little box appeared, thanking me for my subscription. "Click here to continue reading," it said. I moaned and clicked the box.

At the time I chalked this up to nerves. It was her first child, she said, and she wanted everything to go well. She kept asking me if the baby was all right, that she loved her baby without even seeing him. It was very sweet, and she was a remarkably lovely woman, with reddish-brown hair and green eyes. It's the look in her eyes I can't forget, though. Something indefinable that was a combination of loneliness and despair.

So I stayed around, clearly not needed, and held her hand for much of the time. I never knew her name, and her husband, when he came in, shook my hand and introduced himself only as "Lee." He was older than the woman but extremely dashing and charismatic. I was convinced by then that they were Hollywood types who were trying to escape the paparazzi.

They looked vaguely familiar, and I wished my wife were there, because she knows the names of all the movie stars.

At about two in the morning she was ready to push, and I delivered a healthy and beautiful little girl to them; the woman named her Athena. She had been in significant pain, even with her epidural, but the child's arrival seemed to bring a kind of euphoria, and she could not take her eyes from the baby. It was beautiful to see the mother and the child, and the immediate bond between them. The man stood at her side, stroking her hair but also occasionally looking at his watch. The medical staff brought me what seemed to be an official birth record, which I signed and dated, but I have not been able to trace it since that evening, and the local hospital has no record of the birth.

I wasn't particularly concerned when I left that evening; the woman was healthy and happy, and clearly in love with her child. The baby had come with no serious complications, and she was truly lovely, with a full head of dark hair, and little dark eyes like stars. I was discreetly handed an envelope for my services, which I did not open until I arrived back at my hotel, and it contained a ridiculous amount of money for my evening's work. I determined that I would give most of it back the next day, because it is my practice to visit the new mother the day after I deliver a baby, not just for a wellness check, but to answer questions. The woman had seemed a bit nervous, and I wanted to assuage any fears.

I set out the next morning, encouraged by my wife,

who found the whole affair fascinating. I wound through the streets, a bit confused because things looked different in the daytime, but I managed to find the harbor, which had the same sign and the same iron bell on the dock that I recalled from the evening before.

But the yacht was gone. At first I thought it was impossible that something that huge could move through the water at all, but it was entirely gone, and one of the sailors at the dock told me it had left at first light.

I went back, oddly disappointed, because for some reason I had wanted to see the woman and the baby again.

That is probably my most compelling delivery story ever, and I've delivered a lot of babies in a lot of interesting places.

I stopped reading. My heart was still beating and I seemed to be unable to close my eyes, which felt huge in my head, especially because of the last line, in which Dr. Ian Foster provided the most beautiful word I had ever seen.

He had shared the name of the yacht.

AFTER SEVERAL MOMENTS of shock, I was out of my chair and shooting down the hall, screaming for Camilla. I took the stairs two at a time and actually fell down the last four; I landed on my butt at the bottom of the flight, and Camilla found me there, her eyes wide.

"Lena, are you all right? Are you *crying*? Or is that laughter?"

"No. Yes. Both. *Camilla*!" I shouted, wiping at my eyes. She understood in an instant. "You've found them?"

"I've found them. I know I have. We need Doug and Sam, now!"

"Of course," she said, reaching out a hand to help me off the floor. "I'll call him this minute. Take a moment to calm down. Have a glass of water."

"Yes, I will." I watched her walk toward her office and yelled after her: "Camilla! Tell Doug to bring the postcard. The one from Taylor Brand."

20

Joe, in his simple wisdom, warned her not to set her hopes high.

"There are no happy endings," he said. "At best they are ambiguous." Despite his warning, she felt sure that everything, at long last, would be all right.

—From *Death on the Danube*

DOUG AND SAM were there within half an hour; Camilla's house was silent with anticipation. I had printed out the blog interview for everyone to read, and now I passed it out to my three friends at Camilla's dining room table, where the winter light illuminated the hope on every face. "Read," I said.

Sam was laughing halfway through, and Doug yelled "Yes!" while he read. They finished at the same time and slapped each other five; then Sam got up and kissed both Camilla and me on the lips. Laughter was bubbling out of us all and our relief threatened to become hysteria. Doug reined us in with a loud knock on the table. "Let's look at this postcard," he said, pulling out a folder and opening it to reveal the card tucked inside. He pulled it out by one corner with a policeman's reverence for preserving evidence, even though he'd told us there were no fingerprints to find.

There was the scrawled message: .R.Acie.

Doug pointed with the tip of his pencil. "So let's assume those are not periods. That the first one is a tiny letter 'o,' and that the second one is merely there for obfuscation—to throw people off in case her husband or one of his lackeys found her writing it. And the final letter 'i' is in fact not an 'i' at all, but an 'l' that was damaged in the mail, and therefore looks like a dotted 'i.' Then what we would have is—

"Oracle," I said.

"And *Oracle* is the name of the yacht visited by Dr. Ian Foster," said Camilla thoughtfully.

"It's Victoria," Sam said. "You read the description. Reddish hair, green eyes. It's Vic, and now she has a daughter."

"Surely you can find him now, Doug? With the name of the yacht?"

Doug stood up, still looking a bit shocked. "If this doesn't do the trick, Lena, I don't know what will. I will be on the phone before I leave your driveway. But listen—this might take a while. There are various agencies involved, and other countries and their laws. Don't hold your breath."

"Okay," I said, not really paying attention. "Be sure to tell Belinda," I said, "She helped us get on the right track at the very start."

Doug smiled. "I will. She'll want to celebrate with us when this all gets resolved."

"No celebrating yet," said Camilla with some reserve. "Let's find the poor girl. Then we celebrate."

Doug gave us a thumbs-up and jogged out of the house.

The three of us who remained stared at each other, uncertain what to do with ourselves. "Should I go back home?" Sam said, his eyes blank.

Camilla clapped her hands. "No. In cases like this, when people are forced to do some agonizing waiting, they must stick together and distract each other."

"What sort of distraction should we choose?" I said.

"That's the game," Camilla said. "I'll choose our first task, which is to take the dogs for a nice brisk walk. We'll feel better after exercise in the cold air."

We followed her advice because, as always, it was good. When we returned an hour later with two tired German shepherds, we all felt invigorated and slightly less nervous. We sprawled in Camilla's living room and Sam put on the television, where we found an old Grace Kelly movie and watched it for about fifteen minutes before the phone rang and made us all jump. Camilla went to her office, and Sam and I followed. She answered and said, "Oh, yes, Doug. Just a moment—let me put you on speaker phone." She pressed a button and we heard Doug's voice.

"We're all feeling good about the chances right now," Doug said loudly. "*Oracle* is registered to his friend Jon Demetrios; the Feds think that Lazos bought the yacht two years ago and convinced Demetrios to keep the yacht in his own name. Our investigations have told us that there are any number of friends and hangers-on who would be willing to do this sort of thing for Lazos. He's a persuasive man, and he would always have convincing reasons. Demetrios probably didn't think twice."

"So are they questioning Demetrios?" Sam asked.

"They will if they can't locate the yacht based on the name and mooring record alone. Armed with the name of the actual yacht, I don't see how they could fail."

Sam's hand was suddenly clutching mine. I looked at him and was reminded of a long-ago day when I and my fifth grade best friend Andrea Lord were about to go on a rollercoaster for the first time. Andrea had talked me into it, but when we were buckled into our seats, it was Andrea who was terrified. Her face grew white and her expression was one of terror within an existential acceptance. That was how Sam looked now: he was facing the inevitable, but he was afraid.

I slipped an arm around him and said, "It's okay. It's what we want, Sam."

Someone spoke to Doug in the background. He said, "I have to go. I'll call when I can." And then the call ended.

Camilla sent us a bright look. "It's just the waiting, Sam. Waiting is limbo, waiting is purgatory. But eventually you can get into heaven. That's a rather Catholic analogy, but it works here."

Sam nodded. "I could use a dose of God. I've spent the last many months thinking he turned his back on me. Maybe it was the other way around. In any case, whose turn is it to distract us from our waiting?"

"Mine," I said. "And you know what I think you would enjoy? Camilla's new book. Camilla, do I have your permission to read it aloud? It's spellbinding."

Camilla shrugged. "I don't know if Sam wants to—"

"I do," Sam said quickly. "I would love to. Lena, I haven't told you yet, but I just finished *The Salzburg Train*. I loved it. What a talented duo you are."

"It's all Camilla," I said. "I just gave her ideas after the fact. She generated an entire manuscript first."

"In any case, I would be honored to hear the new one."

With Camilla's blessing, I opened the document on my laptop and began to read it aloud. It was something I had never done, and it was surprisingly fun hearing Camilla's narrator talking to us. Camilla liked it, too. "I'm going to jot some notes while you read, Lena."

We all became lost in it for a time: the Budapest night, the waiting boat, the girl in danger, the brooding man with a family secret. Sam actually leaned forward as I reached the end of chapter one. "This is great," he said.

I read chapter two, and part of chapter three, before the phone rang again.

Doug told us, in a clipped tone, that authorities had boarded the *Oracle*. "Somehow the press got wind of it, and there was a horde of them there, like buzzing bees, right at the gangplank. God knows how they knew. Someone blabbed, obviously. But this means you'll see it all on the news, because they were filming as it happened."

"Did they find Victoria?" Sam asked, his voice trembling slightly.

"Yes, Sam," Doug said. "And she's all right. I have to go, but I'll call back."

The line went dead, and Camilla and I, seeing the real distress that had come with what must have been Sam's huge wave of relief, found reasons to leave the room so that Sam could be alone.

I went back after a few minutes, and Sam had composed himself. "My God," he said, reaching for me. "It's like letting air out of a tire. I feel entirely deflated. I hope I don't have to go home, because I don't think I'd make it down the road."

I sat in his lap and kissed his cheek. "You stay right here with the people who love you." I stroked his hair for a while, then said, "You know what? I feel sorry for Jake Elliott. He championed you through all of this, and now he can't be in on the big story."

Sam thought about this and said, "You're right. Hand me the phone, Lena."

He dialed a number that he found written on a scrap of paper in his wallet, and said, "Jake? It's Sam West. I've got some information for you." He told Elliott what had happened, and that he'd probably see it on the news. "But I want you to know that I won't talk to anyone but you about the whole thing. I don't know a damn thing now, but I assume I will eventually, and then you can give me a call. And if I end up seeing Victoria, I'll recommend that she talk to you, as well."

I could hear the loudness of Elliott's joy and gratitude coming through the receiver, and I gave Sam a thumbs-up.

When he hung up, I said, "That was really nice of you."

"It feels good to have control over something," Sam said. "The rest is still all helplessness."

ON THE FIVE o'clock news it was merely called a "breaking story," but they had no real news or footage. But by the six o'clock news broadcast, we got to see it all.

The headline on the screen said *Victoria West Found*, and there was a picture of her next to the lettering. Then the reporter, a striking woman named Callie Forsyth, read a brief statement: "Victoria West, once thought to have been murdered by her husband Sam, has turned up in the Mediterranean on a yacht called *Oracle*. West has been with a wealthy Greek-American tycoon named Nikon Lazos, and it is unclear whether or not she was being held against her will. Authorities are still investigating Lazos and his ties to Ms. West, and police are currently questioning everyone involved. Ms. West did not speak to reporters as authorities led her from the yacht; she was reported to be unharmed, and the mother of a four-month-old child, who was with her as she disembarked."

And as Forsyth spoke, we saw it for ourselves: the gangplank, crowded with reporters and jostling microphones. A woman with a cloud of red hair, wearing a sea-green blouse and a pair of black pants, taking tentative steps out of the yacht. She blinked in the sun and looked almost frightened. At one point, distracted, she looked directly into a camera, her eyes wide and confused, but then, in response to some sound or gesture made by the baby in her arms, she smiled down at it with absolute joy, and Sam said, "Oh, my God. Vic."

She made her way down, flanked by what were clearly Federal agents, and her eyes were on her child alone. The agents batted away any reporters who got too close, and Victoria West, tall and beautiful and intact, got into a black car parked at the dock and was whisked away.

Certain members of Lazos's staff were being detained for questioning, and they indicated that Lazos was away on business. Police were pursuing those leads.

Callie Forsyth, all fake tan and white teeth and blonde hair, grinned at the camera. "Ms. West did not wish to speak to reporters, but we did learn that her child was a girl, and that her name is Athena. Steve?"

Steve looked like a male version of Forsyth. "Thanks, Callie. We tried to reach Sam West for his reaction, but were unable to make contact. West, as you may recall, had long been a suspect in his wife's disappearance, and was only recently exonerated when it was determined that Victoria West was still alive."

Callie looked interested. "And Steve, wasn't the woman who found Victoria West actually Sam West's new love interest?"

"It's true, Callie. The woman's name is Lena London, and she is actually a suspense novelist who has cowritten a book with the famous Camilla Graham. We don't know if it's this special skill that enabled her to find West, but it certainly is an interesting coincidence. My contacts tell me that London was also instrumental in helping to find the yacht, along with an Indiana police detective named Doug Heller, who has been working on the case for a full year."

Callie's face was a picture of fake amazement. "This story just gets more and more complicated, Steve!"

"It does, Callie, and I'm sure we will continue to learn of its complexities over the next days and weeks. West may not wish to talk with reporters, but she will realize soon enough that the world is clamoring for details of how she spent her year, the nature of her relationship with Lazos, and if, in fact, he is the father of her child."

"It's a beautiful baby, Steve."

"It is indeed. We asked our reporter at our sister station in Athens what might be significant about the name Athena, and—" With a flick of the remote, Sam turned off the television.

"That's about all I can take of Steve and Callie," he said lightly.

Camilla studied him. "Sam, are you all right? You can tell us the truth."

Sam shrugged. "The truth is I don't know. The *truth* is, now that I see her, and she's fine, I am reminded of all I endured as her alleged murderer, and I'm wondering, if she was able to send a postcard to Taylor—why not send one to me? All she had to say was 'I'm alive.' But she didn't. I guess that hurts more than I realized."

With a smile of apology, he got up from the couch and left the room.

WE SHARED A quiet dinner, and then Camilla made us some coffee. "I don't know that we can expect to hear anything more tonight," Sam said. "I mean, what are we waiting for? It might take weeks for them to debrief her or whatever it is they do. She'll need time to assimilate. God knows what her mental state is. So—should we just go our separate ways?"

Camilla poured his coffee and pushed it toward him. "She's safe now, and she has ceased to be my concern. This isn't about Victoria, Sam, it's about you. You've been through a great deal, and for a year you couldn't let your guard down because you always had to be ready for the next assault, whatever form it might take. Now, for the first time, you can admit what you feel about it all. You should be around friends during this time. You are, whether you want to think it or not, vulnerable right now. And Lena and I want to take care of you."

He pulled his coffee toward him and took a sip. Then he smiled. "I'm okay with that. Do you have any cookies?"

Camilla laughed, and then said, "You *do* know Rhonda, don't you? She dropped off a whole congratulatory tray about an hour ago, along with a little note."

Camilla brought it to the table—an extravaganza of cookies, tiny cupcakes, fruit breads, mini pies, and chocolate-dipped strawberries. Sam moaned with pleasure as he opened the card from Rhonda. Then he read it and shook his head. "You're right, Camilla, I've had my armor on for a year. And I was pretty sure I hated everyone in Blue Lake. Now I'm being forced to reassess everything. Suddenly the people in this town are looking more positive. But of course I knew Rhonda was great. She's been feeding me here for months without any sign of prejudice."

"Yes, she is special." Camilla took a strawberry and said, "I've had some difficult times in my own life. I have to say that in almost every circumstance, sugar really did help to make things better."

Sam took a strawberry, too, and they toasted across the tray.

AT THE END of the evening, we were installed in the living room, lazily changing channels and trying to focus on something. Camilla told Sam that he should stay over. "Stay in a guest room, stay with Lena, whatever you like. I'm no prude, and I want you to be here with us for a time. I'm sure the reporters are swarming your house despite Doug's barricade, and if they don't know you're here they might leave us alone temporarily."

Sam inclined his head. "Thanks, Camilla. It will be a relief not to go to that empty house tonight, much as I enjoy it most of the time."

I touched his hand, then gathered our empty coffee cups and brought them into the kitchen, where I soaked up the view through the wide window, as I always did.

Blue Lake on this cold winter night was perhaps more peaceful than I had ever seen it—or perhaps the peaceful feeling came from within.

The phone rang, and Camilla called, "Oh, Lena, that's Doug—he said he would check in once more this evening. Would you get it?"

"Sure," I said, and picked up Camilla's landline. "Hello?"

There was a short silence, during which I assumed Doug was breaking away from a conversation or gathering his notes. Instead I heard a tentative female voice—a lovely, cultured voice. "Hello—is that Lena?"

I stumbled through my answer, staring hard at the stars above Blue Lake, and then I ran to the door of the room where Sam sat, looking peaceful and domestic, chatting with Camilla.

"Sam," I said, and his face grew solemn at the sound of my voice. "It's her," I said.

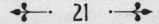

21

They left the police station and wandered into the street, which glittered with soft yellow light under a dark blue sky. "What happens now?" asked Margot. Joe took her hand. "What would you like to happen now?"

—From *Death on the Danube*

WE LEARNED MOST of it later from Sam. Victoria cried through much of the phone call, expressing her vast regret, not only for what happened to Sam in her absence, but about how naïve she had been to fall for Nikon Lazos, a man who had seemed like a dream lover but who had become oppressive and controlling soon after she sailed away with him. She barely even noticed, in her initial euphoria, that her cell phone had disappeared. They were in love and spending a great deal of time in their bed, and when they weren't doing that they were out and about, touring islands, sharing romantic dinners, making plans for the future.

Perhaps a month after they ran off together, she asked what had become of the red phone—he had lent her this in New York, telling her to contact him on it exclusively. Victoria's own phone was left behind, which was why they couldn't track her on it. Nikon told her that they would be unable to get reception out on the water, so the red phone would be useless to her. From that point on she really had no access to the outside world. For the most part, this didn't even bother her. She'd worked hard in New York and her business had still failed. The long hours she'd kept had taken a toll on her marriage. She was ready to start all over again, to see the world, to experience fresh air and nature, and she was rather ashamed of how much time she'd spent on phones, computers, and other electronics.

Nikon encouraged this attitude, calling her his "Nature Girl," and taking her to all sorts of exotic locales, where he photographed her extensively as though she were his personal model. "At first it felt like love, deep love," she told Sam. "It was only after a few months, when I was already pregnant, that I realized it was something different—something obsessive. He framed the photos and began hanging them in our bedroom. Picture after picture of me, as though I was sleeping in a museum of myself." It was then she started wishing to make contact with people at home—her parents, her siblings, Sam. And that was when she found that she could not do so.

First Nikon made excuses about connections—they were in deep water, out of cell phone range. Or he said that she should wait until they knew more about the child, to make sure it was fine, before she told family. And after he got tired of making excuses, he would simply say no, but always in his charming and manipulative way. He would be so loving and doting that she would feel guilty asking him for anything. He lavished her with gifts she didn't really want, took her to the most beautiful places in the world, and yet she longed more and more just to return to New York and the life she left behind. She asked Lazos if he would live there with her, and he always promised that they would do that someday—after they finished their sea odyssey.

Sam had listened with a mixture of pity and disbelief, so crazy did her saga sound. And yet he knew, even with the strangest details, that it was all true.

On that evening he got the phone call, he went into Camilla's study and shut the door. Camilla and I gave him his privacy, but at one point, driven by curiosity and what seemed to be silence in the room, I opened the door to find Sam lying on the floor, the phone against his ear, his eyes fixed bleakly on the ceiling. He said, "But that's the problem. There was blood, Vic. *Your* blood, and a whole lot of it. I couldn't help but think that you were trying to frame me."

He listened, and even from the doorway I could hear the loud distress in Victoria West's voice. She told Sam about Nikon, and his ever-efficient and ever-changing staff. If they needed medical attention, he hired the very best, as he had done for the birth of her baby. One day he had brought a team aboard and said that the local hospital was short of blood; he had promised that everyone on board would donate a pint for the greater good. So they did: Victoria and all the others gave blood, one by one, and yet she realized, in light of Sam's news, that it had been a charade. That he had only wanted her blood, and he had put on that show so that she would willingly give it. She could not have known that he would send someone to Sam's apartment and liberally spill it on the floor. She said bitterly, "Now I don't know if the hospital got the other blood, or if Nikon simply dumped it into the sea."

This had horrified Sam: not only the steps Lazos had taken to make sure no one searched for his secret lover, but how he had manipulated Victoria to believe all of his charming lies. She had been in the web of a spider but had never noticed the danger.

Victoria had spent the last part of the call apologizing. "I can't believe what happened to you, Sam. I had no idea, not ever. If anything, I figured people had sort of forgotten about me, assuming I had run off with my new boyfriend. Everyone knew about him—you knew I was dating someone, and my mother and father knew. I just never mentioned his name, because I was waiting to introduce him to all of you—my big grand surprise. 'Look at my rich, handsome, international boyfriend.' What a stupid fool I was. What a fool. A teenage girl would have more sense than I did, the way I just followed him off into the blue. And by the end I was begging him, begging him to let me go home. He said that I was ungrateful, and that no woman on earth had the things I had. Which was true—so I was tormented on a daily basis. Was I going crazy? Was I a spoiled rich girl, as Nikon suggested? Or was I being victimized? Then, by the time I got really big with the pregnancy, any thoughts of running away went down the drain, and after that I had Athena to think of."

Sam asked after the baby, and Victoria told him that she was fine, beautiful, perfect. "I hope you'll understand, I don't want to be cruel when I say I don't think I ever truly loved someone until I looked into her eyes. She is the love of my life, Sam."

He took this opportunity to tell Victoria about me: how I had stayed by his side when no one else had, how he had grown to love me. She told him that she wanted to meet me, and that she was very happy for us both. "Obviously we need to meet in person, but I need some time to be alone with my baby, to walk on solid ground and just enjoy life. My parents and my sisters are with me, and we're happy."

"Will you prosecute Nikon?" Sam asked.

She hesitated. "The police are asking the same thing, but they're also not exactly sure what we could charge him with. He did not take me against my will, nor did he ever lock me up. He just kept me on the ocean and continued a course of I guess what you'd call psychological intimidation. You'd have to know Nikon—he's so persuasive, it's almost like he hypnotizes you. And it's hard, because a part of me still loves him. They have me talking to a therapist here, and she has made me see a lot of the patterns of abuse, but it's hard to call it that. I never felt abused. But I did feel lonely and afraid. I felt those things quite often."

Sam told her that he would always care about her, and that he would always be here if she needed him. He said he wanted to meet her daughter. Victoria cried then and said that she would make that happen, and soon.

Sam cried, too, as he talked to the wife that the world said he had murdered and heard her say, in a voice once loved and still familiar, that he was blameless.

THAT NIGHT I pulled Sam against me in my big warm bed. Camilla had long since gone to sleep, and Sam and I lay, wakeful and staring at the stars in a dark blue sky.

"She said she would speak to Jake Elliott," Sam said. "He'll tell the story the way it should be told. I feel good about that."

"Meanwhile, the future is clear. Nothing left to wait for, nothing left to fear," I said.

"Right." Sam turned to look at me. "You know I love you, don't you?"

"I do. Do you know I love you?"

"Yes, thank God. So the future is something we have to plan together." His voice, to my great relief, had regained some of its lightness. It also sounded tired and deeply satisfied. He closed his eyes and smiled. "Maybe I'll make you waffles in the morning. I won't have to worry about Doug Heller arresting me, or reporters hunting me down, or Ted Strayer taking our picture."

"That sounds lovely. Go to sleep, Sam West. You're going to wake up a new man."

HE DID. HE was more than cheerful the next day; he kissed Camilla and thanked her for her kindness, then led the way back to his house, holding my hand in his. Some reporters had indeed snuck past the Wentworth Street barricade, and Sam made a brief statement, telling them that he was thrilled Victoria was home, that he had spoken to her and she was in good spirits and surrounded by supporters including her parents, and that they were thrilled to have a granddaughter.

Sam pulled me against him in a dramatic kiss, and the cameras flashed. "Put that on the front page and say that Sam West is in love," he said. "That will be one thing that you got totally right."

His good mood continued inside, where he started on the waffles and flicked through a vast pile of mail. He opened a letter and grinned. "Look, Lena. This is from a little girl in England. She sent me a British pound and a picture of you and me." The picture, drawn with a red crayon, featured Sam West standing next to a table, and me off to one side wearing a bikini. The caption said, "Sam and Lena London."

"I like that one," Sam said. "That bikini is sexy. It's going on the fridge."

I giggled. "You are back to being my playful Sam."

His blue eyes met mine. "Definitely your Sam."

I smiled at him, and he went back to his mail while I set the table. I looked into the snowy backyard, where I had first encountered Taylor Brand. No one had told Victoria about Taylor yet; her therapist had asked her friends and family to hold off until she felt a bit more secure. It would have to happen soon, since Victoria had started to ask about her, and had been looking at her blog.

Despite my happiness at the way things had turned out, and my pleasure in knowing that life in Blue Lake could now get back to normal, a worry nagged at my thoughts. I did not intend to burden Sam with it, and I did not think it had even penetrated his wall of relief and joy.

It was there, though, a subtly sinister fact that remained troublesome even in the light of day.

Nikon Lazos, released from police questioning, had disappeared.

With a sigh I turned back to Sam West, the one-time alleged murderer of Blue Lake, and watched him cook my breakfast.

FOR TWO WEEKS my life was sublime. February came, and for a couple of days the weather grew less cold. Sam and I drove up to Indianapolis for two nights and walked around the city for an early Valentine's Day celebration.

We spent time in our hotel, enjoying room service and our bed, but we also ventured out into the city, happy to be openly together and not dogged by the press. No one knew where we were (except Camilla), and no one cared who we were in the anonymous crush of people on the sidewalks.

On our last night there we walked through the city and paused to window shop at a jewelry store. Sam pointed at some giant sapphire earrings. "Those would look lovely on you," he said.

I laughed. "I'm not a flashy person. I don't wear much jewelry. Just this ring." I took the glove off my right hand to show a small twinkling diamond on my ring finger. "It was my mother's." A bolt of sadness went through me, potent as poison in the blood. I felt it now and then when I thought of my mother and the life we had been deprived of—a life together. She could have met Sam. She could have met Camilla . . .

Sam kissed my hand. "I'm going to find something that's perfect for you. Something that cries 'Lena London.'"

"Okay," I said. "Maybe for Christmas."

"Let's have dinner. Find a place that looks good."

We walked a couple more blocks and I spied a pretty little doorway outlined with Italian lights. "Ooh—that looks lovely."

We moved closer, crossing the street to get to the main entrance, where a large family was filing in, stomping the snow from their feet. "It's Greek," Sam said, peering at the sign. And then, "Oh."

"What?"

"I don't know if you want to go here, Lena."

"Why?"

He pointed at the sign. The restaurant was called the Oracle.

I shrugged. "Oracles delivered good news as well as bad. Are you afraid of evil omens?"

"Not if you aren't."

I studied his face in the warm light. "We found the *Oracle*. We rescued Victoria."

"I know. Just a weird feeling for a minute. Let's go in and have a nice dinner." He took my hand and led me into the warm fragrant interior, where elegant candlelit tables were tucked into booths along both walls, and Greek music played softly in the background.

Sam and I sat down. I remember, in the glow of that moment, that I told him I loved him, and his face brightened.

That was the last happy thing.

WE RETURNED HOME the following morning. It was both comforting and sad to see Blue Lake again. Sam said he had some work to do, but that he would join Camilla and me for dinner.

I went into Graham House to find it empty; Camilla had left a note that she and Adam were out running errands. Her dogs came to greet me, and I took them into the backyard and gave them some frolicking time. Then I let them in and wandered Camilla's house, finally walking into her office and sitting in my purple chair. I stared at her desk; it was odd to see it without her behind it. I hated the idea of change; I wanted everything to remain just as it was with Camilla and Adam and Sam and me, with Doug and Belinda and Allison and John, and my father and Tabitha. I wanted all my friends and family to remain as they were: happy, healthy, in my life. I wanted time to freeze, even as I acknowledged that it was changing at that moment.

I thought of Victoria West, and the way she had followed a dream of love into what had become her prison. The web of fate had wrapped around her and left her isolated, lonely, pregnant with the child of a man she did not truly know. It was Lazos's baby, Sam had assured me of that . . .

Lestrade strolled into the office and jumped into my lap. I scratched his furry head and then kissed it.

When Camilla returned I was still there, sitting in the purple chair.

"My dear, what is wrong?"

I looked up at her and shrugged. "Nothing. Everything is great. I'm just—moody. Isn't that strange? We had the best weekend. And I've been sitting here feeling sad."

Camilla studied me. "Intense emotion can open up other doors."

"Yes. I guess so. Sam said he would come for dinner. Is that all right?"

"Always." She leaned in to touch my shoulder. "Let me go hang up my coat, and then we can talk. We have a book tour to plan, you know."

"Yes! Wonderful."

She moved out of the room; I heard her rustling around, taking off her winter things. Then my phone rang. I took it from my pocket and saw the familiar number: Sam.

"Hello."

"Sweet Lena. I can't come for dinner. Something's come up."

"What's going on?"

"I just got a call—Victoria's here. She's heading for Blue Lake now. She had said she wanted to talk to me in person, and—I mean, she's on her way. I had no time to make arrangements for her, to do anything. In any case, she wants to talk. I want to talk, as well. We have things to sort out, papers to sign."

"Of course you need to talk! You haven't seen her in a year and a half. Can you—would you call me when you know what's going on? I mean, I won't intrude, but—"

"I want her to meet you, of course. But let us talk first. Let me see her alone."

"Yes, I understand, Sam. Just call when you need me, okay?"

"I will. I have to go—she's just minutes away."

"Bye."

I clicked off as Camilla walked back in. "Shall we have a little book meeting?" she asked.

My head was buzzing with Sam's information. There was no way I would be able to concentrate, to look at words on paper. "You know what? That was Sam. He had a quick question for me—something he wants help with in redesigning his kitchen." I was shocked at how quickly the lie came. "Let me just run over there and give my opinion, and then I'll come right back."

Camilla's voice was smooth. "Of course, dear."

I knew that she was watching me as I donned my coat and boots. She was no fool, and she knew that something was happening. But Camilla, ever wise, said nothing.

I gave her a little wave as I left, and an imitation of a

smile. Then I moved down the steps and toward the gravel road. Normally I would have simply marched down the bluff toward Sam's, taking the road that led to his driveway. This time I moved into the trees, stealthy and quiet, staying away from the road even as I kept it in sight. I found eventual shelter under a large pine, just as I had when I saw Ted Strayer try to commit murder.

When the car pulled up I was in shadow. I refused to blink for fear that I might miss her—that after all this time I would be deprived of seeing Victoria West.

The car pulled to a stop next to Sam's house, perpendicular to his driveway. The back seat door opened, and a woman stepped out. I had thought, from pictures and video, that she was very tall, but she seemed smaller in person. Her red hair was tucked partway under a green hat, and she wore a black winter coat with a green collar. She stepped out with booted feet and then turned to retrieve something from the car. She emerged with a baby carrier. I could hear her murmuring to the child, saying sweet nothings to it. In response I heard some happy gurgling. Even from my distance of perhaps fifteen feet I could see that little Athena was beautiful. At one point, as her mother marched toward Sam's door, I thought the baby's dark eyes looked right at me.

I leaned against the tree and heard Sam's door open. "Victoria," he said.

"Oh, Sammy," she cried. I moved closer. She was hugging Sam and saying "I'm sorry—I'm so, so sorry!"

Sam patted her hair, looking slightly uncomfortable, and then she pulled away.

He pointed at the baby. "She's beautiful. She looks like you," he said.

Victoria picked up the carrier and said, "She's much prettier than I am. She's my sweet little goddess."

Sam stepped back. "Come in out of the cold. I made some coffee."

"Lovely," she said. She stepped inside with her carrier, and Sam closed the door. A moment later her driver appeared at the door and knocked. Sam opened the door and I heard Victoria say, "Oh Sam, let him in—I need to pay him."

Moments later the driver reappeared in Sam's doorway; he paused briefly, clearly admiring Sam's sturdy wood door, and then went back to his car, apparently to wait.

I needed to go back to Camilla's, to return to life as usual, but that would have been as hard as pulling metal away from a magnet. Victoria West was just feet away. I wanted to see her up close, touch her hand, talk to her. I wanted her to tell me that she felt happy and free—but then I wanted her to say that she had moved on, that she had no interest in Sam anymore.

After about twenty minutes I decided that it was ridiculous to stand in the cold waiting. Sam had said he would call, and he would be embarrassed and disappointed to find his girlfriend lurking in the trees outside his house instead of waiting in her own warm residence. I eyed the driver who waited for Victoria; he was on the phone inside the car.

I took one tentative step forward, but stopped when I heard the driver get out again. He climbed the stairs and went back to the door. So it had been Victoria on the phone. It had been a short meeting. Was that good or bad?

A moment later the driver went inside the house. He

emerged thirty seconds later holding the baby carrier; little Athena, eyes still bright, seemed to find me again in the trees, and she smiled. I smiled back, though she couldn't see me. So Victoria was leaving; had Sam gotten all the closure he needed? Had Victoria signed the papers he spoke of?

Idly, I watched the driver stow the baby into the back seat. He hadn't bothered to buckle in the carrier; apparently Victoria wanted to do that herself.

He ran back to his side, and that was when I heard the first scream from inside the house. "No," I said, and I moved toward the car, which was already pulling away.

I noted the license number: 2B0NJ7.

Victoria West slammed out of the house, her feet pounding down the porch stairs. "My baby!" she cried. She looked at me without recognition. "What did you see?"

For a second that lasted centuries, we stared at each other. Her beautiful green eyes were wide with terror, but even in my overwhelming pity I felt a spurt of resentment.

I pointed. "The driver. I thought he was carrying her for you."

She looked wildly down the road, and then she ran, screaming her daughter's name as she chased after the car that was gone. Later Camilla would tell me that she heard the screams, and the name "Athena," and that she had known the truth immediately.

In that instant I felt a terrible wrenching inside me, as I watched the mother's grief at being torn away from her daughter. My longing for my own mother welled up so strongly that my eyes filled with tears.

Sam was close behind Victoria; he had a cell phone in his hand. Now he joined me in the driveway, sparing me a look of mild surprise before sending a worried glance toward Victoria, crying pitifully for her child, still running down the gravel road toward Wentworth Street.

"Doug's putting out an Amber Alert," he said. "He won't get far." He shook his head. "That guy taped the door latch. I never thought to—I don't know why, but I assumed we were safe."

"The driver got a call just before he went in; I thought it was Victoria calling. I got a license number. I can give them that," I said.

Our words seemed to blow away on the cold wind, and after several hours, so did our confidence.

Athena Lazos, four months old, had been kidnapped.

22

In the end, it was misfortune, not happiness, which gave her life a clear direction.

—From *Death on the Danube*

CAMILLA SAT WITH Sam and me that evening, watching the fire crackle in her grate. It warmed not just our cold bodies, but our weary hearts. "We know the child is in good hands. Victoria knows, too," she said. "So she won't have to be tormented with images of evil abductors."

Sam nodded. "She does know. She's convinced it's Nikon. Doug says they found the car, deserted in a corn field. Clearly the driver was picked up by someone else. This was an orchestrated abduction."

"But Nikon *is* evil," I protested. "His first wife Grace defended him, and Victoria downplays what he did, as well. And he continues to get away with things. How dare he just steal his own daughter? Poor Victoria. She was just starting over. She called the baby the love of her life."

"And she will have the child back quickly enough. All of the authorities are on the case," Camilla said.

We avoided looking at one another as these hollow words hit home. The "authorities" had been looking for Victoria, too, and it had taken more than a year. Where would Nikon be holed up this time? What friends would he employ to protect him? How long would it be before Victoria would see her little girl?

Sam stood up and stretched briefly, his face solemn. "I want to call and check on Vic. See how she's holding up," he said. He looked at me, and I nodded. I wanted to know how she was, as well.

"Of course, dear," Camilla said. "Lena, I'm getting some more tea. Would you like some?"

"Yes, please." I watched her walk out of the room, and my eyes returned to the fire as my mind returned to the thoughts that had been circling in my head ever since the car had driven away.

In one sense, our drama was over. Life in Blue Lake would return to normal, and Sam had been exonerated once and for all. He was no longer "the murderer" on the hill. He was free, and I was free. Camilla and I would resume our writing, and go on book tours. We would cease to be distracted by real life mysteries. Much as I hated the thought of little Athena's absence from her mother's life, that was not a mystery that Camilla and I, or Doug or Sam, could solve.

And yet, my brain persisted, Nikon Lazos was going to disappear into obscurity once again, and he had arranged to take his daughter with him. I clenched my fists on the arms of my chair, angry about the little dark-eyed baby, about the weeping Victoria, about poor Sam, who was ever present in the center of drama. I thought again of my mother, my beloved mother, long gone but never forgotten. Love between a mother and her child was a bond that could not be broken—not by death, not by distance.

For the third time in my life I found myself vowing that I would find Nikon Lazos, but this time, I fantasized, it would be different.

Someday soon I would meet him face-to-face.

Someday soon I would tell him how many people he had harmed.

Someday soon I would make him answer for it all.

When Camilla came in with my tea, she found that I was smiling.

Keep reading for an excerpt from the first
book in the Undercover Dish Mysteries

THE BIG CHILI

Available now from Berkley Prime Crime!

My CHOCOLATE LABRADOR watched me as I parked my previously loved Volvo wagon and took my covered pan out of the backseat; the autumn wind buffeted my face and made a mess of my hair. "I'll be right back, Mick," I said. "I know that pot in the back smells good, but I'm counting on you to behave and wait for your treat."

He nodded at me. Mick was a remarkable dog for many reasons, but one of his best talents was that he had trained himself to nod while I was talking. He was my dream companion: a handsome male who listened attentively and never interrupted or condescended. He also made me feel safe when I did my clandestine duties all over Pine Haven.

I shut the car door and moved up the walkway of Ellie Parker's house. She usually kept the door unlocked, though I had begged her to reconsider that idea. We had an agreement; if she wasn't there, or if she was out back puttering around in her garden, I could just leave the casserole on the table and take the money she left out for me. I charged fifty dollars, which included the price of ingredients. Ellie said I could charge more, but for now this little sideline of a job was helping me pay the bills, and that was good enough.

"Ellie?" I called. I went into her kitchen, where I'd been several times before, and found it neat, as always; Ellie was not inside. Disappointed, I left the dish on her scrubbed wooden table. I had made a lovely mac and cheese casserole with a twist: finely sliced onion and prosciutto baked in with three different cheeses for a show-stopping event of a main course . It was delicious and very close to the way Ellie prepared it before her arthritis had made it too difficult to cook for her visiting friends and family. She didn't want her loved ones to know this, which was where I came in. We'd had an agreement for almost a year, and it served us both well.

She knew how long to bake the dish, so I didn't bother with writing down any directions. Normally she would invite Mick in, and she and I would have some tea and shoot the breeze while my canine lounged under the table, but today, for whatever reason, she had made other plans. She hadn't set out the money, either, so I went to the cookie jar where she had told me to find my payment in the past: a ceramic cylinder in the shape of a chubby monkey. I claimed my money and turned around to find a man looming in the doorway.

"Ah!" I screamed, clutching the cash in front of my waist like a weird bouquet.

"Hello," he said, his eyes narrowed. "May I ask who you are?"

"I'm a friend of Ellie's. Who are you?" I fired back. Ellie had never suggested that a man—a sort of good-looking, youngish man—would appear in her house. For all I knew he could be a burglar.

"I am Ellie's son. Jay Parker." He wore reading glasses, and he peered at me over these like a stern teacher. It was a good look for him. "And I didn't expect to find a strange woman dipping into Mom's cash jar while she wasn't in the house."

A little bead of perspiration worked its way down my back. "First of all, I am not a strange woman. In any sense. Ellie and I are friends, and I—"

I what? What could I tell him? My little covered-dish business was an under-the-table operation, and the people who ordered my food wanted it to appear that they had made it themselves. That, and the deliciousness of my cooking, was what they paid me for. "I did a job for her, and she told me to take payment."

"Is that so?" He leaned against the door frame, a man with all the time in the world. All he needed was a piece of hay to chew on. "And what *job* did you do for her?" He clearly didn't believe me. With a pang I realized that this man thought I was a thief.

"I mowed her lawn," I blurted. We both turned to look out the window at Ellie's remarkably high grass. "Wow. That really was not a good choice," I murmured.

Now his face grew alert, wary, as though he were ready to employ some sort of martial art if necessary. I may as well have been facing a cop. "What exactly is your relationship to my mother? And how did you even get in here, if my mom isn't home?"

At least I could tell the truth about that. "I'm Lilah Drake. Ellie left the door unlocked for me because she was expecting me. As I said, we are friends."

This did not please him. "I think she was actually expecting *me*," he said. "So you could potentially have just gotten lucky when you tried the doorknob."

"Oh my God!" My face felt hot with embarrassment. "I'm not stealing Ellie's money. She and I have an—arrangement. I can't actually discuss it with you. Maybe if you asked your mother . . . ?" Ellie was creative; she could come up with a good lie for her son, and he'd *have* to believe her.

There was a silence, as though he were weighing evidence. It felt condescending and weirdly terrifying. "Listen, I have to get going. My dog is waiting—"

He brightened for the first time. "That's your dog, huh? I figured. He's pretty awesome. What is he, a chocolate Lab?"

"Yes, he is." I shifted on my feet, not sure how to extricate myself from the situation. My brother said I had a knack for getting into weird predicaments.

I sighed, and he said, "So what do we do now?" He patted his shirt pocket, as though looking for a pack of cigarettes, then grimaced and produced a piece of gum. He unwrapped it while still watching me. His glasses had slid down even farther on his nose, and I felt like plucking them off. He popped the gum into his mouth and took off the glasses himself, then beamed a blue gaze at me. Wow. "How about if we just wait here together and see what my mom has to say? She's probably out back in the garden, picking pumpkins or harvesting the last of her tomatoes."

I put the money on Ellie's table. "You know what? Ellie can pay me later. I won't have you—casting aspersions on my character."

"Fancy words," said Ellie's son. He moved a little closer to me, until I could smell spearmint on his breath. "I still think you should hang around."

I put my hands on my hips, the way my mother used to do when Cam or I forgot to do the dishes. "I have things to do. Please tell Ellie I said hello."

I whisked past him, out to my car, where Mick sat waiting, a picture of patience. I climbed in and started confiding. "Do you believe that guy? Now I'm going to have to come back here later to get paid. I don't have time for this, Mick!"

Mick nodded with what seemed like sympathy.

I reversed out of Ellie's driveway, still fuming. But halfway home, encouraged by Mick's stolid support, and enjoying the *Mary Poppins* sound track in my CD player, I calmed down slightly. These things could happen in the business world, I told myself. There was no need to give another thought to tall Jay Parker and his accusations and his blue eyes.

I began to sing along with the music, assuring Mick melodically that I would find the perfect nanny. Something in the look he gave me made me respond aloud. "And another thing. I'm a grown woman. I'm twenty-seven years old, Mick. I don't need some condescending man treating me like a child. Am I right?"

Mick was distracted by a Chihuahua on the sidewalk, so I didn't get a nod.

"Huh. She's pretty cute, right?"

No response. I sighed and went back to my singing, flicking forward on the cd and testing my upper range with "Feed the Birds." I started squeaking by the time I reached the middle. "It's tricky, Mick. It starts low, and then you get nailed on the refrain. We can't all be Julie Andrews." Mick's expression was benevolent.

I drove to Caldwell Street and St. Bartholomew Church, where I headed to the back parking lot behind the rectory. I took out my phone and texted I'm here to Pet Grandy, a member of St. Bart's Altar and Rosary Guild, a scion of the church, and a go-to person for church social events. Pet was popular, and she had a burning desire to be all things to all people. This included her wish to make food for every church event—good food that earned her praise and adulation. Since Pet was actually a terrible cook, I was the answer to her prayers. I had made a lot of money off Pet Grandy in the last year.

"She'll be out here within thirty seconds," I told Mick, and sure enough, he had barely started nodding before Pet burst out of the back door of the church social hall and made a beeline for the adjoining rectory lot. Pet's full name was Perpetua; her mother had named her for some nun who had once taught at the parish school. Pet basically lived at the church; she was always running one event or another, and Father Schmidt was her gangly other half. They made a hilarious duo: he, tall and thin in his priestly black, and she, short and plump as a tomato and sporting one of her many velour sweat suits—often in offensively bright colors. In fall, you could often spot them tending to the autumnal flower beds outside St. Bart's. At Christmastime, one of them would hold the ladder while the other swayed in front of the giant pine outside the church, clutching strings of white Christmas lights. Pet was utterly devoted to Father Schmidt; they were like a platonic married couple.

As she marched toward my car, I studied her. Today's ensemble, also velour, was a bright orange number that made her look like a calendar-appropriate pumpkin. Her cheeks were rosy in the cold, and her dark silver-flecked hair was cut short and no-nonsense. Pet was not a frilly person.

She approached my vehicle, as always, with an almost sinister expression, as if she were buying drugs. Pet was very careful that no one should know what we were doing or why. On the rare occasions that someone witnessed the food handoff, Pet pretended that I was just driving it over from her house. Today she had ordered a huge Crock-Pot full of chili for the bingo event in the church hall. Everyone was bringing food, but Pet's (my) chili had become a favorite.

I rolled down my window, and Pet looked both ways before leaning in. Her eyes darted constantly, like those of someone marked for assassination. "Hello, Lilah. Is it light enough for me to carry?"

"It's pretty heavy, Pet. Do you want me to—"

"No, no. I have a dolly in the vestibule. I'll just run and get it. Here's the money." She thrust an envelope through the window at me with her left hand, her body turned sideways and her right hand scratching her face in an attempt to look casual. Pet was so practiced at clandestine maneuvers that I thought she might actually make a good criminal. I watched her rapid-walk back to the church and marveled that she wasn't thin as a reed, since she was always moving. Pet, however, had the Achilles heel of a sweet addiction: she loved it all, she had told me once. Donuts, cookies, cake, pie, ice cream. "I probably have sweets three times a day. My doctor told me I'm lucky I don't have diabetes. But I crave it all the time!"

Pet reappeared and I pretended that I was about to get out of my car to help her. I did this every time, just to tease her, and every time she took the bait. "No," she shouted, her hand up as though to ward off a bullet aimed at her heart. "Stay there! Someone might see you!"

"Okay, Pet." She opened my back hatch and I spoke to her over my shoulder. "It's the big Crock-Pot there. Ignore the box in the corner—that's for someone else."

"Fine, fine. Thank you, Lilah. I'm sure it will be delicious, as always." She hauled it out of the car, grunting slightly, and placed it on her dolly. Then, loudly, for whatever sprites might be listening, she said, "Thank you so much for driving this from my house! It's a real time-saver!"

I rolled my eyes at Mick and he nodded. Mick totally gets it.

I waved to Pet, who ignored me, and drove away while she was still wheeling her prize back to the church hall. My mother played bingo there sometimes and probably would tonight. We were church members, but we were neither as devout nor as involved as was Pet. My mother called us "lapsed Catholics" and said we would probably have to wait at the back of the line on our way to heaven, at which point my father would snort and say that he could name five perfect Catholics who were having affairs.

Then they would launch into one of their marital spats and I would tune them out or escape to my own home, which was where I headed now.

My parents are Realtors, and I work for them during the day. I mostly either answer phones at the office or sit at showings, dreaming of recipes while answering questions about hardwood floors, modernized baths, and stainless steel kitchens. It isn't a difficult task, but I do lust after those kitchens more than is healthy. I have visions of starting my own catering business, experimenting with spices at one of those amazing marble islands while a tall blue-eyed man occasionally wanders in to taste my concoctions.

Mick was staring at the side of my face with his intense look. I slapped my forehead. "Oh, buddy! I never gave you your treat, and you had to sit and smell that chili all through the ride!"

Mick nodded.

We pulled into the long driveway that led to our little house, which was actually an old caretaker's cottage behind a much larger residence. My parents had found it for me and gotten me a crazy deal on rent because they had sold the main house to Terry Randall, a rich eccentric who had taken a liking to my parents during the negotiations. Taking advantage of that, my parents had mentioned that their daughter would love to rent a cottage like the one behind his house, and Terry had agreed. My rent, which Terry didn't need but which my parents had insisted upon, was a steal. I'd been in the cottage for more than two years and Terry and I had become good friends. I was often invited into the big house for the lavish parties that Terry and his girlfriend liked to throw on a regular basis.

I pulled a Tupperware container out of my tote bag— Mick's reward whenever he accompanied me on trips.

"Who's my special boy?" I asked him as I popped off the lid.

Mick started munching, his expression forgiving. He made quick work of the chili inside; I laughed and snapped his picture on my phone. "That's going on the refrigerator, boy," I said. It was true, I doted on Mick as if he were my child, but in my defense, Mick was a spectacular dog.

I belted out a few lines of "Jolly Holiday" before turning off the radio and retrieving Mick's now-clean container. I checked my phone and found two text messages: one from my friend Jenny, who wanted me to come for dinner soon, and one from my brother, who wanted me to meet his girlfriend. I'd met lots of Cam's girlfriends over time, but this one was special to him, I could tell, because she was Italian. My brother and I, thanks to a wonderfully enthusiastic junior high Italian teacher, had developed a mutual love of Italian culture before we even got to high school. We immersed ourselves in Italian art, music, sports, and film. We both took Italian in high school, and Cam went on to get his PhD in Italian, which he now taught at Loyola, my alma mater. We were Italophiles from way back, but Cam had never met an Italian woman. It was I who had won the distinction of dating an Italian first, and that hadn't ended well. But sometimes, even now, when I found myself humming "*Danza, danza fanciulla gentile,*" I could hear Miss Abbandonato saying, "*Ciao,* Lilah, *splendido!*"

She had told us, in the early days of our classes, that her family name meant "forsaken," and I had remembered it when I, too, was betrayed. *Abbandonato.* How forsaken I had felt back then.

I turned off my phone and smiled at Mick, who was still licking his chops. We climbed out of the car and made our way to the cozy little cottage with its green wood door and berry wreath. Home sweet home.

I grabbed my mail out of the tin box and unlocked the door, letting Mick and me into our kingdom. We had hardwood floors, too, at least a few feet of them in our little foyer. The living room was carpeted in an unfortunate brown shag, but it was clean, and there was a fireplace that made the whole first floor snug and welcoming.

My kitchen was tiny and clean, and between my little dining area and the living room was a circular staircase that led up to a loft bedroom. Every night I thanked God for Terry Randall and his generous heart (and for my savvy parents, who had talked him into renting me my dollhouse cottage).

As I set my things down, my phone rang.

"Hello?"

"Hi, honey." It was my mother. I could hear her doing something in the background—probably putting away groceries. "Are you going to bingo with me tonight?"

"Mom. Bingo is so loud and annoying, and those crazy women with their multiple cards and highlighters . . ."

"Are what? Our good friends and fellow parishioners?"

I groaned. "Don't judge me, Mom. Just because I get tired of Trixie Frith and Theresa Scardini and their braying voices—"

"Lilah Veronica! What has gotten into you?"

"I don't know."

"Sweetie, you have to get out. Dad thinks you have agoraphobia."

"I don't have agoraphobia. I just happen to like my house and my dog."

"What song is in your head right now?"

My mother knew this odd little fact: I always had a song in my head. There was one in there when I woke up each morning—often something really obscure, like a commercial jingle from the nineties, when I was a kid—and one in my head when I went to bed at night. It was not always a conscious thing, but it was always there, like a sound track to my life. My mother had used it as a way to gauge my mood when I was little. If I was happy it was always something like "I Could Have Danced All Night" (I loved musicals) or some fun Raffi song. If she heard me humming "It's Not Easy Being Green," she knew I needed cheering up. Nowadays my musical moods could swing from Adele to Abba in a matter of hours. "I don't know. I think I was humming Simon and Garfunkel a minute ago."

"Hmm—that could go either way."

"Don't worry about it, Mom."

"You haven't spent much time with young people lately. You need to get out on the town with Jenny, like in the old days when you two were in college."

"I'm planning just that next week. We've been texting about it. But, Mom, I'm not in college anymore. And neither is Jenny. She's busy with her job, I'm busy with my jobs—plural. And if you are subtly implying that you want me to meet men, I am not ready for that, either."

My mother sighed dramatically in my ear. "One bad relationship doesn't mean you can't find something good."

"No. It just means I'm not *interested* in finding a man right now. I think I'm a loner. I like being alone."

"I think you're hiding."

"Mom, stop the pop psychology. I have a great life: a growing business, a nice house, a loving family, and a devoted dog. People who saw my life would wish they were me."

"Except no one sees your life, because you hide away from the world in your little house behind a house."

"Right. With my agoraphobia," I said, choosing to find my mother's words amusing instead of annoying. She had found me this house, after all.

"Come with me tonight. I heard that Pet will be making her chili. It's my favorite," said my mother, who was one of only three people who knew my secret.

"I guess I'll go," I said. "But only because I'm hoping your crazy luck will rub off on me and I'll win the jackpot."

My mother had won two thousand dollars at bingo six months earlier. She came home beaming, and my father groused about the fact that she went at all. Then she pulled out twenty hundred-dollar bills and set them in his lap. Now he didn't say much about bingo, especially since they'd used the money to buy him a state-of-the-art recliner.

What I could do with two thousand dollars. . . .

Connect with Berkley Publishing Online!

For sneak peeks into the newest releases, news on all your favorite authors, book giveaways, and a central place to connect with fellow fans—

"Like" and follow Berkley Publishing!

facebook.com/BerkleyPub
twitter.com/BerkleyPub
instagram.com/BerkleyPub

Penguin
Random
House

1844